For a Keg of Good Brandy…

Also by the same author:

A Rum Do! Smuggling in 18th century Robin Hood's Bay
Lady Mary's Journal (with Mary Neads)
Making Ships in Bottles (with Léon Labistour)

The author has lived in an old sea captains house dating from
1824 in Robin Hood's Bay since 1967. She is an experienced local
historian and lecturer, holding a Certificate in Regional Maritime
Studies. Her other interests include family history research,
modelmaking, needlecrafts, and classical music.

For a
Keg of
Good Brandy...

To Gill,

Best wishes

Pat Labistour.

Patricia Labistour

MARINE ARTS PUBLICATIONS

First published 2004 by Marine Arts Publications.
'Seascape'
Robin Hood's Bay
North Yorkshire, England. YO22 4SH

ISBN 0-9516184-8-2
For a Keg of Good Brandy...

Reproduction by
Redpress
14 Queen Street
Redcar
North Yorkshire
TS10 1AE

Cover illustration Robin Hood's Bay,
lithograph by Francis Nicholson 1821

For Cath, Mat and Anna

'My father and mother once happy did dwell
In a neat little cottage not far from the shore.
My father did venture his life on the sea,
For a keg of good brandy he was bound for folly.'

'The poor Smuggler's Boy'........traditional folk song.

Preface

This is a story based on historical facts. In the eighteenth century, smuggling was rife all along our coasts.

Britain had been undergoing a long period of political unrest and expense; money had been poured into supporting the army in its failed attempts to keep America, and there was now a serious risk of invasion during the Napoleonic Wars. Napoleon had 200,000 troops lined up on the French coast ready to attack. 'The English do not know what awaits them. In twelve hours Britain could be no more,' he boasted. This menace was so real that naughty children were threatened that 'Boney' would come and get them if they did not behave.

The money to fund the forces came largely from the heavy taxes placed on imported goods, and as this affected the ordinary person who, in most cases, did not understand the reason, smuggling escalated to such an extent that it became a national industry involving almost half the population of the British Isles in one way or another. This alarming statistic is easily proved if a piece of contraband is followed on its 'run'. Most items sneaked into our East coast ports and harbours originated in Holland and France, where often a member of the British gentry would arrange and pay for the merchandise. Contact made with reliable sea captains ensured the safe transport of the cargo across to our coasts, where fishing communities were on hand to quickly and efficiently unload and hide the goods until they could be moved on. Local farmers provided horses and carts or pony teams for transport over the moorland tracks to the nearest towns, where the illegal imports eventually ended up in the drawing rooms of the rich eighteenth century folk who could afford their bits of tax-free luxury – wines and spirits, silk, lace, velvets, snuff and tobacco, tea, coffee and chocolate to name but a few. Careful planning and competent organization was essential at every stage of a run.

The fishing village of Robin Hood's Bay was an important centre for the smuggling trade on the Yorkshire coast. With its remote geographical location, hidden away in a deeply recessed coastline, its close-knit population of men and women with a life-time's knowledge of the dangerous tides, currents and rocks, and its unique higgledy-piggledy architecture, it was ideally situated to be a valuable and successful landing place. Although smuggling could be - and often was - violent, in many instances discretion became the better part of valour, and violence gave way to cunning and stealth which actually enabled greater quantities of goods to be moved in secret, and made life even more difficult for the Preventive service, who were vastly outnumbered, strangers to the area, poorly paid, and highly unpopular, lonely men.

Many of the events portrayed actually happened, though the main characters in the story are fictitious. Although they are not intended to represent any individual persons alive at that time, they do bear both Christian and surnames common in the village. A jealous rivalry was inherent for many years between the Storm family and the Dukes, so an event such as Thomas Duke's betrayal of Reuben could well have occurred.

Historical evidence suggests that other characters - Constable Jos Clarke, Riding Officers Peter Herbert and James Maxwell, and Captains Whitehead, Gillie, Ogilvie and Mitchell of the Revenue Cutters did actually exist, as did

Stoney Fagg, David Pinkney, Silas Biddick, Sandy Kellock, 'Big Isaac' McGraw, and Jiddy Vardy. Corporal Casseldine was later killed in a skirmish at Runswick Bay.

The sea battle in 1777 involving the *Kent* actually took place further down the coast, off Filey Brigg, but for the sake of added drama, has been located in Robin Hood's Bay, where there were many conflicts between smuggling vessels and Excise cutters.

John Wesley's visits, his words and thoughts, are adapted from his original Journals.

To assist in the recreation of an eighteenth century atmosphere, I have drawn extensively on local folklore, customs and superstitions that were widely believed in at the time. The text is mainly in narrative form with a minimum of dialogue, as excessive use of the local dialect of the time would be difficult for the reader of today, and to 'modernise' the speech would, I feel, lose the essential nature of the characters.

Patricia Labistour – Robin Hood's Bay – 2004.

Part One

Sleep just would not come. Damaris tossed and turned, counted sheep, recited poetry, but still could not settle. She sighed and rose from her tumbled bed, tiptoed over the chilly floor to the small dormer window, climbed onto a chair and knelt, leaning her arms on the window sill. Carefully drawing aside a corner of the bedroom curtain she gazed into the starlit sky, hoping the soothing and hypnotic movement of the gently heaving sea below would calm her overactive mind. From her small attic room in the stone cottage high above the waves she observed her own secret world, and considered the events of the day just past.

Her window commanded a view of a broad sweeping bay, enclosed on either side by great protective headlands. Northwards, the gentle arms of Bay Ness cradled the curve in which the village clung precariously to its cliff-edge setting. To the south, the contours of the spectacular promontory of Raven Hill reminded her of a sleeping lion. She had never actually seen a real one, but a woodcut illustration in a borrowed book had made a keen impression on her young mind. Her imaginary beast lay, benevolently somnolent, head resting on outstretched paws, though sometimes he snarled and foamed angrily at the mouth as winter storms raged over his feet and sent thundering spray showering skywards, but in summer's calm he slept peacefully, undisturbed by turbulent waves.

When gales howled outside so ferociously and roaring seas hurled themselves shore-wards, the juddering force of their impact on the cliff below her window rattled the handles on her furniture, and sent small stones and fragments of seaweed streaming down the glass. On many such occasions Damaris had become sleepless with anxiety for those sailors caught in the violent anger of the great sea god, Neptune. Salty blood of generations of seafarers coursed through her veins, instinctively stirring within her the anxious empathy and deep concern for their safety and well-being that was inherent in all Baytown women. Even the youngest were strangely uneasy during rough weather, and female babies slept fretfully until the storm had abated.

Propping her elbows on the windowsill and cupping her chin in her cold hands, Damaris glanced towards her lion's slumbrous profile, touched with the silver moonlight, and felt reassured. Although it was winter, the darkness was peacefully still and he slept quietly, so all was well.

Night was one of her favourite times for privately observing the world from her window. This evening, the whole earth seemed at ease. The sea was calm and beautiful in its tranquility. There was a sparkling sharpness in the air that somehow deepened the enchantment. A frosty full moon cast a shimmering silver path leading to the invisible space beyond the horizon. Slivers of silvery light spangled the tiny wave crests as they gently lapped and twinkled on the shore far below. On the horizon, the mast-head light of a schooner swayed gently on the swelling sea. Maybe it was one of the smuggling ships which often sailed into the Bay – perhaps the notorious *Kent* captained by the fearsome Stoney Fagg, of whom even her father stood in the greatest respect.

She would have stayed longer, fascinated by the awe-inspiring splendour of the moonlit seascape, but the night air chilled her and eventually the cold and tiredness coaxed an unwilling yawn. Reluctantly dropping the corner of the curtain, Damaris quickly crossed the cold floor on tiptoes and cuddled down under the cosy quilt, tucking her feet up into the folds of her long flannel nightgown, and enjoying the sensation of warmth gradually creeping up her cold legs. She carried on counting the sheep, and by the time the fiftieth ungainly animal had struggled its way over the imaginary fence, Damaris was fast asleep.

In summer time, she awoke to glorious golden mornings when the blazing orb of the sun rose majestically out of the sea, coruscating in a riot of colour, painting her world in the brilliant and vibrant hues that only the palette of nature can furnish without appearing tawdry. On such beautiful mornings she could barely wait to rush down to the shore and gambol in the freshness of the tiny toe-tingling wavelets as they chased her nimble feet in their playful game of catch-as-catch-can up and down the new-washed sand.

On bitter winter mornings, however, she coaxed herself unwillingly from her warm bed to scrape a small space in the delicate tracery the frost had engraved on her windows during the dark hours of the night. While she slept that magical artist, Jack Frost, created for her eyes alone scenes of a fabulous winter wonderland of fans and ferns and fairy forests. Her warm breath clearing a space, Damaris could peer through into the blinding purity of whiteness that overnight had transformed her world. From the eaves of her small dormer window hung great icicles resembling the great jagged teeth of sea monsters, evoking one of the familiar stories her father read from the huge family Bible. She knew such creatures existed, for there were some very scary pictures in the Bible, and she knew that the Bible did not lie.

On Sunday evenings Zack gathered the whole family round the table, the warm candlelight illuminating his rugged face, to listen to his deep fisherman's voice reading again all the greatly loved words of comfort and assurance. Some stories held excitement, and appealed to a vivid imagination, as did Damaris's own particular favourite, the tale of Jonah. When he had peered out from within the belly of the great whale, had he looked through a toothy barrier such as the one that confronted her on these icy cold mornings?

The heavy Bible was already a hundred years old, and its brown leather binding showed the signs of much wear. Its pages were well thumbed and dog-eared, and it fell open naturally at some of the most frequently read passages. Grubby marks underscored many of the longer words which had proved hard for less well educated ancestors to decipher. Damaris's sensitive mind recoiled at this unwitting desecration, yet at the same time understood the problems of unfamiliar reading. One of the lucky ones to have a basic schooling, Damaris physically felt the fingers of her forebears tracing these difficult words, syllable by syllable. Small treasures such as faded pressed flowers and little hand written notes hid within its venerable pages.

Inside the front cover, carefully and painstakingly inscribed in childlike and amateurish handwriting, were the names and birth and death dates of several generations of the family. The most recent name was Matthew's. Before the year was out, it was more than likely a new entry would be made, but whether this would be a birth or a death, no-one yet knew.

Damaris needed a good sleep, for the previous night had been seriously disturbed.

It must have been well past the witching hour of midnight when she was awakened by the subdued click of a carefully closing door. The slight sound was, however, enough to jar her from slumber, and alert her keen young ears to further disturbances - muffled voices, soft feet on cobble-stoned street outside, and secretive knockings and whistlings. She raised her head from the pillow and accustomed her eyes to the darkness. A faint light from the moon shone through the open curtains, silvering the room with stark cold shadows. Fully awake, Damaris got out of bed and crept on chilly bare feet into her younger brother Matthew's room. Matt was sound asleep in the traditional seafarer's box bed, occupied long ago by the uncle after whom he was named; the Matthew Storm who had died in tragic circumstances on board the Royal Navy ship, *Marlborough* back in 1746. His father, Zachariah Storm, had lost both his older brothers following their capture by the Press Gang and enforced service on board His Majesty's ships. The news of Christopher Storm's death on board *Lennox* in 1741 heralded much sad news for their parents. Isaac and Rebecca feared greatly for the safety of their one remaining son, Damaris and Matt's father, Zachariah.

Young Matthew dreamed often of his brave sailor uncle, drifting off to sleep imagining that this bunk bed that bound the two Matthews close in spirit was a great ship setting sail on the wide oceans of the world on dangerous voyages of discovery. He was far away on the high seas of dreamland, a tumbled heap under the warm patchwork coverlet whose multi-coloured fabrics, holding man memories of past generations, covered the sleeping boy in his storm-tossed slumbers. When they were both younger, brother and sister listened enthralled as their mother identified the scraps which made up the quilt. With dreams in her eyes she always let her fingers rest lovingly on one special patch of pale blue figured with pink rosebuds. 'This is the dress I wore when your father asked me to marry him. That was such a happy day! This is part of my wedding dress, and that your grandmother Rebecca's Sunday skirt. This,' she pointed to a startling scarlet satin of gipsy hue, 'belonged to Jennet when I first knew her,' and so on, the reminiscences fascinating the two young children.

However, just at this particular moment, Damaris had no thoughts of the past, for the present was far too exciting.

'Matt! Psst! Wake up!' Damaris shook his shoulder urgently, and hastily pressed her finger on his protesting lips. 'Listen, Matt!' Damaris's sky blue eyes held Matt's, deep brown and fathomless as the rock pools they loved to explore. Both harboured hidden wonders in their depths; the pools held secrets of fish and sea anemone; Matt's eyes guarded the mysteries of his own private thoughts.

He too could hear the muffled whisperings downstairs. Pulling the quilt from his bed, he and Damaris crouched, huddled with ears close to a crack in the floor, hugging the coverlet, still warm from his disturbed slumbers, tightly round their shivering bodies. Shivering not only from the penetrating cold of the winter night, but with excitement. Both were old enough to know exactly what was going on down below, and too wise to ask awkward questions. Neither would they comment on the footprints in the fresh snow which led away from their front door first thing in the morning when no member of their own family had yet been outside. The gathering down in their cottage parlour was none other than a clandestine meeting of smugglers.

During the daytime village life carried on with its humdrum tasks of fishing or farming, shopping and trading, but when night fell and enveloped the isolated community in its veil of secrecy, life changed dramatically and dangerously as undercover activities got under way. The business of bringing goods ashore silently and secretly to avoid the heavy and unpopular taxes, was honed to a fine art on this lonely stretch of coast. Yorkshiremen were known for their ingenuity and were well versed in the practices of the smuggling trade. Damaris's own village was at its very heart.

Indistinct muffled voices, shufflings, heavy thuds, indicated that such a gang was meeting at that very moment, right there in the house of Zack Storm. Brother and sister stealthily moved across and uncovered the trap door hidden beneath a small rug on the bare pinewood boards of Matt's bedroom floor. Carefully rolling back the rush mat they exposed the concealed fastener of the heavy wooden hatch-cover. Silently the two children eased it back to reveal a dark, gaping hole, empty now, but frequently containing all manner of strangely shaped parcels and boxes. At the bottom a beam of pale candlelight flickered faintly through a chink in the ceiling boards.

A strong whiff of tobacco drifted up in the candle smoke. Damaris and Matthew could now identify at least two of the voices conferring in subdued tones immediately below.

One was undeniably the familiar gruff voice of their father, Zachariah Storm, a voice they both loved and feared. Zack was a man of fickle moods, as changeable as the sea that gave him his livelihood; at times all calm and sunny and laughing, then with little warning, storm clouds could gather and they would be lashed with his anger. Matthew and Damaris had long since learned to read the signs in their father's facial expressions and behaved accordingly. Zack was well surnamed. His stormy moods were definitely best avoided.

A lighter, younger, more gentle voice floated up through the chink in the ceiling. Damaris was glad of the darkness that hid the faint blush which, unbidden, suffused her fair cheeks as she recognised the voice of Reuben Granger. Reuben was a sturdy, strikingly good-looking young man, a direct descendant of the bold Viking race which had once invaded this part of the coast; big, ruthless strangers, landing from fearsome dragon-ships, wearing great horned helmets on their arrogant heads. People fled in fear of their lives from these tall and terrifying aggressors. Dwellings were moved to safer places inland, where hidden amongst the hollows and trees on the hillsides above the Bay, they could look out across the wide waters to the distant horizon and have warning of these devastating attacks. In due course peace returned and the villagers could once again go back to their homes by the shore, close to their work, and live in comparative safety. However, traces of the Nordic culture still lingered in the local dialect, with Scandinavian words forming parts of the everyday speech. The rocky 'scaurs' still jutted out to sea, 'Staup' Brow was just as steep, and the ancient manor of Fygeling still stood central to the life of the farming community, although it took its name from the Scandinavian for the taking of the sea-fowl which featured large in their diets. Their heritage of the long-ships lingered in the design of the traditional fishing boat, the coble. With its clinker-built bulging curves for stability, its proudly rising prow, and its twin-keeled flat bottom, it was ideally suited for beaching in the shallow waters of these sandy shores. The visible Viking inheritance remained in the people, a handsome fair-haired, blue-eyed race, rightful descendants of the fierce but handsome invaders.

Reuben was such a one, his fair good looks being the cause of many a wistful sigh from the young women of the village. Damaris was just becoming old enough to feel disturbed by her attraction to the handsome man in the room downstairs. She didn't want this uncomfortable beating of her heart and the embarrassing flush that flamed like fire on her young cheeks every time she saw him. She wanted to stay free of such feelings and retain her childhood innocence, but nature was taking its unstoppable course and undoubtedly Damaris was growing up. One of the physical consequences was the effect of her attraction to young Reuben. A wave of unreasonable jealousy swept through her as she recognised amongst the hubbub of male voices the low, sultry, very feminine laugh of Jiddy Vardy. Matt heard it also and poked Damaris violently in the ribs. If Jiddy was there, then serious business was afoot.

Jiddy's dark, exotic beauty and the mysterious circumstances surrounding her arrival in Baytown created a romantic charisma that provoked mixed feelings of admiration and resentment. The fair-haired maidens of this cold northern land envied Jiddy's glossy long hair, black as a raven's wing, her sloe-dark eyes, sun-warmed Mediterranean skin, and tall athletic figure. Married women eyed her with suspicion, issuing their husbands with dire threats if they became involved with this bewitching gypsy. Many Baytown men stoically suffered their wives' displeasure as they defiantly continued to associate in the company of this extraordinary and brave woman. The jealous ones may have curbed their anger if they had only understood the real nature of Jiddy's friendship with their men folk. Could they but have known the true facts, many would have indeed realised that they owed their husbands' very lives to Jiddy's courage and ingenuity.

Her sudden arrival as a young girl in the home of an elderly childless couple had caused tongues to wag in an unprecedented flurry of speculative gossip. As far as could be established, her childhood had been both eventful and sad. Her dark Latin good looks were inherited from her mother, a beautiful Italian girl named Vardarelli, who had arrived in England as companion to a French noblewoman on a visit to the Court of King George II. The lovely Signorina had caused quite a stir in the palace of the King. When plans for her secret elopement with a wealthy English Count were discovered, the man was banished on some trivial mission, and Signorina Vardarelli left behind with a baby daughter. The King's Court being no place for a squalling baby, the infant was promptly removed to an orphanage from which she was apparently kidnapped and held to ransom by someone who had discovered her unusual background. Plans going awry, mystery hung over the intervening years until her unexplained arrival in the area some time later. The elderly couple with whom she now lived would never speak of how they came to take her in as a housemaid. One thing was certain, however, that it had been a favourable wind that had blown her in to the lives of the people of Baytown, and there they let the matter rest.

Jiddy's aristocratic background had bred in her an instinctive feel for the better things of life. Quickly developing a natural skill with her needle, she was in great demand in all the big houses for dressmaking and sewing jobs. Her astute mind learned to listen discreetly, thereby gaining her much secret and useful knowledge.

Contented living with the kind old couple, she was more than happy that her earnings with needle and thread enabled her to supplement their meagre income. Jiddy grew tall and fit and very athletic, caring not a toss for the attentions of the men folk, though she would flirt and tease them with the other village girls in their playful games. She was well aware of her sexual attraction, but knowledge of the plight of her mother had hardened her against becoming too involved with men.

She developed a fierce loyalty to these people and many of those deeply involved in the smuggling activities had cause to be grateful to her keen ear, sharp eye, and wise discretion.

Damaris frequently chatted with Jiddy when she brought her beautiful off-cuts of fabrics left from her sewing of fine garments. Damaris had a quick skill with her own needle and these scraps became useful gifts for her mother and dresses for her own favourite doll, a stiff, wooden creature with a flat face painted with a staring expression, full of character but certainly no beauty. She envied the daughter of the local Squire who proudly showed off an exquisite porcelain doll from France, bedecked in silk and fine Valenciennes lace, just like the rich ladies at Court. Emma Farsyde was very smug about her doll, boasting that it was a present from her father, smuggled in from France and given as a reward for keeping quiet about his involvement with the 'Gentlemen.' Damaris thought, 'Mm, she's not keeping very quiet about how she got that doll. Just as well we all know about her father, anyway!'

Young though she was, Damaris had long ago learned the wisdom of discretion.

She would certainly need to be discreet in the morning, and keep the knowledge of their night's eavesdropping strictly between herself and her brother. Although much younger than his sister, Matt's loyalty was unquestioned and Damaris was grateful for his close and trustworthy companionship. Physically, the brother and sister were as different as the proverbial chalk and cheese. Matt, like his father, was tough, dark-haired and chunky, Damaris blue and gold and pretty as an angel, the apple of her father's eye. Zack puzzled over the fair beauty of his daughter, for her mother was also dark like himself. Obviously way back, Scandinavian blood ran in the family, and this maybe partially accounted for Damaris's strong attraction to Reuben, almost as if in a past life they were close blood kin.

Below in the parlour the candlelight flickered on the scrap of paper Jiddy produced from her pocket and laid on the table before Zack, Reuben, and a third man, a local sea captain, David Pinkney. Jiddy's dark eyes looked piercingly at David, who whistled through his teeth as he read its contents. David's wife Abigail was Jiddy's closest friend, so she felt especially thankful to bring this important information to his attention.

That afternoon Jiddy had been sewing at the home of Mrs. Clarke, wife of the Constable of Baytown. Although a good customer who paid Jiddy generously and promptly for her services, Arabella Clarke was still on the other side, that of the Revenue and Preventive men stationed in the village. During her session of sewing and mending, Jiddy had been asked to repair a tear in the uniform coat of Constable Clarke which had certainly been caused by a scuffle with an escaping smuggler. Feeling something stiff in the pocket,

Jiddy removed it. Glancing guiltily towards the door, she quickly unfolded the parchment. Her eyes opened wide at the words of the boldly written heading, '*Warrant for the Arrest of David Pinkney.*'

She silently blessed her ability to both read and write, a fact perhaps overlooked by Arabella Clarke who had left her alone with her work. Not many ordinary girls were so educated, but then, Jiddy was no ordinary girl.

Dated 6 January 1774, the condemning document stated that Pinkney was to be prosecuted for 'obstructing the Officers of the Revenue in their duty.' The accompanying letter informed that Pinkney was now at his home in Robin Hood's Town and should be apprehended and sent for trial without further delay. Jiddy's quick eye scanned this information before she carefully folded and replaced the paper in Constable Clarke's pocket. In her sewing bag, Jiddy kept her own note-book in which she sketched her customers' fashionable requirements and entered up their accounts. At the back were several pages in a special secret code which made sense to Jiddy's eyes alone. Here she made a coded copy of the information just revealed, and hastily re-buried the notebook under a pile of silks and cottons. It was the transcription of this vital note which now lay on the table before Pinkney's own astonished eyes.

Constable Josiah Clarke sat at an imposing oak desk in the front room that served as his office. He lived in a large property in the better part of Baytown as befitted a man of his important status. His house, like most of the others was built from sandstone, carried down by horse and cart from the quarry in the north cliffs, each stone carefully dressed with the herring-bone pattern so familiar to local stone masons. The strong roof timbers and heavy ceiling beams had sailed the seven seas before the ships from which they had been salvaged were wrecked on the rocky shores of the Bay. Three storeys high and built on rising ground, the attic rooms gave Constable Clarke a useful viewpoint over much of his territory. The house was neat and well kept and exuded an air of prosperous authority which reflected his position of Town Constable. Mrs. Clarke was proud of her husband's efforts in attempting to exercise some control over the lawless smuggling community amongst whom their current duties lay. She held herself aloof and greeted the village women with a disdainful sniff.

Constable Clarke drummed his fingers impatiently, idly traced the heavy grain of the old oak surface, and looked at his watch with an annoyed frown. They were two minutes late already. Jos Clarke demanded total dedication to duty and punctuality was high on his list of priorities. He turned back to the Warrant spread out before him and smoothed it with his stocky fingers. David Pinkney. At last! High time that trouble-maker was put away. For years Pinkney had cunningly avoided all Clarke's efforts to have him apprehended. Here, surely, lay the Warrant which, if carried out competently, would rid him of this sea-faring pest for some time at least if not, hopefully, for ever. A shadow of doubt flickered momentarily across his furrowed brow. 'Efficiency' was the key word in his thoughts. Would his men bungle the arrest yet again?

A firm knock resounded on Constable Clarke's front door. Voices exchanged greetings, and feet stamped to remove snow from boots. Footsteps approached down the flag-stoned hallway. A firm rat-tat on the office door heralded the arrival of the two men Constable Clarke awaited with such impatience. He welcomed them with restrained courtesy. The task ahead of them all would not be easy, and he needed their full support.

'Ah! Maxwell. Herbert. Come in.' Slowly and deliberately he took a large watch from his straining waistcoat pocket and looked at it rather pointedly. 'You are a trifle late, but no matter. Sit ye down and have a look at this.'

The Riding Officers pulled out two stout chairs, knocked the remaining snow from their high leather boots, flicked out their uniform coat-tails and sat down at the other side of Constable Clarke's impressive desk. He pushed the Warrant for the Arrest of David Pinkney towards them with a gesture that combined satisfaction with a degree of anxiety.

Jos leaned back in his chair, tipping it precariously on its two rear legs towards the blazing fire. Placing his stocky hands together, stubby fingers resting thoughtfully against his lips, he observed the two men now poring intently over the document.

Peter Maxwell and James Herbert did not have an easy time of it in this wretched place, and neither did he, thought Jos Clarke. He was comfortable enough in his nice home with a pleasant and obedient wife who ran his household smoothly. They both fed well and grew plump as Christmas chickens from the presents - he refused to recognise them as bribes - which he frequently found on his doorstep with cryptic little notes, some of which gave him more information than the anonymous sender intended. After many years of experience in such matters Jos Clarke had become very expert at reading between the lines.

But the fact remained that he and the two men now facing him were employed by the hated Revenue department. Their job was to prevent smuggling, seize contraband goods, and seek to arrest the perpetrators of this illegal activity. Constable Clarke's very position meant that he had to maintain a degree of aloofness from the rest of the community, so he and Arabella his wife led largely lonely and self-centred lives.

Maxwell and Herbert were somewhat more impervious to their situation as they were not confined to the one place. As Riding Officers they each had a wide area to cover and hostile terrain most of it was, too. The countryside which they patrolled was bleak, especially in winter with the already treacherous moorland's numerous bogs swathed in impenetrable mists, scythed with icy winds which cut through the warmest cloaks, or obliterated into a blinding Arctic wilderness of deep snow. Such roads as traversed the inhospitable environment were merely tracks; narrow delves hardly wide enough to accommodate the wheels of a cart. At best, the stretches of pack horse road were lines of flagstones, only one paver wide, which carried the trains of pannier ponies to and from the principal places in the transportation of goods, legal or otherwise.

Already in use for several hundred years, these pack roads and ancient monks' trods were in a sad state of disrepair, causing danger to both horse and rider especially during the hours of darkness which was when the Riding Officers most often found themselves in this bleak wilderness in pursuit of their duties. Many times had they written complaining that their lives and those of their horses were frequently endangered. Certainly their territory was not an easy one to patrol. The land was hostile and the villages under their supervision equally problematical. Many were almost impossible. Rabbit warrens of narrow cobbled streets and steep slippery steps often led to dead-ends or to the very edge of the cliff where a fast-running man could easily plunge to his death. Maxwell and Herbert had been stationed around Baytown for long enough to have discovered the most serious hazards, but for a newly appointed officer without that local knowledge, it was veritably a potential death-trap.

Maxwell looked up from the Warrant in front of him and cleared his throat with a discreet cough that jerked Constable Clarke back from his wandering thoughts.

'Err...hmm. Well, gentlemen? Have we got him at last? We have this Authority, certainly, but have we the means to carry it out? At present, as you will be only too well aware, there are just the three of us in this god-forsaken spot. The Dragoons that I have sent for from York will not be here for some days yet, and this matter cannot wait that long. We must act tonight or the slippery character will dodge us yet again.'

The officers consulted together. They would certainly have preferred to delay the arrest of Captain Pinkney until armed reinforcements had arrived. From time to time, when the smuggling activities were at their worst, the local Preventives were assisted by soldiers from the barracks at York. These men were billeted in the villages and it was one of Constable Clarke's awkward duties to ensure that the officers were accommodated comfortably in the homes of local residents. As most were up to the neck in the current illegal activity, they were not over pleased to suddenly find a military man at their dining table.

Maxwell and Herbert could hardly speak their inner thoughts in front of Constable Clarke, but they exchanged significantly knowing glances. In each other's eyes they read the unspoken thought that the arrest of David Pinkney would be virtually their affair alone. They were young active men, kept fit by their daily rides and pursuits round a countryside that was a formidable training ground for the fleetest athlete.

Not so Constable Clarke who spent much of his day behind his desk, fed far too well and was consequently too fat for fast chases round the steep alleyways of Baytown. The successful arrest of the devious Captain Pinkney depended entirely on secrecy and cunning. He was a violent man, not easily physically overcome and not easy to discover alone, which they must do, otherwise they would be outnumbered and overpowered. This campaign would need very careful planning indeed and more than a modicum of good luck.

The three heads bent together to devise a plan. Each realised the importance of executing this Warrant, but all of them appreciated the dangers and difficulties this would entail. Pinkney was not a character to be trifled with lightly, and the scheme needed to be carefully thought out.

It was not until some time afterwards that they rose from the table, grasped each others hands in farewell, and arranged to meet later that evening at the hour when they anticipated Pinkney and his friends would be leaving their favourite public house, The Mariners Inn in the Square, hopefully somewhat unsteady of foot after an evening of hard drinking.

The door closed behind the Riding Officers, their dark blue cloaks merged quickly into the dusk, and Constable Clarke sat down to the substantial tea that Arabella had so competently provided.

The home of Captain David Pinkney reflected the sea-faring background of its owner. In his garden the remains of an old upturned boat, no longer seaworthy, served as a chicken hut where Abigail kept a flock of plump brown hens, lorded over by a proud and colourful cockerel who woke the entire neighbourhood with his bold morning crowing. By the door a couple of oars lay propped in a corner, an old ship's figurehead from a vessel wrecked on the treacherous shores of the Bay adorned his front porch, and a brass porthole, polished to a gleaming shine by Abigail, winked back the pale gold beams of the wintry sunlight and gave those within a circular view of the world on the other side. The door itself, of stout mahogany, had once led to a cabin on some beautiful white-sailed ship that had traversed the globe before meeting its doom on the rocks below Captain Pinkney's home. Abigail's bright curtains were spotlessly clean and the old blemished glass in her windows sparkled with the care of a proud housewife's hand. Colourful pot plants adorned her windowsills, peeping between the curtains in curving poses of curiosity. David Pinkney may be a rough diamond but his home bore the stamp of a man of some fair fortune and it was no secret how he came by his money.

This late January afternoon the light was fading rapidly. Smoke began to rise from fires being stoked up to provide a cosy warmth on this cold winter's evening. Tall chimney pots and roof tops were starkly silhouetted against the strong colours of the setting sun. A crisp nip in the air foretold an early frost.

The home of the swashbuckling sea captain was a hive of noisy activity. In the back yard young Reuben Granger busily sawed large chunks of wood from a stack in the corner. To unsuspecting eyes he was merely preparing firewood. Any keen observer would notice that he was cutting to given measurements. From time to time Zachariah Storm emerged from the cottage and carried inside the pieces

Reuben had sawn up. Sounds of hammering echoed down the alleyway where Pinkney's house was closely surrounded by his neighbours.

A pleasant smell of warm bran wafted from the steaming pan of hot mash which Abigail carried into the darkening garden to feed her chickens.

'Now then, Abigail!' called out Mrs. Baxter from next door. 'What's goin' on? All that bangin' and hammerin'! A body can't think straight for all t'noise an' commotion.' Mrs. Baxter was well known for her inquisitive nature. You didn't find things out unless you poked your nose into all your neighbours' affairs and her notable curiosity was certainly keenly aroused this particular afternoon.

'Why, Ah'm sorry tha's bein' disturbed, Ah'm sure, Mrs. Baxter. But it's like this, y' see.....Davy is away back to sea on the mornin' tide, and he nivver got me new cupboards fitted - and if they'm not finished by t'time 'e sets sail timorrer, gawd knows how long he'll be away, and Ah shall be fallin' ovver bits of wood for weeks on end, so Reub an' Zack 'ave come to give 'im a hand ti get t'job fettled.' Abigail felt quite smugly pleased at the way this plausible story had fallen so naturally from her lips, smiling with quiet satisfaction as Mrs. Baxter nodded her head and turned to go indoors. 'So tha sees, Mrs. Baxter, it'll all be done wi' very soon, and tha won't be disturbed to'neet.'

Abigail was not to know that the latter statement would be proved not quite correct.

Near chaos reigned inside the normally neat cottage, as the three men hurried to put the finishing touches to the barricades. The windows were firmly nailed and heavy furniture piled against the door. No-one would enter David Pinkney's home without a struggle.

On cold winter nights most cottagers closed the shutters over their windows, both for safety and to keep out the piercing easterly draughts which blew directly at the village straight across the German Ocean, so no one thought it strange when, as the last of the daylight faded, Zack and Reuben came out and closed the shutters firmly, calling out loudly, 'See thee at t'Mariners, Davy, aboot eight o'clock!' This was part of their careful plan, that the neighbours were to believe that David had gone to the inn as was usual on his last night before a long sea voyage, whereas he would actually be safely in his barricaded home alone with his brave young wife.

David and Abigail sat companionably together by the fire and waited. Thanks to Abigail's friendship with Jiddy Vardy, David knew exactly what fate had awaited him. He now felt forewarned and ready for anybody and anything.

'Tha's gotten a reet grand friend in Jiddy, Abbie! It were a fair good job that owd Jos ripped his coat. Ah'd like to think that Arabella knew nowt about t'Warrant bein' in his pocket all t'tahm.' He nodded his head in approval, and grinned cheekily. 'My, she's a reet sharp lass is Jiddy, and canny too, to read an' write, and put all them notes down in secret code. Pity Ah'm married ti thee – she'd mek a fair wife, would Jiddy!' He winked at Abbie. David's admiration for Jiddy was all too evident, but Abigail was not one of the jealous young wives who feared faithless philanderings.

According to plan, Constable Clarke met Peter Maxwell and James Herbert in a dark corner of The Square, in sight of the doorway of The Mariners Tavern. Hidden from view, they pulled coat collars high round their ears, partly for concealment but mainly to ward off the piercingly bitter winds which penetrated every fibre of their beings. Maxwell had never been so cold in his life. His nose felt like an icicle, his fingers were numb and he had long since forgotten that he'd ever had any feet at all. After an hour or so, Constable Clarke relaxed his rigid rules of duty and produced a hip flask full of neat brandy. Maxwell and Herbert exchanged amused glances. Here they were, freezing to death on duty, waiting to catch a brandy-smuggling sea captain yet drinking the stuff themselves. The ironic humour of the situation caused a wry smile in spite of their discomforts and they declined to query Constable Clarke's possession of the illicit spirit, but drank gratefully, feeling its comforting warmth slowly penetrating their frozen insides. They pushed aside growing feelings of envy for the drinkers within the merry public house, warmed by the blazing fire and cheerful in their companionship. The time passed unconscionably slowly as the three officers waited patiently for the revellers to leave and weave their unsteady ways homewards. Gradually, one by one they departed, each one keenly scrutinised by the watching officers who were now completely on their guard, alert and ready to rush forward and grab their victim. In the narrow alleyway leading from the inn, they would have no trouble in cornering him and pinning him against the wall, as long as they were quick and silent, and took him completely by surprise. Each of them knew Pinkney well by sight and would have no difficulty in identifying him even at this distance and in the dark. A faint glow, casting sufficient light to recognise familiar faces, spread itself across the snow-laden ground every time the door opened as a seafarer decided it was time he staggered home to his bed. In their concealed corner, Clarke, Maxwell and Herbert closely observed the features of each departing drinker. Not one of them was Pinkney.

Midnight passed and the last customer had gone. The publican closed his doors and extinguished his candles and lanterns. The three officers were plunged into total darkness as he doused the final light. Well! Dammit! They turned angrily on one another, furiously disbelieving that they had stood so long in the perishing cold to no avail. Numbed anger overtook reason as each accused the others for losing concentration and letting him slip through their fingers. It dawned on them that Pinkney had not been in The Mariners at all, but must have been at home all evening. They would have to act quickly for it was an early tide that morning. Whilst they had been idiotically standing freezing in the darkness Pinkney might well be already on his way to catch his ship to sail on the morning ebb, craftily dodging them yet again. What utter fools they felt, all too conscious of how he must be laughing up his sleeve.

Annoyance roused the three to action. Furiously they charged down the dark narrow alleyway to where Pinkney's house stood firm and square, end on. Jos held up a warning hand, and James and Peter flattened themselves against the wall, as they carefully closed in on their target. All was suspiciously quiet within. Maxwell's keen eye detected a slight movement of the curtain at the bedroom window. Moonlight glinted momentarily on the cold metal barrel of a shotgun. Before he had time to warn Herbert and Constable Clarke, a tremendous flash and explosion shattered the silent blackness of the night. The three men dived for cover, and instantaneously Mrs. Baxter's astonished face appeared at her window. Her lantern illuminated an incredulous face topped with straggly grey hair done up in curling papers so as to be fashionably smart at church on Sunday.

James squealed as a bullet grazed his cheek. Clapping his handkerchief over the stinging wound, he shook his fist angrily, and shouted, 'I'll have thee for attempted murder – then thou'll hang, thou blaggard!'

Jos Clarke was the first to emerge from his undignified position behind Abigail's chicken hut, the startled occupants fluttering indignantly and clucking wildly within. Remembering his position of authority and his confidence boosted by the feel of the official parchment in his pocket he dusted himself down, cleared his throat and called out in his most officious and self-important voice, 'Captain Pinkney! I have here a Warrant for your arrest. In the name of His Majesty King George, you are commanded to come forth and deliver yourself into my keeping.'

Pinkney replied with a further defiant barrage from his shotgun, an invective of blistering language and a challenging, arrogant laugh. 'Come and get me, then! What's keeping thee? Art afraid?' he taunted. Bang! The gun went off and more bullets whizzed past the cowering officers.

An agonized squawk, a battering of panicked wings in the chicken hut, and a flurry of feathers from the hole in the roof indicated that Pinkney had made a kill, but not as he intended. Abigail would be upset, but he might have shot the enemy. Perhaps as well for him that his shot misfired, or he would be up for murder. At that moment, however, he was so incensed that he did not care. He fired again, this time more carefully.

Peter Maxwell and James Herbert, highly embarrassed, had had enough of this farce. Miraculously still alive and uninjured, they preferred to stay that way. Although under the orders of the Town Constable, secretly they each wondered whether Jos Clarke was truly aware of the significant danger in which his pomposity had placed them. Captain Pinkney had proved time and time again that he was not a character to be trifled with. Stumbling across the garden, keeping close under cover, they joined Constable Clarke and agreed that to stay endangered all their lives. If they were blasted to pieces that would do no one any good, least of all themselves. They had suffered a near miss, James had been injured and mopped the blood from his cheek. Wisdom, caution and a degree of relief prevailing, they retreated with as much dignity as they could muster, to the Constable's comfortable office where the three of them drafted a face-saving letter to their superiors in London. David Pinkney's arrogant abuse followed them until they were out of earshot. The last they heard was a very coarse laugh, and some very insulting language, referring to their cowardice and their dubious parentage.

Safely out of gunshot range, the three officers regained some measure of composure, and in the comfort of Jos's home, where Arabella offered a warming drink, confidence returned, and they discussed their report.

Jos Clarke dipped his quill pen in his ink pot and boldly wrote the words 'Warrant Not Executed' across the fateful document and thus began the letter which explained that Captain Pinkney had already put to sea, therefore he was unable to deliver the summons, and recommended that a new Warrant be made out to await his return. By that time the Dragoons would have arrived from York, so next time they really would get him. Behind the safety of his desk, a roaring log fire warming his back, Jos Clarke was filled with a new and determined courage.

James and Peter bade Jos goodnight, and left with a feeling of frustration. With the proper strong support they could have got Pinkney, they were quite certain. This was an ignominious failure, and they would have to face the sniggers from the rest of the village, as for sure, the tale would spread and become wildly exaggerated. Still, they shrugged their shoulders philosophically. It was all part of the nature of the job.

Abigail's chickens shuffled their feathers and settled down to roost, some still clucking in a complaining fashion, and in their own way grieving over their dead comrade. Mrs. Baxter extinguished her lantern and returned to bed, delightedly anticipating the tale she would tell in the morning, and David and Abigail raised their glasses in a toast to the resourceful courage of Jiddy Vardy.

Damaris and Matthew had both been woken out of their sleep with a startled, heart-thumping jump. The explosive sound of Pinkney's shot-gun reverberated throughout the close-packed village, rousing everyone except the very old, stone deaf, and the past generations now sleeping their long undisturbed rest in the ancient churchyard on the hill.

Curiosity made further sleep impossible for some time, as they lay in the dark in their warm beds, imagining the scenes outside, wondering what was happening.

Impatiently Damaris waited for the long hours to pass until the faint grey dawn gradually lightened the black sky behind her curtains and the homely sounds of early morning activities began in the kitchen below, where Elizabeth now occupied herself with cooking the family's breakfast.

Zack was already preparing for the day's fishing. His workshop held piles of nets, lobster pots, fishing gear, tools, and many more useful and interesting things. Beneath his piles of clutter was concealed the trapdoor which led down to the cellar, a mysterious place whose contents changed most noticeably and frequently. Matt and Damaris were not supposed to know too much about the subterranean room. Zack wisely believed it was safer that way. He was unaware how much knowledge of his activities his children really did have. Realisation would have caused him intense worry, for the children's awareness could make them very vulnerable, and the thought of them being harmed for his sake was unbearable.

Damaris finally decided she could get up. She jumped more eagerly than usual from under her warm quilt, wincing as her bare feet touched the chilly uncarpeted floor. She quickly pulled on a pair of thick hand-knitted stockings, before dabbling her face and hands in the freezing cold water that stood in the pretty rose-patterned jug and bowl on the delicate little pine wash-stand in the corner of her room. It was far too cold for a proper wash - besides, exciting news awaited her downstairs. Anticipation dulled her sense of discomfort as she removed the flannel night-gown and pulled a warm petticoat and soft woollen dress over her head. The quick fingers of one hand smoothed her corn gold hair, tucking the long strands neatly behind her ears, whilst the free hand fumbled clumsily with the laces in her black ankle boots. Why did the wretched things always knot themselves when she was in such a hurry? Impatiently she tugged and pulled and finally tied the laces in a neat bow and clattered excitedly down the stairs.

The sounds of her parents' guarded conversation greeted her as she entered the warm kitchen with its glowing fire and glorious smell of fresh baking bread. Elizabeth worked domestic magic in that small oven, and her family were always well fed and well kept. Their subdued laughter was cut short as they regarded the figure of their daughter in the kitchen doorway. An awkward silence was only momentary, as Elizabeth turned to Damaris and gave her a quick good-morning hug. Zack turned away to busy himself at the table and to hide the wide grin that would not be suppressed.

Damaris could wait no longer to ask her question. 'What was that shot in the night, Da? It woke me and Matt and we couldn't sleep.'

Zack turned to his daughter, the smile now controlled, but the irrepressible twinkle still in his eye. 'Why, lass, nowt for thee to worry about. T'would only be somebody shootin' vermin.' Zack patted Damaris on the head, and burst out laughing at his own joke. 'Hear that, Liz? Shootin' vermin! Good, eh?' and he thumped the table in his delighted glee. There was no question that Zack knew just what had been going on and no doubt whatever as to whose side he was on.

As James and Peter knew only too well, and often to their embarrassment, Baytown was notorious for its gossip and rumour. Tales frequently grew wildly out of hand in the re-telling from neighbour to neighbour. The truth of the gunshots of the past night was only known to those immediately concerned but the curious Mrs. Baxter had seen enough from her bedroom window to assert her complete authority in the entire matter, so this bright, sharp Sunday morning she revelled in being the centre of attention. Her best black bonnet with its waving feather nodded vigorously as she repeatedly related her adventures to a growing group of fascinated listeners. By the third telling Mrs. Baxter was well into her narrative stride. With each telling the story gained new facts from her fertile imagination. By the end of the morning it was more than likely she would have all participants rumoured shot to death.

The buzz of excited conversation hushed, and the jostling group of gossips scattered guiltily as the preacher was observed arriving on his horse to begin the Sunday morning service. Rapidly gathering decorum, they obediently entered the small chapel, took their customary places and bowed their heads in prayer. Sneaking sideways glances across to where Constable Clarke and Arabella sat with stony faces and averted eyes, a few sniggers were hastily turned into coughs, muffled with gloves and handkerchiefs and hidden behind prayer books which suddenly appeared to take on an unusual degree of interest. Arabella Clarke's long nose proudly raised itself in one of her customary disdainful sniffs. What if her husband had failed in his duty - yet again? He was, in her eyes at least, a very brave man to even attempt tackling these lawless hooligans single handed. Maxwell and Herbert's part in the matter meant little to Arabella, and she felt a sense of triumph as she glanced round the assembled congregation. Abigail Pinkney, the impudent hussy, had not dared show her face. Arabella did not know that the courageous Abigail was still removing the barricades from her home, the slight damage they had caused being a small price to pay for David's safety and freedom. Thanks to Jiddy's invaluable information, by now David's ship was away on the high seas and far from the threats of Constable Clarke and his unexecuted Warrant.

Arabella felt an indignant smart as the memory of her discomfort still rankled. On her way to chapel this morning, a few of the bolder young women had insolently offered either their sympathy on the serious shotgun injuries or their admiration of Constable Clarke's unimaginable bravery. One neighbour, believing Mrs. Baxter's now wildly exaggerated 'eye witness account' had even genuinely approached Arabella with condolences on the death of her husband. 'Such a gallant, brave man,' she had commiserated, mopping the tears from her eyes with a somewhat grubby handkerchief. Arabella was outraged. It was all just too much. She was vastly relieved when the preacher entered the pulpit and announced the singing of the sailors' Psalm 'They that go down to the sea in ships and do business in great waters, these see the works of the Lord and His wonders in the deep,' with which they traditionally began their morning worship, and many anxious prayers flooded from the congregation for the safe return of those in peril on the sea.

Jiddy, Zack and Reuben exchanged glances from under their lowered eyelids. It was plain with whom their thoughts lay this Sunday morning.

The salty blood of seafarers had flowed through the veins of many generations of Bay folk. A close-knit community drawn together by the trials and tribulations of their perilous occupations, they wrested a hard living from the treacherous northern sea which could give generously of its rich harvest of fish, and just as easily take with casual vengeance both man and boat. An unpredictable environment at the best of times, at its worst the sea was a formidable opponent. Bay's fishermen learnt to read its subtlest change of mood and treat it with the greatest respect.

In the good times, a reasonable living could be made from the catch and sale of the plentiful fish, and an air of cheerfulness pervaded the village. The strong odour from fish hanging on racks on the fronts of cottages to dry for supplying long-voyaging vessels indicated prosperity.

In the bad times, the community drew close in its adversity. Tragedies hit not only the immediate families concerned, but the entire population, with grief shared, support generously given and gratefully accepted. Almost all Baytown families had their share of sadness caused by accidents at sea, whether close in shore or on world-wide voyages from which many of the men never returned. Their losses, as borne out by the poignant inscriptions on the ancient tombstones in the churchyard, were stoically accepted as a hard fact of life and death.

Matt and Damaris had grown up to share in this mutual understanding of their neighbours. It was a strange binding together, one which could be at one moment warm and loving, yet change with the swiftness of the wind with a thoughtless word or careless action into jealous feuding. A breach which miraculously healed when need or trouble enveloped a family. There was, however, an enduring hostility between Damaris' family, the Storms, and their rivals, the Dukes, an aggravation which sometimes blazed into bitter quarrels and at others merely niggled with petty jealousies.

However, this Sunday morning, the community had drawn together in support of their own kind against the unwelcome intrusion of the Preventive men.

Damaris and Matthew enjoyed Sundays, pleasantly spending the hour after morning service before the mid-day meal in the company of friends. Matt and the boys rushed to the flat, sandy shore to race, chase and scuffle, Damaris and the older girls retreating to their favourite corner behind the fishing boats drawn up safely out of the way of the rushing seas, which at high tides charged right up the launching slipway like a boisterous animal wanting to play.

But like an unpredictable animal it could be dangerous, as a strong undertow could sweep the unwary off their feet and out into the sea.

From their semi-concealed position they could keep a vigilant eye on their younger sisters at their childish games, and at the same time a speculative eye on the older village boys who lounged nonchalantly against the wall of the Watch House. These youths were making the natural progression up towards the balcony which ran round this important building, set strategically in the corner of the very sea itself and affording clear views to the distant horizon. A place on the balcony was the prerogative of the older men, who gathered under its sheltering walls to gossip and share a pipe of contraband tobacco, the pipes often hastily and dangerously concealed in a pocket if Peter Maxwell or James Herbert wandered by, and their keen noses frequently detected a faint whiff of smoke on the salty air of the strong sea breeze. But the rigidly innocent faces above the rugged grey beards gave them no indication as to the culprits, the only clue being a revealing grimace from the owner of a painfully smouldering pocket. Two centuries later, the smell of tobacco still lingered from their ghosts.

Damaris observed young Reuben Granger in the centre of a group of handsome fishermen, and hugged to herself with some smug satisfaction the knowledge that he had been in her house a couple of nights ago, feeling great pride in his part, humble though it may have been, in the escape of David Pinkney. This absent hero was the toast of the village this fine bright morning, but Reuben and Zack kept their part, and Jiddy's, a close secret, and the identity of the 'informant' remained unconfirmed, though suspected. Even amongst good friends, such knowledge was safest unspoken.

As the wintry sun grew towards its mid-day zenith, the groups gradually dispersed, each to their respective homes, where the one group missing from the sociable mid-morning gathering, the housewives, had returned straight from church and had been busy in their cottage kitchens dishing up the dinner.

Zack beckoned to his daughter, shouted to his scuffling son, and together the three of them strolled homewards up the narrow cobbled alleyway. Zack felt exhilarated. Life was good to him, but the nagging fear that never totally left his mind, reminded him that life was dangerous, and happiness a fragile and easily broken dream.

Zack was, like most fisher folk, a God-fearing man, and their Sunday meal together began with a simple, thankful grace, spoken in his deep, musical Yorkshire accent.

With the good food inside them, and grateful thanks expressed to Liz, Damaris and Matt cleared the table and washed the dishes. Matt's morning job to fetch the day's supply of water from the village pump at the bottom of his street was one he sometimes did unwillingly, especially on icy mornings when the steep street froze and he slipped and slithered with sloshing buckets. A huge pan of hot water simmered constantly on their fire, and this Damaris now carefully lifted and carried to the rough stone sink in the corner of the kitchen. A small pot of carefully gathered wood ash stood by the bowl, for scouring stubborn grease from the plates. Liz picked up her knitting and worked companionably by the fire; Zack retired to his workshop, ostensibly to potter with his fishing gear, but most probably he would be found down below in the cellar, making preparations for the next smuggling run, which, rumour had it, would be on the first moonless night which fell mid-week. Zack's cellar held many ingenious secret places, known only to himself. Loose boards in the floor and ill-fitting stones in the wall were not signs of careless maintenance, but led to concealed places where contraband could be inconspicuously stored. False bottoms set in fish boxes and barrels, hollows in ceiling beams, aided by the pitch blackness of the windowless cellar, all of which would need the beam from an extra bright lantern to distinguish from the normal.

Zack was a brave man, but no sensible smuggler was entirely fearless. Over-confidence could lead to carelessness, and the nagging apprehension which lurked in the minds of most, ensured absolute care, total discretion, and above all, loyalty. Their fear was by no means suggestive of cowardice, involvement with the smuggling rings being highly dangerous, the consequences affecting not only the man concerned but having far-reaching repercussions on his family and friends.

Penalties for being caught were severe, the convicted culprit being offered an unattractive choice; five years service in the Royal Navy, or a term of imprisonment and seizure of all his possessions. Conditions aboard many of His Majesty's battle-ships were so terrible for the ordinary seaman that few joined up voluntarily. When crews got short, through death or desertion, the notorious Press Gang roamed coastal towns and villages, capturing fit-looking young men and bundling them unceremoniously on board. Baytown had had its fair share of this unpleasant activity, and tales were still told of how the gallant women hid their men and beat off the Press Gang with saucepans and rolling pins. Drums were kept in readiness for beating a warning signal, and ears always keenly alert and listening for the ominous threat. A term of imprisonment was no pleasant prospect, as jails were dens of dirt, disease, overcrowding and starvation, and the confiscation of possessions badly affected the remaining family.

As yet, Damaris was unaware of Thomas Duke's malevolent jealousy, the result of which was to affect her so badly before the year was out. In innocence, she enjoyed the last few months of fleeting childhood with happy abandon.

Up in her lonely cottage in the hills above the Bay, old Jennet, the 'wise woman,' read the signs of looming tragedy in her crystal ball, regarded Damaris with pity, and kept her own counsel.

With the week's domestic chores completed, Liz looked forward to a quiet Sunday afternoon by her fireside. Maybe a friend would call round for a chat, or maybe she would just enjoy the rare, luxurious peace of solitude after the hurly-burly of the past week. Living in such a small cottage, with a physically big and clumsy husband and two lively, growing children, a couple of hours of space and quietness were to be savoured. She could hear Zack thudding about below, but left him to his own devices. She knew better than to be full of curious questions when he emerged for his tea, dirty and dusty, beard and hair covered in cobwebs.

Damaris and Matt had already left on their weekly visit to their grandparents at the far side of the village. Isaac and Rebecca Storm dwelt in a neat cottage on the banks of King's Beck, a clear, sparkling stream which had its source high up in the moorland and fell, bouncing and bubbling over its stony bed in its haste to pour itself into freedom in the sea. The stream was a useful supply of clear water for domestic use, and in their creaking old age, Isaac and Rebecca were grateful for its proximity.

King's Beck held interests of widely varying kinds. Damaris and Matt had explored its upper reaches on spring and summer excursions into the wild hinterland. It was the habitat of many wild birds and flowering plants, and harboured fresh water fish in its deeper pools. Overhanging tree roots sheltered other things, too; things which were not intended for the prying eyes of children; strange boxes and small barrels which Damaris and Matt hastily concealed if they accidentally stumbled upon them. They knew that within a few days these hidden goods would have disappeared and be on their way on the next stage of the smuggling run, on the backs of pack ponies with hooves muffled in sacks to deaden the sound of their passing. Baytown children learned young to keep secret such unexpected finds.

The lower reaches of King's Beck flowed through a dank, dark tunnel which ran under a large part of the village. It was a masterly feat of engineering, with its arched stone ceiling and strongly built sides. The tunnel had originally been constructed so that the Beck could be built over, and several cottages stood on the flat ground over the top. Building space was scarce in Baytown, most of the village being set on the sides of a steeply sloping ravine which ran down to the stream at its base. Terraces were levelled out of the hillsides and from a distance Baytown looked as if its red roofed cottages had been neatly stacked in rows by the hand of a giant model maker.

Over the years the Beck tunnel had proved itself one of the most useful places for the smuggling community. Outwardly innocent-looking homely cottages built on its top held deep underground secrets, as their cellars had small connecting passages which led directly into the culvert. Through these, contraband could be unloaded and stacked at leisure, when the goods were run ashore into the tunnel entrance near the beach. The network of underground passages had saved the lives of many an endangered smuggler who used its dank recesses as an escape route.

Deep underground, near the centre point of the flat open area where the villagers congregated and the boats were hauled up, a second tunnel led into the main branch, running deep inland. Emerging into the wild countryside of Marner Dale, where the Beck ran at the deep base of a narrow valley, covered with overhanging trees and thick bushes, it became an ideal hiding place on a dark night. This side branch of the tunnel was much lower, only two or three feet in height, and users had to crawl under the floor joists of the houses above, which could clearly be seen, and felt, by unwary heads.

Zack and Reuben would be finding themselves in uncomfortably close companionship in these murky depths before many more days had passed, and young Matt was soon to learn to fear the tunnel for himself.

However, this particular Sunday, Damaris and Matthew had no time for such explorations. The stream would most likely be frozen in parts, its surface thinly sealed with a glassy coating of ice beneath which the waters struggled for freedom. Some winters the ice had been thick enough to bear their weight in the fun of skating and sliding, but then they had not been bursting with news as they were today. Both were anxious to reach the warmth of Isaac and Rebecca's welcome, and to share the exciting events of the past few days.

A special relationship existed between these smugglers' children and their paternal grandparents. Both had lived through many dangerous moments and Damaris and Matt trusted them implicitly, confiding details they dared not tell their parents. In return, Isaac and Rebecca instinctively understood the emotional anxiety that was unspoken in their grandchildren's minds. Isaac's stories of his own smuggling days had sent thrilling tingles through Damaris and Matthew for as long as they had been old enough to learn and be trusted with old Isaac's secrets.

Matt and Damaris knew that life had not always been so comfortable for their grandparents. In his young days, Isaac had toiled hard and honestly at his fishing and earned enough to give them a basic living, but when the children started arriving, things were not so easy. Both he and Rebecca respected the teachings of John Wesley, and managed to avoid being caught up in the smuggling that so many of their friends were involved in. It was hard for them, as their neighbours often shunned them, and talked in muted whispers when Isaac was around his boat, afraid that he may hear things not intended for his ears. However, things changed one very cruel winter. The seas were so rough that Isaac could not go fishing, and gradually the food and fuel ran out. The weather was bitterly cold, and the little family huddled together for mutual warmth. One day, little Zack, a mere toddler, sought Isaac's hand with icy cold fingers. 'I'm so cold, and so hungry,' he cried. '*Please* can I have something to eat?' Isaac and Rebecca's eyes met sadly, and they shook their heads. There was nothing they could give him. Isaac sighed, released Zack's little hand, and silently left the cottage.

When he returned, he nodded to Rebecca, who accepted his decision with reluctance. She knew where he had been.

Next night, he was absent from home for some time, and when he returned, he handed Rebecca a small handful of coins. Zack had finally, through sheer desperation, joined the smugglers, and accompanied them on a run.

Rebecca was fully aware of the danger they were now in. Zack knew the identity of the men he had worked with, he knew the contraband that had been run, and he knew who was hiding it and where. He was in possession of vital knowledge, and until it was proved that he could be trusted, any leakage of information would be laid at his door. His life was threatened, as was that of Rebecca, but what else could he have done? At least now, his children would not starve.

Matt's early love for his grandfather had developed over the years into a deep respect for his cunning and bravery, and he, like his sister, listened enthralled as the white-bearded old man shared his best stories. Isaac had always possessed a great sense of humour, and still chuckled with deep-throated laughter at some of the pranks he had played on the Preventives.

A favourite of both of them, Isaac from the point of view of the teller, and Matt the avid listener, concerned a young inexperienced Preventive, newly stationed in Baytown.

The *Kent* had been expected some time during the night; no one quite knew the exact time, and Isaac and his friend Black Jake assigned to watch duty. Black Jake had taken the first long spell on the cliffs overlooking the Bay, and had arranged for Isaac to take over in the early hours of the morning. Isaac had had a particularly hard day's fishing, and replete with a large helping of Rebecca's splendid rabbit pie and vegetables, had nodded off by the fire. At Rebecca's insistence, he turned in for an early night and a few hours good sleep. To be more comfortable he had undressed and put on his long white nightshirt and fallen asleep as soon as his head touched the pillow. The next thing he knew was

Rebecca's firm hand shaking him awake. He had completely forgotten his poor old friend out on the lonely cliff top. He realised by the position of the moon in the sky, that he was very late indeed. Wasting no time in dressing, Isaac merely stuffed his nightshirt into his wide-topped trousers, dragged his gansey over his head, and, hopping into his heavy boots as he scrambled down the stairs, he was off and away. Running up Flagstaff Steps to the cliff path to relieve Black Jake, Isaac was horrified to observe the tall, dark-cloaked, tricorne-hatted figure of the new Preventive silhouetted against the moon. The path was narrow and lined with sharp-spined gorse bushes. The open edge dropped sheer to the beach far below. Isaac did not know how to get past him unobserved.

Suddenly he chuckled. He had a wonderful idea. He would frighten the life out of that silly young fellow, or his name wasn't Isaac Storm! Pulling the long white nightshirt out of his trousers, and stripping off his gansey, Isaac crept towards the unsuspecting Preventive, arms flapping his nightshirt in the breeze. Coming close behind the man, Isaac cupped his hands round his mouth and in a deep, hollow voice intoned, 'It's a fine night for the dead to be walking abroad!'

The Preventive was shaken rigid with terror; the hair prickled on the back of his neck and he turned and fled, pushing past the 'ghost'and fleeing down the steps for dear life, his tricorne hat spinning on the path behind him. Isaac met up with Black Jake, hardly able to explain for laughing. Black Jake should have been annoyed with Isaac for being so late in relieving him of his duty, but found his excuse so hilariously funny that he forgave him. For years afterwards, their eyes would meet over a tankard of ale, and the froth would splutter as they remembered the sight of the terrified man. Isaac had retrieved the hat and kept it as a souvenir of his adventure. As a small boy Matthew liked nothing better than to snuggle up on his grandfather's knee and be allowed to wear the shabby old tricorne as Isaac told the tale yet again.

Isaac and Rebecca Storm jerked out of a quiet Sunday afternoon doze by their warm cottage fire as running feet approached down The Bolts. Not an unusual sound, for the aptly named alleyway, leading straight into the concealing depths of countryside, was the escape route of many a panting man, hotly pursued by Preventive Officer or Press Gang. This peaceful Sunday afternoon, the running footsteps were light and accompanied by peals of youthful laughter.

Two pairs of sleepy eyes caught each other with an amused glance as the door burst unceremoniously open and their excited and breathless rosy-cheeked grandchildren hurtled in, accompanied by an icy blast of air. The peaceful Sunday afternoon atmosphere was shattered and lost forever.

'Fer goodness sake, come in and shut t'door. We'll freeze ti deeath,' grumbled Isaac in mock reproof. Rebecca shifted her arthritic bones uncomfortably in an attempt to rise and make room by the fireside. 'Sit still, lass. There's room for them two as well. They're as thin as rakes, not takin' up all t'space like some folks.' He prodded the plump Rebecca playfully. Matt picked up the two small hand-made stools which Isaac had fashioned for each of them when they were both much younger. Now somewhat small and low for their fast growing limbs, Matt and Damaris nevertheless still regarded the little cracket-stools as their own special seats and would take no other. Tucking them underneath, the two children hitched forward, closer to the glowing fire, and held out their cold hands to the welcome warmth.

Rebecca indicated the constantly simmering kettle on the hob and produced a small shiny key from the depths of her pocket. 'As 'tis Sunday, we shall all have a bit of a treat. You two look as if a hot drink wouldn't go amiss. Matt, pass me that box off the mantel, and Damaris, you get four nice cups. Not the very best ones, I save those for when Mr. Wesley takes tea with us, but the ones with the blue pattern will do nicely.' These were Damaris' own favourites; she remembered from very early days her grandmother telling her the story of the little Chinese people who walked across the bridge and stood under the blue willow tree. 'I can see from your faces you've got something special to tell your grand-dad and me, so let's just get oursens settled and then you shall tell all.'

Matt handed Rebecca a small polished mahogany box. She fitted the key into the smoothly operating lock and opened the lid to reveal two compartments with perfectly fitting flat tops, each with a little carved acorn for a handle. Damaris held the china tea pot whilst Rebecca carefully measured the precious aromatic leaves, and poured on just the right amount of boiling water. She imagined herself the mistress of a prosperous household as she sipped the luxurious golden liquid, for tea was normally only affordable by the well-to-do, because the heavy duty imposed on its legal importation put it beyond the pocket of the average person.

Smuggling had its 'perks' and the occasional treat of tea drinking was certainly one of them. Damaris raised enquiring eyes to her grandmother, but Rebecca tapped the side of her nose with her forefinger and touched her smiling lips in the age old gesture indicating secrecy. 'Best we don't know too much, lass,' she warned. 'What we don't know we can't be made to tell.' Damaris accepted her grandmother's wise advice a little reluctantly. Her youthful curiosity was avid; perhaps Reuben had smuggled this tea ashore … She cradled the delicate cup in her hands, gazed into its tawny depths and became lost in daydreams.

When they drank tea at their other grandmother's, she swirled the dregs around, upturned the cup, and told fortunes from the signs she read within. Rebecca would not have approved. She was a strictly God-fearing woman and did not hold with all the strange goings-on in grandmother Jennet's house. It was strongly rumoured that Jennet was a witch. Certainly she had a reputation for all kinds of strange cures, and a few effective curses as well, if need be.

Rebecca felt a little anxious that the impressionable Damaris did not fall too much under the undesirable influence of her maternal grandparent. Straight-forward cures were well enough, she supposed, but when it came to spells and love-potions and the like, Rebecca held strongly disapproving views of meddling with the supernatural.

She was jerked back to the present by Matt's urgent tugging at her apron. 'Gran!' he reproached. 'Tha was noddin' off agin, and Dam and me 'ave got summat to tell thee!'

Rebecca smiled apologetically and affectionately patted Matt on the shoulder. 'Ah'm sorry, lad. Ah'm a foolish, dozy old biddy. Me mind were miles away.' She leaned towards him, placing gnarled hands on plump knees, her blue eyes twinkling with a gesture of anticipation. 'Reet, now. We're all ears. Tell us what's on tha mind before tha bursts wi' excitement.'

Matt needed no more prompting, and the whole story, from the eavesdropping in the night, the sound of the gunshots, to the final safe escape of David Pinkney, tumbled from his eager lips.

Isaac and Rebecca cackled with laughter at the discomfort of Constable Clarke, and even more at the wild rumours of death and destruction spread by the notorious Mrs. Baxter. 'Tha should 'ave 'eard 'er, Gran. It were that funny!' Matt giggled as he imitated Mrs. Baxter's vigorously nodding bonnet. ''Er big black feather were wavin' aroond that 'ard, Ah thowt she were aboot ti tek off!'

The short January day was closing in, and the cottage room grew even darker with the gathering snow clouds that approached over the hill top opposite. Damaris moved over to the window and glanced anxiously upwards as the first snowflakes came gently floating down and began to settle on the frozen pathway outside. A bitter wind whistled cruelly down the narrow alleyway, whirling the fast falling flakes into a flurry of bewildering whiteness. Pressing her nose against the cold glass, Damaris grew dizzy with watching the white specks hurtling towards her eyes from the darkening sky and turned back to her grandparents' fireside.

Rebecca looked up at the densely swirling snowflakes and exclaimed, 'Well, Mother Carey is pluckin' her chickens again!' an age-old story to explain why snow fell in soft white flakes like floating feathers. Many unexplainable facts were re-told as folk tales, and one of Matt's favourites was the story of their local saint, Hilda, inspired to build a monastery at the place then called Streonshalh, or the 'white bay' from which Whitby was named after the rolling breakers which foamed in great lines like charging horses towards its shore. When Hilda arrived at the chosen site, the land was infested with snakes. Legend told how Hilda had taken a whip and driven the offending creatures from the cliff top, whipping off their heads and rendering them harmless as they curled up tightly and turned into stone as they plummeted to the beach. That explained why hundreds of fossil ammonites were found on the shore below the abbey cliff. Matt and Damaris had one of these 'snakestones' in their treasure box, and they would dearly have loved that spectacular story to have been the truth.

'Well, tha can't go home yet awhile, that's for sure. Snug up ti t'fire and keep warm, but before tha sits down, pass us me pipe and that bit of rope off the mantel, there's a good lass.'

As Damaris handed the pipe to Isaac, Matt remarked, 'Poof, Granddad, tha's not going to smoke that owd rope, is tha?' Isaac merely smiled and began to unravel the end. Inside the rope was the contraband tobacco.

'Ah'm not that 'ard up yet, Matt!' he remarked as he proceeded to fill the pipe, and light it with a strip of tightly rolled paper which he poked into the fire. A few concentrated puffs and the pipe was well alight, filling the air with the fragrant smoke of good tobacco. Much more pleasant than old rope. This was a new one on Matt, who thought he knew quite a bit on secret smuggling devices. 'This 'ere owd bit came from Holland, Matt, all twisted up ti mek tobacco look like thick rope, and wi' all the miles you need for riggin' on a sailin' ship, naebody is goin' to guess that a few scratty owd ends are not what they seem. Mind you,' he added with a wink, 'you 'ave to be sure what you've got; Rebecca there doesn't care overmuch for t'smell o' burnin' rope!'

The snow still fell thickly outside. Rebecca rose stiffly from her chair by the fireside, limped to the cupboard from which she took a loaf of fresh baked bread and a knife, and unhooked a couple of long-handled shiny brass toasting forks which hung at the side of the fireplace. Matt and Damaris each stuck a slice of the fragrant bread on their forks and held them before the glowing embers until they turned golden brown and crisp. On Fridays, the country people came in to Baytown with supplies of fresh farm produce, butter, eggs and milk, and a variety of fresh vegetables, which were much appreciated as few Baytown cottages had gardens large enough to grow much. The impromptu markets were well attended; Baytown people bought what they needed and the country folk often went home with a few luxuries purchased discreetly from the smugglers. So all went home happy and satisfied with their day's trading.

Rebecca smiled as she unwrapped a block of butter, glistening and golden as the dew covered buttercups in the lush meadows. Firm hands had patted it with ribbed bats into a neat square on which was impressed the distinctive mark which identified the farm from which it had come. The salty butter soaked, succulent and golden, into the slices of hot toast, and fingers were licked noisily as the melting liquid escaped.

Damaris cheekily pretended to wipe her greasy fingers on Isaac's gansey. 'Hey, give ovver!' Isaac gave her a playful slap. 'That's me best bridal shirt!' The garment referred to was now some fifty years old, and had stood the test of time, as had Isaac and Rebecca's long and happy marriage. The gansey still fitted Isaac's sturdy body as well as it had done when he was the young, handsome man for whom Rebecca had affectionately knitted it. It was the tradition for a prospective bride to knit her bridegroom a special gansey in his family's own distinctive pattern; one which he would wear at his wedding, on Sundays and special occasions, and finally be buried in. The young brides pushed the latter thoughts from their minds for few were fortunate enough to have their husbands as long as Rebecca had had Isaac, for many died tragically early, often leaving young widows and small, fatherless children to cope the best they could. Families helped, naturally, but many young women had a hard time bringing up their children. Prospective brides prayed that they were not knitting early sorrow into the betrothal garment.

Rebecca leaned over and fingered Isaac's gansey critically. 'Aye, it's worn better than thou has!' she smiled at her grey-bearded, weather-beaten spouse.

'Maybe,' retorted Isaac, 'but it's only been worn of a Sunday. *Ah've* been worn oot seven days a week!'

There was no answer to that, and Rebecca let the conversation drop.

Rebecca fiddled in her knitting bag and checked out the remaining quantity of wool. She would soon need some more winding from the hank. Rebecca never worked on Sundays. It was the Lord's Day and the Day of Rest. 'Six days shalt thou labour' said the Bible, and that was enough for anybody, avowed Rebecca firmly.

The wool was supplied in large loose hanks and had to be wound into tight, neat balls for ease of knitting. To avoid spending boring hours when he had better things to do than hold the oily hanks for Rebecca to wind, Isaac had made her an ingenious wool winder which clamped to the table, expanded to hold the hank tightly, and whizzed round like a demented windmill, leaving him to enjoy his pipe in peace. With her arthritic hands she was slow and clumsy, dropping the ball which ran across the floor, unwound itself, and tangled all round the furniture legs, and if the neighbour's cat decided to call in for a game of chase, chaos reigned and Isaac's temper frayed. Winding the wool was always done in the hours of daylight, enough being prepared for the whole evening's knitting. Superstition declared that winding wool during the treacherous hours of darkness would 'wind' a ship onto the rocks.

Older Bay women never forgot the time when a new bride, coming from farming stock and marrying into the fishing fraternity, disregarded this old wives tale with a toss of her head, and carried on winding her wool in the late evening. During the night, a fierce storm had suddenly blown up, catching the unwary fishermen. Next morning, the remains of her husband's fishing boat were found smashed on the rocks. His body was never found.

Rebecca put her knitting bag away, rubbed her hands, smooth and soft from the natural lanolin absorbed from years of contact with wool, and chuckled as she began to recount yet again the adventure in which her knitting, and regretfully, her rheumatism, had once fooled the Preventive men and probably saved her from a heavy fine or unpleasant jail sentence.

Rebecca's story was one which Damaris and Matt had heard so many times they knew it word for word, but the old lady loved to re-live her moment of real excitement. Her grandchildren would not deny her that pleasure for anything; the look of mischief that twinkled in her eyes as she recounted the oft-repeated story transformed her wrinkled old apple of a face.

Isaac and Rebecca had been involved in smuggling adventures all their lives and in younger days shared many exciting experiences, but old age was not always dull, as Rebecca well remembered.

Their cottage at the end of The Bolts was close to the escape route into the wild countryside beyond. One night a large cargo of contraband had been safely run ashore, and most of it already tucked away in cellars, under floorboards and behind beds. Plans had been agreed for the first load of brandy kegs to be secreted up King's Beck and on to the backs of the pack ponies waiting patiently in the bushes. So far the plan had worked pretty well and most of the goods were stowed, when sounds of a distant scuffle alerted the smugglers and running feet clattered along the cobbled street outside Rebecca's house, accompanied by the rumbling sound of a fast-rolling barrel. Breathless voices shouted a hastily made decision. Rebecca's door flew open and rough hands dumped the barrel unceremoniously inside with the terse instruction: 'Get rid of it! Quick!' and they were gone. So there she was, a solitary old lady, left with the condemning evidence. Isaac was out. She had neither the time nor the strength to roll the barrel to their cellar trap door and drop it within. Preventive men were on the alert. What to do?

Should she lock and bar the door? Her first instinct was to do so, but as soon as her hand touched the lock she paused. No. A locked door would immediately arouse suspicion in this place where doors were always open to neighbours. Besides, a plan was forming in her mind, and to have to get up and go to open it when the unwelcome visit took place, as it most certainly would, would give the game away completely.

Quick thinking and even quicker action was called for. With a struggle, the gallant old lady dragged the barrel over to her fireside, took up her knitting and, spreading her skirts wide, sat herself down on it, trying to convince herself it was comfortable. Her heart thumped uncomfortably in her chest, partly from the sudden exertion and partly from anxious excitement and a degree of shock as, without ceremony, a heavy boot struck the ancient oak timbers of her door, bursting it open yet again, and slamming it violently back against the wall. The sudden reverberation shook the dresser on which the prized Staffordshire figure of John Wesley had stood, but now lay shattered in pieces on the stone flagged floor. Silhouetted against the dark night sky, lantern held high, in the open doorway stood the blue-coated figure of Peter Maxwell.

He attempted to maintain a degree of civility as he apologised for the intrusion.

Maxwell held his lantern high. Its beams reflected from the polished surfaces of the neatly kept cottage. Lifting a corner of the hearthrug and moving a picture or two to ensure no hidden openings revealed tell-tale hiding places or trap-doors to deep cellars, he completed his token search. He didn't really feel convinced that the outwardly respectable Rebecca could possibly be guilty, but you never knew with these Bay folk. Peter Maxwell had a soft spot for old Rebecca and had made sure he was the Officer to carry out this search. Some of his colleagues may not have been so easy-going, and could wreak havoc when conducting a full inspection. He would not inflict that on her if he could possibly avoid it.

He touched his hat in a gesture of apology. 'Sorry to have troubled 'ee, Rebecca. I'll bid 'ee good night.' He closed the door and paused a moment, his hand still on the doorknob. Rebecca's eyes had been unnaturally bright, her cheeks pink from exertion, and her breathing a little hurried .... how long had she been sitting there trying to compose herself into some attitude of peaceful normality? He shook his head with a smile. Poor old lass, he'd give her the benefit of the doubt. She was a brave old soul and despite the ruthless nature of his job, a streak of compassion underlay his conscience. He couldn't possibly be responsible for her punishment, and in any case, the brandy, if it had been there, would be gone by the morrow and none but he, and Rebecca, would be any the wiser. He resisted the temptation to peer through the chink in her curtains just to make sure. It was better not to know.

The echoes of his departing feet died away. Rebecca put down her knitting and stretched her aching back with a broad smile. 'That foxed him,' she thought. 'Just wait till Isaac gets back. He'll nivver believe me!' But Isaac had no doubts as to the bravery of his dear old wife. Quick thinking and totally reliable even now, her youthful courage remained undiminished, for in her old age she still would not have escaped some form of punishment.

Sadly, Rebecca bent stiffly, and picked up the pieces of the shattered china figure. In her hand she held the head with its chipped nose. The painted eyes, still bright, seemed to gaze back at her reproachfully. 'Oh, Rebecca!'

'Aye, she's a grand lass is your gran. Allus has been a good 'un,' said Isaac with a look of pride and affection in his clear blue seafarer's eyes.

'Well now, you two. Snow's easin' off. High time you was trottin' home-along. Liz will be gettin' anxious, wonderin' what tha's up to.'

Isaac lit Damaris and Matthew a small lantern, gave them an affectionate hug, watching fondly as two pairs of boots made parallel tracks in the new fallen snow. As the light of their lantern dimmed into a faint glow in the distance, he turned and closed the door, rejoining Rebecca by the glowing fireside. 'Eh, lass. Ah wish we was as young as them two, and knaw what we do now.'

'Aye, wisdom only comes along of old age, that's the sad part of it,' agreed Rebecca wryly.

Zachariah Storm shivered as he shrugged his coat collar further up round his ears and pulled down the faded rough red woollen cap which covered his head. Although he stood in the lee of his cottage wall, a bitter, unrelenting east wind penetrated every gap in his clothing. Further along the exposed cliff top, stationed at strategic intervals, a number of very cold men waited impatiently, raising telescopes to streaming eyes, scanning the horizon for the mast heads of the long awaited ship.

Down by the slipway cobles were deceptively being made ready for the fishing. Crews knew that this day they would be certain of a profitable 'haul.' Like their companions on the bleak cliffs, they too awaited the signal that the eagerly expected schooner, *Kent*, was on her way. The *Kent*, a fast-sailing ship, heavily armed with sixteen four-pounder carriage-mounted cannon and twenty swivel guns was a familiar vessel in the waters of the Bay. Her Captain, 'Stoney' Fagg, a brave, swashbuckling buccaneer, and his crew of some forty equally desperate men, armed with blunderbusses and muskets, were not seriously threatened by the smaller, more lightly armed Revenue cutters manned by the Customs department. For years, Stoney Fagg had arrogantly ruled the high seas and run contraband with scornful defiance.

Suddenly an excited shout of 'Sail ho!' passed along the waiting men when the most observant first spotted the tall masts of the *Kent* breaking the horizon. Zack turned back into his house and called Matthew. 'Matt!' he bellowed. 'Get thissen down t'boat and tell Reub and t'lads not ti wait any longer. Tell him ah'll see him later as planned, ... and dean't run and mek a clatter aboot it,' he added. 'Walk down, normal like, and tell him quietly. He'll knaw what ah wants him ti do.'

Matt knew too; the appearance of normal fishing preparations and activities were important for everyone's safety in the coming hours. Even in this close-knit community it was best not to be too trusting. Matt restrained his footsteps with a great degree of impatience as he sauntered, whistling nonchalantly, down to the boats. Looking over his shoulder carefully to ensure he was not being watched, he casually strolled, hands in pockets, over to where Reub was baiting his lines. 'Now then, Reub.'

'Now then, Matt.' They exchanged the commonplaces of a traditional Baytown greeting, then Matt leaned with his elbows on the bulwarks of the boat, and swinging his legs out behind him, leant forward and calmly delivered his father's message to the waiting Reuben with a secretive wink.

'Right-ho. Thanks, Matt lad.'

Heaving himself up on his elbows before jumping back to the ground, he whispered, 'Good luck! Come back safe. Our Damaris'll be all of a dither if she finds tha's gone out to the *Kent*,' he added with an impish grin.

'Dinna thee fret, Ah will.' Reub brushed away his surprised amusement at the affectionate concern of Zack's lovely daughter and concentrated on making the final preparations for launching his coble into the waiting sea. This was the unspoken signal to the rest of the fishing boats which were to be engaged in that particular day's activity. One by one the remaining crews made ready to launch up. Plenty of boxes and piles of nets lay in the boat bottoms, not so much as to catch and store fish, but to conceal a more valuable cargo. Lug sails lay ready to hoist as soon as strong, willing hands had oared the boats out into deep water and soon, to the satisfaction of the shoremen, a flotilla of small boats was heading out towards the 'fishing grounds.'

There was time for a meal and a hot drink before Zack and his team finalised their arrangements for the safe landing and stowage of the incoming cargo. From past experience Zack knew just what to expect. The *Kent* sailed from the port of Flushing in Holland, one of the main smuggling supply ports for the east coast trade. Kegs of French brandy, Dutch geneva or gin, and wooden crates of tea and spices imported from the Dutch East Indies, would form a large part of the 'run,' along with neat oilskin-wrapped parcels of fine silks and laces and packs of tobacco. He must keep a bit of that back for old Isaac who would smoke it with double enjoyment, thought Zack with an inward smile. The old fellow had done his bit in his day and Zack enjoyed refilling his tobacco box when he wasn't looking. Isaac never questioned the constant replenishment of his supplies, but exchanged a knowing look with his son when he lit up his pipe. Their eyes said it all. There was no need for words.

Matt returned with the news that the cobles were all safely off for the days 'fishing.' Zack prodded him in the chest with a firm forefinger. 'Reet! Now thoo keep out o't way when they gets back. Understood?' Matt nodded. He understood all right, but he had no intention of missing the fun and excitement, and retired to his room to make his own plans.

Baytown appeared small and distant to the men in the cobles as, with dark red lug-sails filling with the stiff offshore breeze, they sailed swiftly towards the *Kent*. Signals indicating 'safe to approach, no Revenue cutters in the area' being given, the distance between the vessels closed rapidly. The small cobles lowered sail as they bobbed over the choppy surface and drew in under the lee of the *Kent's* towering bulwarks. From their low position close to the sea's surface, Reuben and his crew craned their necks uncomfortably to converse with the desperadoes on the deck high above them. The *Kent's* hull was thickly tarred for protection against sea water. Dense black colour overall totally concealed her illicit presence in the hours of darkness. Without lights she was almost impossible for the Revenue cutters to seek out. Stoney Fagg was a practical man, and saw no advantage in decking out his vessel with fancy paint work. He was safe in the knowledge that she was heavily armed, and had no need to feign she had cannon on board, unlike many of the small trading vessels he sailed arrogantly past, with their decoration of black squares on white or yellow bands, faking dummy gun-ports to pretend they were armed when they were not. Stoney Fagg regarded these *'ruses de guerre'* with a sneering contempt. They were easy prey for piracy.

This cold, grey morning, however, Stoney Fagg's concentration lay in delivering his cargo quickly and sailing on his way. The Baytown cobles were all alongside. Eager hands outstretched to guide the lowering boxes and kegs safely aboard. The sea this particular morning was reasonably calm and the small boats only bumped somewhat annoyingly against the tall ship's side. When the sea was too rough to enable the safe transference of cargo, Stoney's crew would need to 'sow a crop,' to tie the contraband firmly on ropes, attach a marker flag or float, and drop them overboard to be 'harvested' when the seas abated. In winter, bad weather could last for days, causing much valuable cargo to be lost or damaged, or worse still, broken loose from their moorings and washed up on the shore right into the hands of the Preventives. It was strange how a sudden urge for beach-combing flourished after a storm.

The coblemen concealed their illicit cargoes in the bottom of their boats, began to man the oars and drew off away from the *Kent* to engage in a spot of genuine fishing. A whole fleet of empty boats returning together could certainly arouse the suspicions of Maxwell or Herbert if they just 'happened' to be around when the fleet came in. Or the inquisitive eyes of Arabella Clarke which missed nothing, would ensure that a message reached the Constable; it would be not only their wives who were on the slipway to welcome the returning men.

Patience was essential, as the small cobles dispersed over the fishing ground. Lines which had been carefully baited and coiled on basket skeps by their womenfolk, were 'shot.' Weary crews rested and enjoyed a quick tot of warming brandy and a pipe of duty free tobacco. Drinking of spirits on board was rigorously disciplined. Any dulling of wits could spell disaster; celebratory drinking would come later that night, for some. Others were destined to spend an uncomfortable evening, but luckily they were unaware of events to come.

Bay coblemen knew where the largest shoals of fish would be feeding. Years of experience had instilled an instinctive knowledge of where to most successfully shoot their lines. This day they were lucky, and within a few hours knew that they could confidently return to shore with a doubly valuable cargo, part of which at least would arouse no suspicion.

Dusk was falling early this grey winter day. Dim lights already twinkled welcomingly in the distant cliff top windows as the fishermen hauled their lines, unhooked and packed the incoming catch neatly into the waiting boxes, and set sail for home. It had been a long day, but a profitable one in both respects, and the men were anxious to return. One or two might not have been quite so eager if they had foreseen what lay ahead in the fast-approaching hours of darkness.

Matt crouched behind his bedroom door, listening for the tell-tale click as the door closed behind Zack as he left the house. Liz had not questioned his action, and he was grateful for her silent understanding. Some of the other men's wives were too curious. Liz had merely given him a quick hug and whispered a caring word of caution.

A thick grey mist crept shorewards as the boats were hauled up the slipway, enveloping all in its cold clamminess. These sudden 'haars,' rolling in thick clouds across the surface of the water were a mixed blessing. At sea they were treacherous, obliterating all sense of direction, but on shore shielded the activities of the illicit traders who vanished silently into the concealing fog.

Zack approached Reuben with an air of casual nonchalance. 'Made a good catch, then, Reub?' he enquired loudly, but with a secretive wink.

'Oh, not so bad, Zack. Could've been better without this damn cold fog. Ah'm nithered. Give us a hand wi' these boxes, then Ah can gan along home. Ma's gotten a good hot fire an' Ah'm longin' to toast mi toes.' Willing hands heaved the legitimate catch ashore to be cleaned and salted ready for transportation and sale.

Just then the dumpy figure of Arabella Clarke emerged from the grocer's shop nearby. She paused, as her inquisitive eyes roamed intently over the newly landed boats. Zack was certain she could determine the lumpy packages still concealed under the piles of nets in the bottom of the boat. 'Hold on a bit, Reub,' he muttered. 'Wait until that busybody's gone.'

'Evenin,' Mrs. Clarke, ma'am. Been a nice day.' He greeted her with a sarcastic grin.

Arabella ignored him, and head in air, walked up nearby Tyson's Steps with a conscious dignity, fully aware of the hostile attitude of the men behind her, but with a satisfied smirk on her plump face. She had seen quite enough.

Close by the slipway where the boats were hauled, the seaward entrance to the tunnel loomed dark and foreboding. King's Beck flowing through it made it an uncomfortable place after heavy rains swept down in flood, but tonight it trickled normally and appeared ready to play its part in yet another drama.

The day's catch of fish dealt with, the task ahead of the cobles' crews was a dangerous one that must be accomplished quickly and unobtrusively. The design of the coble, inherited from its Viking predecessors, with its flat bottom and finned keel, enabled it to be beached on the sandy shore and remain almost upright, a feature which proved useful when engaged in legitimate work or, as this evening when some of the boats were running their contraband ashore further along the beach under the shadow of the overhanging cliffs, where ropes hung ready to haul the goods silently upwards and stow them safely away in the secret recesses prepared in the cottages above.

Squeezed into a dark corner by the doorway into the old inn which overlooked one side of the slipway, affording a good view of the gaping tunnel entrance, Matt concealed his presence and watched with growing excitement as faint lights glimmered and quiet voices gave orders for the speedy stowage of the goods. Matt clearly recognised his father and Reuben amongst the group of men, hastily and efficiently passing kegs and boxes from hand to hand until they disappeared from view. From his hiding place on the corner of a small overhanging balcony, Matt peeped cautiously, leaning over the wooden fence railings. The last keg had been stowed and the light from the lanterns now glowed faint in the tunnel's darker depths as the men retreated with their treasure far into its damp nether regions.

Matt was undecided whether to go back home before his presence was missed and Liz came calling for him, or whether to risk his father's stormy anger and follow the smugglers into the tunnel. Matt had always suspected that there were many secret hiding places within its dank and clammy interior, but his own secret explorations had so far revealed nothing to his inexperienced young eyes. Tonight would be a rare opportunity for discovery. But, if observed, Matt knew his father's anger would be terrible indeed. Indecision kept him hesitating which way to go. Fate was to make his mind up for him within the next few vital moments. In the distance, but still out of sight, his keen ears detected the sound of marching feet.

Matt froze into immobility against the wall, all senses quivering alertly. Cautiously he peered into the darkness as a swinging lantern, faint at first, but rapidly growing brighter with the approaching tramping feet, spasmodically illumined the unmistakable features of Riding Officer Peter Maxwell at the head of a group of Dragoons, the dreaded soldiers who had marched from York, at the request of Constable Clarke, to deal with these impertinent smugglers.

Matt's mind was made up. He knew what he must do. Thoughts of the men's safety far outweighed the fear of his father's angry reaction. Silently Matt swung himself over the railings, dropped onto the sandy shore below and cautiously entered the gaping blackness of the tunnel.

The lanterns of the smugglers were now far ahead of him. Any faint light from the moon behind him receded quickly as Matt struggled on, stumbling in the darkness, hand out-stretched to touch the cold and clammy wall that was his only guidance. Trying to keep to the dry sides, in his hurry to reach the men with his warning, Matt slithered and slipped on the slimy stones, tripped, and plunged headlong into the running stream. Bruised and bleeding, dripping wet and white faced with anxiety, he presented an alarming appearance when he suddenly turned a corner and the light of Zack's lantern fell full on his face.

Zack lifted his arm in an instinctive gesture of anger, his face black with fury. 'Come 'ere, you disobedient little varmint,' he began, as he grabbed Matt's collar, but Matt bravely grasped his father's upraised wrist before the broad hand could swipe him off his feet.

'Da! Wait! Tha doesn't understand! Listen to me! *Da! Listen!*' he shouted frantically as Zack's anger rose further and he wrenched himself roughly from Matt's grasp and flung him back against the wall. 'Da! Oh, Reub,' he appealed desperately. 'It's t'sodgers! They're comin'! I had to warn 'ee somehow!'

Zack's angry fist unclenched, his sudden stormy anger abated and he rested his rough hand on Matt's shoulder in a gesture of forgiveness and understanding. 'Ah'm sorry, son,' he reproached himself. 'Ah didna realise. Tha's a reet brave lad.'

'There's no time to waste. Hide!' whispered Matt urgently. Word passed up the tunnel to where the foremost men had already stowed almost two hundred small kegs of brandy up the narrow passageway into the cellar of the Fisherman's Arms which lay directly above them, and where the publican was already neatly stacking them against the walls.

On the roadway immediately above the tunnel where the smugglers were hastily attempting to dispose of the remaining telltale goods, the Dragoons sprang smartly to attention and gathered round Constable Clarke for instructions. Arabella's suspicions had been correctly aroused, and Constable Clarke was certain that tonight the military action would at last result in his returning a favourable report to his superior officers.

'Surprise is the secret of success, men,' declared Constable Clarke pompously. 'They'll have no idea we've discovered their plans.' He had outlined the scheme and sent the soldiers on their way. He himself would hang about above ground; he convinced himself that he would only be in the way. He was too old and plump for chasing up tunnels.

Peter Maxwell was well known in Baytown and had an unnerving habit of appearing in the wrong place at the right time. He was not of the usual character that one expected to find in a Preventive man, coming from a fairly wealthy family background with a good education, where it was customary for one son to enter the armed services with a commission, one to become a lawyer, and one to enter the ministry of the church. Peter, from an early age, felt the strong pull of the sea, and found it hard to swallow his disappointment when refused entry to the Royal Navy due to less than perfect eyesight. A life in the Preventive Service would, he realised, at least keep him in sight of his beloved sea and ships, but it was unusual to find someone of his gentlemanly background in the company of the tough

Preventive men who dealt with the rough smugglers in a ruthless fashion. Turning his inborn good breeding to best effect, though, Peter Maxwell soon found that a subtle and gentle approach to the folk he found himself dealing with often brought great rewards. They were inclined to treat him as a bit of a soft touch, consequently guarding their tongues less than when in the company of his fellow snivs. Thus he frequently learned of secrets casually dropped in careless unguarded words.

Off duty, he enjoyed a pint of ale in the bar of the Fisherman's Arms, and this night a cunning plan entered his mind. Removing his uniform hat and drawing his cloak tightly over his blue jacket, Peter Maxwell declared his intention of uncharacteristically relinquishing his duty and going in for a drink.

His idea was to draw the publican into a long conversation whilst Herbert led the Dragoons into the tunnel below.

He ducked his head as his tall frame entered the low doorway and cautiously looked around him. A strangely uncanny emptiness pervaded the normally busy inn parlour. Maxwell thumped his fist on the bar counter. 'Landlord!' he bawled.

The small door leading to the cellar opened and Richard Tindale emerged covered in dust and cobwebs. 'Quiet in here tonight, landlord,' Peter observed.

'Aye, indeed sur. Bit early for 'em yet. They'll still be gettin' fish ready for market. They've had a good catch today,' he smirked as he served the ale with scant courtesy. Maxwell carried his brimming tankard over to a wooden settle beside the blazing fire.

'Bring one for yourself, landlord, and join me. I'm in need of company.' Richard glanced anxiously towards the cellar door as he pulled himself a pint of ale and reluctantly joined Maxwell by the fire. He was cleverly trapped, for to have opened the stout wooden door would have invited discovery, as Maxwell's keen ears would certainly pick up the give-away noise of activity below. Quietly though the men worked, the occasional thud and bump were unavoidable, and of course, they were not aware of the situation in the room above their heads.

'Not on duty tonight, then, Mr. Maxwell?' Richard licked his dry lips and nervously opened the conversation. Maxwell slowly stretched his long legs luxuriously before the blazing log fire, the light of the flames flickering off his highly polished leather boots.

'No, there'll be nothing doing tonight, Richard, otherwise I'm sure we would have heard about it. We have very reliable sources of information, you know.' Maxwell tapped the side of his nose with a confidential wink, raised his tankard, sipped the excellent ale sparingly, and glanced through lowered eyelids at the publican sitting uneasily opposite. 'Your good health, landlord,' he toasted.

'And yours, Mr. Maxwell.' Richard raised his glass in reply and drank a little more deeply, rolling it round his mouth until it warmed and gave off the full rich flavour. He was proud of the quality of his ale, and appreciated the chance to savour it. He was beginning, if a little unwillingly, to relax. Maxwell smiled. His plan was working nicely, and very pleasantly too, on this cold and foggy wintry evening. He stretched his long legs further towards the fire and sighed with smug satisfaction.

James Herbert knew all the obvious nooks and crannies of Baytown. Several years of official duty in this difficult place had armed him with a highly useful local knowledge which stood him in good stead on occasions such as this, as he beckoned the Dragoons to follow him.

'Remember, the secret of success is surprise, so tread quietly,' he ordered.

Holding one hand up behind him to signify caution, then beckoning them forward, he silently and stealthily led the soldiers toward the tunnel entrance. Dense swirling fog swept up from the sea as they approached the slipway and enveloped them in its damp and chilly grasp. Cloaks were pulled close for warmth, and feelings of distaste niggled at the backs of their minds as they thought of their comrades, back in comfortable Barracks in York. What had they done to deserve being deployed to this dreadful place, freezing cold, and just to apprehend a few ruffian smugglers; a far cry from their glorious exploits on the battlefields of Europe. Their distaste for the job increased as they entered the dank, slimy tunnel, feet splashing in the rushing black water which charged relentlessly towards them. What a foul place this was.

Round the bend in the tunnel which concealed their activities from their yet unseen and unheard enemies, Zack and Reuben directed the stowage of the remaining kegs up the passageway into the cellar of the Fisherman's Arms. The passage was narrow, and since the unexplained disappearance of Richard, whose hands had been receiving the kegs at the cellar end and neatly stacking them, it was becoming blocked. Only a small space remained between the barrels and the top of the passageway, too small for any grown man. Zack suddenly remembered Matthew, waiting in subdued excitement until his father's work was done and they could return home together. Zack hated to involve his young son, but there was no alternative, for only a body as slim and lithe as Matt's could possibly squeeze through that gap.

'Matt!' Zack called quietly. 'Come ovver 'ere an' give us a hand.' Matt nodded eagerly as he listened to his father's terse instructions. Zack was a man of few words at the best of times and tonight was no exception. Reuben held the lantern high as Zack gave Matt a heave up. His wriggling body squirmed and disappeared painfully over the top of the kegs, and shortly, keen ears could detect the sound of them being dragged out of the passage and into the cellar. The kegs, though small, were heavy for someone as young as Matt, and he sweated as he struggled to heave the awkward shapes into place. In his urgency, he dropped one heavily on the floor, and to his dismay a crack appeared in the wooden side, becoming discoloured as the dark contents oozed out. Matt stacked it with the rest and carried on systematically clearing the tunnel.

Up above, the thud of the falling keg was clearly audible to both Richard and Peter Maxwell, who each heard the noise with very different feelings; Richard with anxiety, and Maxwell with an air of satisfaction. Proof that his plan was working well. With admirable presence of mind both men outwardly appeared to ignore the thud, and attempted to behave normally, their awareness only betrayed by a momentary, undisguised flicker of the eyes, and a slight twitch of Peter Maxwell's lips.

In the warm and cosy inn parlour, the Excise man engaged the publican in uneasy conversation. Richard was finding it impossible to concentrate when his mind was definitely elsewhere, and he spasmodically gulped his beer nervously. Maxwell sipped his sparingly; he would need all his wits about him shortly.

'Here. Buy yourself another one, on me!' offered Maxwell generously, as he slapped a silver coin down on the table in front of Richard.

Without appearing churlish he could not refuse. Maxwell smiled inwardly. His hip flask was full of best brandy. All he needed was the opportunity to slip a good measure into the landlord's ale, and he would soon be well away.

'Why, thank 'ee, Mr. Maxwell, I will.' Richard was beginning to relax just as Maxwell had planned. Not only did loosened tongues tell many secrets, but relaxed bodies offered little resistance.

Peter settled himself more comfortably in his chair, and waited for events to take their course.

Deep in the earth below the light from the Dragoons' lanterns illuminated an extraordinary scene. Alerted so suddenly by Matt's brave warning, the smugglers had to make a hasty decision; to stay and hide the goods and risk being discovered, or to save their skins and leave their valuable cargo. Vainly they had hoped to do both but time was not on their side that evening,

Herbert's exhortation to silence had paid off. Even their careful footsteps echoed in the hollowness of the tunnel and voices carried easily. The smugglers were not so cautious, and the noise of shifting contraband obliterated the sound of the approaching Dragons until it was too late.

Suddenly the light from the lanterns blazed into Zack's eyes, and he was not only taken by surprise but temporarily blinded by the glare which bounced off the darkness.

Reub impetuously grabbed the fisherman's knife from his belt and hurled it at Herbert. His thick uniform protected him from serious injury, but Reub could have kicked himself for not taking more careful and considered aim. His knife was sharp enough to have seriously scarred Herbert's handsome face for good.

With an angry roar, Herbert broke silence and shouted orders to his men to attack. Total confusion broke out, as man to man, smuggler and soldier struggled in the slippery darkness. Zack and Reuben put up fierce resistance against capture but strong though they were, they were unarmed except for their fishing knives and the Dragoons were trained fighters. Smugglers who had hidden themselves returned to assist their companions, and soon the narrow confines of the tunnel echoed with the sounds of fierce struggling. The local men were heavily outnumbered and although they put up brave resistance, were soon tied up tightly, gagged, and propped against the tunnel walls.

Officer Herbert straightened his uniform and issued his orders. 'Well done, men. Now leave 'em to cool off, and come with me.'

Tramping feet disappeared back down the tunnel, light from the lanterns dimming as they retreated, leaving Zack, Reuben and their associates in total darkness.

The Dragoons emerged into the clean fresh air with expressions of thankful relief. Herbert mustered them into an orderly group, and led the way to the doorway of the Fisherman's Arms.

'Wait there until I call,' he commanded.

Herbert opened the door and entered the bar parlour where Peter Maxwell gave him a broad wink and a wide grin of greeting. The landlord dozed contentedly, head resting on folded arms on the table top, his empty tankard laid beside him. Maxwell and Herbert tied him firmly to his seat. 'He'd not get far in that state, anyway, but best make sure. Right, now bring in your men.'

The door banged back against the wall as the eager Dragoons entered. In the cellar, Matt heard the noise, and with beating heart, quickly concealed himself behind the stacks of brandy kegs. His nose twitched at the dank smell which permeated the walls. Years of storing beer and spirits had left a strong aroma of wood and yeast in the damp plaster. Matt felt that he could soon become dizzy with the fumes if he inhaled too deeply. He knew he must keep his wits about him, so tried to keep his breathing measured and shallow.

Maxwell and Herbert approached down the long dark stone stairway into the cellar, and whistled in amazement as they observed the size of the haul. There must have been a good two-hundred ankers, worth a small fortune. No wonder the smugglers had resisted arrest. A casual search with the lanterns revealed no human presence, though Matt felt sure they must hear the thud-thud-thud of his heart which sounded deafening in his own ears. He resisted the temptation to sneeze as the settling dust tickled his nostrils. Herbert shone the lantern down the narrow passage way down to the tunnel. 'No one in there,' he called. .'................in there,' came back the faint echo. The cargo should be safe until morning when the officers would decide what to do with the captured contraband. The trussed-up smugglers in the tunnel could also wait until morning. It would give them chance to cool off and reflect on their impending punishment, thought Herbert cynically. Meanwhile, it would be prudent to set a guard. These smugglers were a crafty bunch, not to be trusted.

Herbert selected two Dragoons, gave them a lantern, and banished them to the cellar for the night. The rest were dismissed with a word of praise for a job well done.

'Come, Maxwell. Let's go home. Leave sleeping beauty there.' Herbert gently lifted Richard's head and let it drop back onto his folded arms. 'Dead to the world,' he smiled. 'He's no company for anyone tonight. Now I fancy a bite to eat at my own fireside. Come along with me, and we'll discuss our plans for that lot down there.'

In friendly companionship the two officers quietly closed the door of the Fisherman's Arms and departed up the silent street to the comfort of James Herbert's warm fireside and the prospect of a tasty supper.

The two Dragoons appointed for guard duty glanced round them in distaste. Why them they grumbled? There was nothing they could do about it, however. Orders were orders, so they'd just have to make the best of it. They settled down for a long night.

Behind the kegs, in his cramped hiding place, young Matt resigned himself to a long and uncomfortable night, too. Worrying thoughts about his father and Reub, for all was very quiet down below, and of Liz fretting back home, not knowing where he was, all nagged in a confused jumble in his mind. But whilst the Dragoons remained in the cellar, Matt was stuck.

After a period of desultory conversation, the Dragoons fell silent. The two were not particular friends and had little in common to talk about. In the ensuing silence, a regular, slow dripping sound became audible. The light of their raised lantern revealed the dark stain spreading across the dry wood of the cracked barrel. The brandy was leaking and filling the confined air with a pungent aroma.

The men were feeling cold and bored. Temptation was great, they were in a pub after all, even though supposedly on guard in the cellar. All their mates had been released from duty. Life just wasn't fair. A glance of mutual agreement passed between them. Corporal Casseldine took the lantern and ascended the stairway to the bar. His coat tails brushed the hand of Matt as he passed closely by where the boy was hiding. Matt recoiled in terror. A couple of glasses lay handily by on the table, just put ready for the occasion, he thought wryly. Grasping the glasses, he retreated back to join his colleague, Matt holding his breath as the officer's clothes touched him for a second hair-raising time.

The rich, golden, aromatic liquid dripped tantalisingly slowly at first, and the Dragoons waited impatiently until enough had gathered in both glasses to toast each others' good health and fortune. By Jove; it was good stuff! James Casseldine savoured it, swirling it round his mouth appreciatively. No wonder those wretched smugglers were keen to risk all to save it; it was worth a mint of money. Eager to taste more of a drink, the quality of which had never passed his lips before, Casseldine carefully inserted the point of his sword into the crack and persuaded the reluctant liquid to flow more generously.

Soon the evening's atmosphere had changed from a cold, boring guard-duty job with a virtual stranger, into a pleasant evening spent drinking in the company of a good friend. The two soldiers soon felt as if they had been mates for life. Leaning against each other, tears streaming down their laughing faces, they hiccupped and related experiences which now took on a degree of helpless hilarity. Their voices raised in barrack-room songs, some with words that enriched young Matt's vocabulary as he listened, alarmed and wondering, behind his barrel.

Gradually, though, the singing abated, as the two slumped into a drunken stupor, and snores echoed round the damp cellar walls. Matt waited until he was certain they would never wake until morning, then stretched his painfully aching limbs and cautiously tiptoed silently past the sleeping bodies. The light from the guttering lantern finally extinguished itself as he groped his way into the narrow passage and began his long crawl back to the main tunnel.

'Hello! Anybody there?' called Matt in a subdued voice. All was very quiet, and very dark. A faint murmur was just audible.

'Mm-mm. Mm.' Matt cocked his ear and listened. His eyes, becoming accustomed to the dark, picked out a very faint glimmer of light some distance away down the tunnel. Creeping forward very cautiously, Matt suddenly stumbled and fell over a pair of outstretched boots.

'Ahh! Mm!' Matt guessed rightly that the owner of the boots was tied and gagged, so speaking softly, his hands groped upwards until his fingers touched a rough beard.

'Da?' he queried.

'Ahh! Mm!' grunted the unintelligible voice in reply. Matt's exploring fingers touched the gag, and finding the knot at the back of the head, fumblingly untied it.

'By gum! That's better! Good lad!' Zack shook his cramped head. 'Now, Matt, feel down into me pocket; me fishin' knife's in there. Oppen it oot, an' cut these 'ere danged ropes round me wrist, then we can see aboot rescuin' t'others. Wish we had a bit more light, though,' he grumbled. Matt found the knife and hacked his way painfully through his father's bonds. Two pairs of hands were now free to release Reuben. Reub had a tinder-box and re-kindled the lantern which had fallen from its hook in the wall in the scuffling. The welcome beams shone on a group of battered, rough faces, eyes glinting angrily above their gagged mouths.

The released men were eager to hear of Matt's story of the happenings above. 'Are them Dragoons really hard asleep, Matt?' enquired Reuben.

'Oh, aye. Snorin' like pigs.' chuckled Matt.

'Reet!' said Zack with a grin. 'We'll fox 'em yet! How's this for an idea?'

Matt carefully crawled back up the narrow passage into the cellar. Reub followed close behind. 'All clear,' Matt whispered. He cocked his ear and inclined his head. 'Listen to 'em!'

Reub crept across the floor and lifted the first keg. Matt eased it down the passage into the waiting hands of his father. Zack passed it on to his companions and waited for the next.

'Here we go, Matt. This'll be a long and heavy job, lad,' warned Reuben.

'Dinna worry, Ah can do it, Reub,' replied Matt proudly. 'Ah'm a real smuggler toneet.'

'That thoo is fer sure. Tha's a reet grand chap.' Matt glowed with pride at Reuben's confident praise, ignoring the painful grazes on his bleeding knees and the splinters in his hands, as between them they carefully cleared the cellar. They would not ask where Zack and the other Bay men had finally taken the kegs. True smugglers, born and bred to a dangerous trade, each did his own job and asked no questions. It was always safer not to know too much.

With the final keg safely removed, Reuben and Matt exchanged triumphant glances, man to man, wiped their gansey sleeves across sweating faces and, smothering a snigger as they imagined the stupefied awakening of the Dragoons the next morning in an empty cellar, returned back down the tunnel to their waiting companions.

Zack laid his hand on the shoulder of his gallant young son, and Matt glowed under his fatherly praise. A new bond of paternal relationship had been forged between the two. Matt had grown up tonight, and Zack was inwardly very proud of him. Matt had proved he could be trusted, and in a very different frame of mind from that in which he had entered the tunnel with his message of fear, left the scene of his adventure with head held high. In adult companionship, father and son set off home to the promise of a welcome hot supper.

James Casseldine and his companion slouched in surly silence in front of the two Riding Officers who stood, smart and imposing, on either side of Jos Clarke. Completely unaware of the events that found them standing in the Constable's office, with thick tongues and heads that felt like kicked footballs, they slumped untidily, staggering against each other to prevent an undignified falling over. For the life of them, they could not recall the events of the previous evening, and stared stupidly at Jos Clarke with glazed eyes. James Herbert was furious. The two incompetent idiots before him would suffer for this, he swore, for it was James who would have to write the report to his superiors. If he wrote the truth, for certain he would lose his job, and that he did not want. He was nicely settled in Baytown and valued his friendship with Peter Maxwell, which went beyond the field of duty. Peter, too, was uneasy, but, benefiting from his superior education, found it possible to reconstruct the events in an alternative way without diverting too far from the truth. He began to smile, cupped his hand round James' ear and whispered 'Get rid of these two drunken fools. Reprimand them, but get rid. Now!'

The two dragoons lurched from the Constable's office, bemused at Herbert's anger with them. They still had no idea what they had done to make him so furious. A pair of strong hands bundled them through the door and into the path outside, where they promptly sprawled down the short flight of stone steps which led from the Constable's house onto Fisherhead.

'Right!' Peter Maxwell took control of the situation and outlined his thoughts to Jos Clarke, whose final responsibility would be to endorse James Herbert's 'eye witness' account. 'This place is a long way from York,' he remarked. 'Those two useless clods out there will remember nothing at all, and the rest of the soldiers were not involved at that point but could corroborate what happened earlier. For certain the smugglers won't say anything, so it's up to the three of us to *really* say what happened – if you get my drift,' he added with a knowing smile.

'James wants to keep his job here, and I for one would be more than sorry to see him moved on. It was not his fault what happened later – in fact the earlier part of the action was most highly commendable and bravely executed. Headquarters knows what a rough job we have here, so let's tell them a nice little entertaining story.'

Peter took up Jos's quill pen, dipped it in the ink pot and after a few moments thought, began to write. Soon he was totally absorbed in his narrative, and James and Jos had to wait patiently until the quill stopped scratching across the paper. Peter picked up the sander and liberally sprinkled the wet ink. Shaking the loose particles from the parchment, he took it up and began to read aloud the courageous exploits of his colleagues, how they had fought and tied up the smugglers, and captured several boxes of pistols, blunderbusses and ammunition. Jos looked puzzled, but James knew that this evidence could be 'produced' from their own personal stores if need be.

Jos added his signature with a flourish, replaced the pen, and sealed the document with his official wax stamp.

He noted that Peter Maxwell had deliberately omitted to state what had happened to the two hundred kegs of brandy!

Part Two

Spring came early that year. Winter had passed. The weather had not been too bad, and the community thrived reasonably well. More fishing than usual had been possible, runs of contraband had been successful and profitable, life had felt good. Bright mornings gave off a sense of optimism. The smuggling fraternity, lulled into an unusual sense of false security planned the next run with a little less care and precision, not knowing how close this lack of attention to one small detail would bring them to a disaster – an avoidable disaster threatened by one man's sheer carelessness, the situation saved by unnecessarily involving Reuben, an event that began his downfall. When things ran smoothly, as they had done for the past few months, it was easy to fall into a mood of casual acceptance that all would be well. It only needed one small slip for many lives to be endangered. Within weeks, one man was to make that vital slip. Although relatively trivial at the time, the repercussion of his negligence was to have far-reaching effects on many lives, notably those of Zack and his family. Fortunately, for the time being, they remained unaware.

One morning, Damaris awoke to an unexpectedly clear blue sky with white clouds scudding across in the temperate April wind. Even before she flung up her sash window, she sensed that the air would be mild and sweet and full of the promise of the forthcoming summer.

After the seemingly interminable succession of freezing cold winter mornings when rising and dressing was an uncomfortable experience, the sheer physical delight of the touch of bright warm air gave her a feeling of enormous well-being and joy.

Leaning on the sill by the open window, the gentle April breeze wafting corn-coloured hair across eyes as blue as the sky, Damaris took stock of her world. The last time she had done this, her outlook had been framed by vicious looking icicles hanging from the eaves, and she had observed a cold white winter landscape. This morning, her world was green with new spring grass and golden with sunshine glinting on the polished petals of celandines. The soft flowers of shy primroses in their nest of fresh green leaves snuggled close to the earth in the small patch of garden she tended as her own. Beyond the sheltering wall, very little grew on the bleak cliff top between her home and the sea. Biting east winds laden with salty spray blighted all but the roughest and toughest plant life, so Damaris' little plot was a specially treasured haven. She rejoiced that her garden also brightened the days and gave pleasure to her hard-working mother.

Up Marner Dale and the upper reaches of King's Beck, Damaris knew that a whole pale golden carpet of primroses would now spread across a landscape she and Matt had last seen covered with a fluffy white blanket of snow. Emerging from their winter coverlet, wild flowers of every hue painted the ground with a palette of pastel colours and birds nested in the burgeoning hedgerows. She resolved that this coming Sunday, she and Matt would pack up a parcel of food, and after visiting Isaac and Rebecca, make their springtime pilgrimage into the countryside.

Damaris opened what she called her 'avalanche cupboard' to search for the small wicker basket which each year she filled with primroses for her mother. Elizabeth's rough, work-worn hands delighted in arranging the delicate blossoms in small china vases, feeling their cool softness against her skin, and spreading them around the cottage, so for several days to come the rooms were pervaded with the delicate perfume of spring.

The sweet fragrance of the primroses may, however, have been overpowered this particular morning with the appetizing smell of baking turfcakes and frying ham that wafted tantalizingly up from the kitchen. A temptation to even a failing appetite, to the young and healthy Damaris it was totally irresistible. The delicious aroma, mingled with the pungent smoke from the peat fire, assailed her nostrils even up in her bedroom. Elizabeth had been up and busy for some time, as the first turf cakes were almost ready. It seemed an interminable period of time, however, until Elizabeth declared herself satisfied with the perfection of her baking, or perhaps she deliberately held out on her hungry children for as long as she dared.

Proper turf cakes as the women of Elizabeth's generation made them, were exquisite culinary delicacies. Rich country butter, rubbed into the flour and mixed to a stiff paste, rolled out and folded over more dabs of butter, cut into rounds with a teacup, and finally placed in the special deep, straight-edged frying pan with a high lid. The hot pan containing the cakes was hung on the 'reckon' and a slice of peat or turf placed on top, so that the cakes were baked top and bottom to a golden perfection. Only when the cook declared the moment was right were they split and buttered and served with traditional Yorkshire ham and fried eggs, a feast fit for the King himself, declared Elizabeth, had he been fortunate enough to have lived in Yorkshire.

Peat was an excellent fuel. Coal was scarce and expensive and only delivered in Baytown infrequently by the boats from the Tyne. These collier brigs were rough ships, ill-maintained by their owners who cared little for the safety of their crews and drove both men and vessels literally to death. Fresh in Damaris's mind was the wreck of the *Richard*, which, in the previous October's fierce gales, had foundered on the rocks in the Bay. Fortunately all the crew had been saved, but Damaris would long remember the white faces and terrified expressions of the rescued men as they came dripping ashore. Some were especially afraid, as they feared capture from their knowledge of the great hoard of contraband tobacco that was hidden between the double skin of the hull. That cargo was an extremely valuable one, and as yet, the ship had not started to break up and reveal its secrets. When it did, and packs of tobacco began to float ashore, there would be a flurry of delighted activity among Zack and his friends, for yet another rich and unexpected bounty from the sea.

Coal was bought at a heavy price, not only in money but in lives. Damaris had heard horrific stories about the miners who worked like moles deep under the earth and was glad her father was a fisherman. She could not bear to think of the bold and free-minded Zack being holed up underground. Even more unbearable to her sensitive mind was the thought of the exploitation of women and small children, and the pit ponies which went blind from being permanently in the darkness underground. The freedom of fresh clean air and bright sunshine seemed doubly precious to her this beautiful clean spring morning.

Like many cottagers, Zack owned rights of 'turbery' up on the moors, a valuable asset asserted in the Deeds to their properties, which permitted the holder free access to the moorland to cut his own supply of fuel from the peat formed by the soil and roots of the heather. Special sharp spades were needed to slice through the tough roots and cut neat slabs which were stacked to dry in the strong moorland winds. Many families owned a donkey or pony for carrying nets and fishing gear to the boats. At the end of the turfing season, teams of the patient animals would make their sure-footed way across moor and beck with panniers laden with winter fuel. Familiarisation with the treacherous and boggy terrain stood the animals in good stead for their night time activities, as many of them frequently found themselves picking careful tracks across the rough country in the darkness, with panniers laden with smuggled goods.

Peats were difficult to light, but once afire, smouldered aromatically and economically and a pile always lay on the hearthstone to replenish before the fire went out. Many cottage peat fires had, it was said, been kept alight from generation to generation, even in the heat of summer, because an open fire or peat-fuelled oven provided the only means of cooking.

Damaris and Matthew always preferred the gentle glow of the peat fire, with its sweet aroma of earth and strong fresh air, to that of the luxurious coal which smelt of tar and blazed with leaping, garish flames, conjuring up pictures of the fires of hell which had once terrified their young minds. Damaris had never forgotten one dark Sunday night when the family had attended chapel to hear a visiting preacher. Not a gentle, kindly grey-haired man like their own minister, Edward Brown, or even the famous Mr. Wesley who visited Baytown sometimes in the summer, but a Bible-thumping demon who ranted and raved and shouted until his congregation was cowering, wide eyed with fear, at his threats of eternal damnation in the fires of hell if they did not mend their evil ways. Bemused, these ordinary people searched their minds for their sinful doings. The only bad thing they ever did was to cheat the Government of a bit of revenue from the contraband brandy, and surely that was not wicked enough to condemn them to such a fearful end?

'The Devil Temptation stalks these very streets,' roared the ranting preacher in strident tones which bounced in a reverberating echo from the quivering chapel walls. 'Tonight he waits out there for thee!' He brought his fist down with a crash that almost lifted them from their seats, and thumped the Bible until the pulpit shook. Damaris and Matt dived under the pew seat in terror. Hands over ears, they huddled together, paralysed with fear until Elizabeth's comforting and protective hands on their heads and gently patting fingers restored some degree of reassurance. But Damaris never forgot the courage it had taken her to come out from under that seat and enter the dark street which she knew lay between the chapel and the safety of her own fireside. Heads hidden under the warm folds of Elizabeth's cloak, they had peeped out fearfully as the perilous journey was finally accomplished. Inexpressible relief that the Devil had not impaled them on the sharp prongs of his long fork flooded their emotions. Safe behind their own door which solidly protected all within that comfortable cottage room, the trembling panic gradually left them, as Elizabeth explained what this new preacher had been trying to tell his congregation.

'There's a group of preaching men who call themselves Ranters,' she told the children, 'and they think the only way to preach the forgiveness of God is by frightening people out of their bad habits.' Elizabeth gathered her children close, and they crouched by the glowing fireside, their heads on her warm lap, her loving hands comfortingly on their shoulders, gentling and calming away their fears.

'But,' had said Matt with a sniffle, 'what about that Devil out there?' It was still horribly real to the small boy, who nodded apprehensively towards the street door.

'There's no such person,' reassured Elizabeth. 'The only 'devil' is in peoples' minds, and in wrong or unkind actions. Do not fear him, my son. Always look for the good and kind, and you will not meet him.'

Matt felt much better. With a final wipe of his gansey sleeve across his tearful eyes, 'Ma,' he said with a twinkle coming back which was not only the brightness of recent tears, 'can we make some turfcakes for supper?'

The path through Marner Dale led steeply upwards, twisting and turning as it followed the line of the stream now far below, almost hidden from sight by the thick undergrowth. Little sunlight penetrated, even on this bright spring day, as Damaris and Matthew headed towards the open country beyond. The denser parts of Little Wood were spooky at the best of times. A dank earthy smell pervaded the air where damp-loving ferns and sinister fungi grew in profusion. Cracks and holes in tree trunks shaped grotesque faces, grinning sardonically at those who queried them. Overhanging branches caught and snagged at hair and clothes, as if the trees reached out with skeletal fingers to prevent them penetrating too far into its secret depths. Little Wood was an eerie place, unvisited at night by the faint hearted. Its ghostly reputation protected its deepest secrets, where overhanging tree roots concealed hidden contraband from prying eyes. A short way into the wood lay the entrance to the Marner Dale tunnel, arched and well concealed by tangled weeds, a convenient way in and out to the secret part of the narrow valley.

Beyond the stile at the end of the path through the wood the country opened out into a more pleasant and comfortable landscape. Blackthorn bloomed in snow-like profusion, and from the depths of a thick bush the beady bright eye of a female blackbird, snug on her well-hidden nest, gleamed anxiously. Matt's curious but gently probing fingers alarmed the bird into a position of frozen immobility. He did not disturb her, but drew the branches close, and wished her well with raising her family.

From the hill top where sheep grazed contentedly with their new black-kneed lambs gambolling in the joyous spring air, Damaris and Matt turned to draw breath and look back on the picturesque village of their birth. Up here was a new world, full of open space and a sense of freedom rarely experienced within the confines of the narrow alleyways of Baytown.

Yet even up on the high hill top, thoughts of the sea were never far away, as the strong yet mild spring wind chased across the expanse of long grass, bending and silvering in rippling waves evoking the smooth heaving movement of the ocean.

In the autumn they would return to gather the luxuriant crops of rich, juicy blackberries which loaded the hedgerows, but which must be picked before the devil had touched them and turned them bitter with his passing. But time enough for that; today the harvest of spring flowers lured them on to their destination.

Brocketts Wood clustered on the sides of the valley of Mill Beck, a stream a little south of the village, so named from the water mill which gathered power and energy to grind corn from the nearby farms into fine, white flour. Damaris recalled with a grin how she had, in her babyhood days, regarded the miller as a ghost. Elizabeth had taken her there to collect flour for her baking, and Damaris still held a clear picture of the large man in breeches and long apron, covered from head to foot in the fine white flour dust. The interior of the mill was a wonderful sight. A tremendous sense of power emanated from the creaking wooden machinery which turned the huge round grindstones; energy from the stream that began as a trickle high up in the moorland, and gathered force as it tumbled towards the sea. A large dam had been built to confine the water and guide it through a narrow channel to pour onto the slats of the great wooden wheel that worked the machinery inside until, at end of the day, the miller lowered the sluice gates to close it down for the night. Damaris and Matt had on several occasions witnessed the starting of the great mill wheel, slowly and creakingly at first as the newly released water made little impression, but gradually gaining momentum until the whole mechanism was working smoothly.

The mill pool was a fascinating place in its own right, though dangerous as its waters were deep and its sides steep. Migrating salmon could be caught in its murky depths at the right time of the year. Matt determined to return and try to catch one, though he would have to be very wary not to get caught himself. The salmon 'belonged' to the Squire, and poachers were severely punished. But the mill pool was a lonely place, and chances of discovery slight.

Beyond the mill pool, the rivulet sparkled over the stones in its bottom, and Damaris peered through its clear waters searching for coloured pebbles. The streambed contained a treasure trove of semi-precious stones, like the red and green jaspers which, she had been told, had travelled all the way from Scotland in the ice age, when the great glaciers had carved their way through Britain, carrying debris from far afield. Greatest treasures of all, however, were the cold green emeralds and rich glowing amber carnelians, most easily discovered when a low, head-on sun coincided with a newly receding tide. At such times, these jewels leapt spectacularly to the sight from their mundane bed of sand.

Bird life was rich in this part of the stream. The children paused awhile to observe the comical antics of wagtails as they bobbed and dipped like clockwork toys, and the handsome black and white dipper as he searched the stream for food. In summer they had occasionally seen the brilliant blue-jewelled flash of a kingfisher, a rare and unforgettable sight.

However, today they were here to gather primroses, and climbed away up the banks from the stream to where the cheerful flowers carpeted the ground in thick profusion. Even with so many, they picked carefully, never taking too many from one single plant. Once the basket was full they would rest and refresh themselves with their packed tea. Elizabeth had wrapped fresh, crusty-crisp bread rolls, with pats of golden country butter, a piece of farm cheese, a juicy red apple and some homemade ginger biscuits, which in the fresh air and with keen appetites was as good as a banquet.

They had almost finished and were throwing the remaining crumbs to the chattering chaffinches that had appeared hopefully as soon as the food was produced, and which now jostled and scuffled with pushing wings and flying feathers for the scraps thrown to them, when a movement in the undergrowth attracted their attention. A little distance from where they sat, a hare broke cover.

As a rule, this would not have been unusual enough to cause comment, but this hare was different. It was very large, and, it was white. White hares or rabbits were very unlucky, and were believed by the country people to be the foretellers of misfortune and even death. What was more alarming, their maternal grandmother, Jennet, who lived just a little further upstream in a small, strange cottage, and was reputed to be a witch, was also said to be able to turn herself into a hare. Damaris was sure that it was with Jennet's distinctive and unusual greeny-gold eyes that the hare gazed straight at her.

The white hare turned, and lolloped a few paces before turning again, paws raised almost beckoningly, and stared piercingly at them once more, before turning to bound away over the fields in the direction of Jennet's cottage. After a short distance it paused, and glanced briefly behind it, to make sure they were following.

Matt and Damaris were now quite sure it was Jennet, and she wanted them to come. They never quite knew what to make of this peculiar old woman. Her eyes would look straight through you with an absent-minded expression as if she were seeing things far beyond. She also said and did some very strange things, but were these simply the results of a lonely old age? She was, in fact, not their true grand-mother, but their step-grandmother. After Elizabeth's own young mother had tragically died, her father had married Jennet, then a very beautiful if somewhat peculiar girl and an excellent cook, though she did seem to use a lot of strange herbs in her recipes. Jennet had cared for the child in a rather offhanded way, but after her step-daughter's marriage to Zack and the death of her husband at sea, Jennet saw Elizabeth only on rare occasions, though Matt and Damaris did visit from time to time, but mainly out of curiosity rather than real affection. Jennet was so different from the lovely old Rebecca, whom they both regarded as their real granny.

By the time they had cleared the woodland and were out into the open fields again, the hare had quite disappeared. Over in the far corner in a small clump of trees, the smoke rose from Jennet's cottage, curling upwards into the blue sky. Once a shepherd's hut, Jennet had made the small stone building into a cosy if unusual home. Since her widowhood many years before, Jennet had preferred her own company. However, she was not always alone as she had many secret visitors, villagers coming for advice, or her herbal cures for all kinds of ailments, or magical potions and even spells to cast on troublesome neighbours. No, Jennet was not always alone.

The ricketty wooden gate creaked a little as Matt cautiously opened it and they entered the untidy, sweet smelling herb garden. A heady scent arose as their feet crushed the plants which sprawled untidily across the narrow garden path. Jennet had the nine mystic herbs growing in her untidy patch of land; pungent marjoram and sage, fragrant rosemary and lavender, hellebore, comfrey, wormwood and vervain, and rue, the herb of grace.

A large, rather battered black cat with one eye and fight-torn ears luxuriated in the spring sunshine that warmed its dusty fur as it lay sleepily sprawled in joyful abandon on the warm stone doorstep. Damaris stooped and rubbed her forefinger up and down its throat. It purred noisily and lazily stretched its neck for more. Reaching over the cat, Matt knocked on the door from which the paint peeled in flakes and blisters. As a small child he had loved popping them and now, as no-one had ever repainted the door, there were only the scars left.

'Hello! Anybody at home? It's Damaris and Matt.'

'Come in,' croaked a faint voice from the other side of the door. Damaris clenched her right fist with her thumb thrust firmly between first and second fingers in the age-old gesture of charming away a spell, just in case. Like crossing your fingers for good luck, it had never failed her. So far.

Jennet sat, dishevelled and a little breathless, in her rocking chair by the fire. Had she just arrived home from chasing across the fields, or was she merely suffering one of the heaving bouts of asthma which not even she could cure for herself? A heap of books and papers with strange writing lay scattered on the untidy floor; an ancient long-handled broom made from a bunch of birch twigs was propped against the wall, and open cupboard doors revealed rows of neatly labelled bottles and jars. Were these the signs of her mysterious calling or merely the possessions of an eccentric old woman?

One fact was undeniable, though; her unusual golden-green eyes looked at Damaris with a strange and knowing understanding, as she nodded and said, 'Welcome, my children! I knew you would come today.'

A buzz of excited conversation passed around the female population of Baytown that spring as the rumour that Jane Moorsom, who had been keeping company with William Barnard, a well-to-do young farmer, had finally fixed the date for her marriage. A village wedding, especially one into a family of some substance, was an event to be anticipated with great enjoyment. The prospect of a grand feast and free-flowing ale, jollifications and rumbustious games, folk dancing and fun, lit up the days ahead and preparations began in many homes. Jane was a popular young woman and William's parents fully intended welcoming her into their family in grand style. Wardrobes were raided, best garments refurbished, and husbands pestered until they dipped into their pockets and provided money necessary to buy new trimmings. Baytown wives were thrifty creatures who spent little on themselves, but the forthcoming grand wedding gave them an excuse to indulge in a little vanity. After all, their husbands wanted them to look their best, surely, they argued?

Jiddy Vardy's dressmaking skills were in demand as never before and she worked tirelessly from morning till night. Traditionally the bride's friends made the wedding dress and Jiddy was determined that Jane would rival any fine lady on this, her special day. Damaris was proud and delighted that Jiddy should have sought her especial help. Already Damaris had learned much from Jiddy's friendship. She had a natural artistic flair for design and the two of them had already spent hours closeted in Damaris' room, much to the amusement of Zack and the disgust of Matt, who disdained weddings and all the attendant fuss, but all the same, he'd be sure not to be missing the feast afterwards.

Later, Jane's other friends would be given parts of the dress to sew, but just for now Damaris and Jiddy kept their design completely secret. Jiddy was well fixed for obtaining the finest materials. Her reliable and trustworthy relationship with the smuggling fraternity was now generously rewarded. Her request for fine Lyons silk and Valenciennes lace, the very best from France, was met unstintingly. For Jane, especially. She was a lovely and popular girl and Baytown men were proud to help deck her out in her wedding finery.

Damaris' blue eyes opened wide as Jiddy arrived with a large bundle under her cloak and in the privacy of Damaris' room, shook out the rustling folds of the softly sussurating silk. As it drifted and settled in a cream cloud on her bed she touched it with tentative fingers. It was the finest silk she had ever seen, and could not help feeling a twinge of envy as she imagined Jane walking to her wedding dressed in such unimaginable quality. Jiddy's dark eyes twinkled with amusement. 'This'll make that snooty Arabella Clarke's eyes pop!' she remarked, and Damaris' hint of jealousy disappeared in a smothered giggle.

Very carefully they placed the pattern pieces on the priceless silk. Damaris held her breath and averted her eyes as Jiddy expertly sliced away with her scissors. The offcuts were gathered up and Damaris was allowed to keep enough to make a replica of the dress for her doll. The battered old wooden face, though, would make a mockery of the fine garment. Still, her old Dutch doll would have a dress as good as Emma Farsyde's fine French *poupée*, even if she wasn't as pretty, and no one could deny that. Damaris held that character was more important than beauty, anyway.

With the main pieces pinned together, Damaris and Jiddy settled down to the long job of sewing. Jiddy was very good company and the hours sped by, enlightened with her hilarious tales of how she had misled the Preventive men.
It was still a matter of embarrassment, and every time she encountered Peter Maxwell, Jiddy felt slight pangs of guilt when she recalled how she had almost caused his death in his early days of duty in Baytown - now some years back, but still keen in the memory of both, and if truth be known, a healthy respect and regard had that night been sown between the two of them. They had got the measure of each other in no uncertain terms.

It had been on a dismal November day when Jiddy had been visiting friends in a nearby village. She was just about to leave, when a horse came clattering into the yard. Mounted was a very handsome young Preventive officer – Peter Maxwell, new to duties in the area. He began questioning her, but Jiddy skillfully turned the conversation. Always a bit of a tease, she had sidled up to him and fluttered her eyelashes alluringly, in the hope of extracting some information from him about his presence there.

'Oh, just meeting some friends,' he replied to her question.

'Wives ….or sweethearts?' taunted Jiddy.

'Just friends,' he retorted, sharply.

'New round here, aren't you?' asked Jiddy, and pulling her shawl tight round her voluptuous figure, she sidled up to his horse, and posed a few very cleverly worded questions. Peter was very taken by her, and blushed to feel stirrings of sexual attraction. As yet, he had no idea who she was, but he would certainly like to know her better. Swaying seductively and brushing her breasts against his legs she drew him into conversation, and gleaned more than enough information about his current errand. Running her hands swiftly over his thighs, she tossed her hair back over her shoulder, slapped the horse hard on the rump, and said 'Goodbye, handsome! See you around!'

'That you will!' retorted Peter, but he did not know how soon, or where they would meet again, much to his discomfort.

Jiddy had extracted enough details to confirm her suspicions, and set off, fleet of foot, to warn the Baytown men that the Preventives were suspicious of the coming night's run, and that they must rapidly change their plans.

As darkness fell, Jiddy and a couple of men left the village carrying lanterns. When they reached the boggy moorland, they lit the candles and walked backwards and forwards, waving the lanterns high, and then lowering them out of sight to give the impression of a number of men moving in a line. Peter and his men fell for the ruse and followed on. Craftily Jiddy lured Peter right into a deep bog, where he floundered helplessly. She let him wallow there for a while, but remembering the way he had looked at her, she felt it would be a shame that such a handsome fellow should ignominiously drown in a lonely moorland bog. Putting on the accent of a farm boy, she called out of the darkness, and offered help. Her team of men spread heather over the bog, and Peter gradually hauled himself onto firm ground. He was a very different sight now, from the handsome, smartly uniformed officer she had met earlier in the evening. Covered in slime and smelly mud, he reached safety. Jiddy could not resist lowering her lantern and shining the beam in his face. 'Well, hello handsome! We meet again!' She extinguished the light with a laugh and disappeared from his sight. Meanwhile, the Baytown men had taken another route, and the contraband was safely on its way.

Jiddy certainly led an exciting life.

In happy companionship they stitched away until the light faded, and they suddenly became aware of stiff necks and tired eyes. The first stages of their handiwork was surveyed with satisfaction, before being carefully folded, packed in clean papers and cloths, all evidence tidied up and stowed in the secret compartment of Damaris' wardrobe. A neat sliding panel closed over the gown, and hid all trace of its existence.

Some days later, Jane was brought to Elizabeth's house for tea and to be fitted for the gown. Jiddy blindfolded her. She was determined Jane would not see the dress until it was complete in all its elegance. Jane did, however, feel the quality of the cool soft silk as it slipped over her smooth bare shoulders, and already she felt like a queen. She was the happiest girl in Yorkshire, and with difficulty resisted the urge to twirl and dance, so joyous did she feel in the warmth of William's love, and in the beautiful dress which made her feel so special.

Jiddy cut and pinned the long tight sleeves which would be handed to other friends to sew. Then, when all had finished, they would meet together to complete the dress and sew on the trimmings of priceless lace, which would fall from the collar, flattering Jane's graceful neck and small, neat head.

The length decided upon, the final touch was for each girl to sew up part of the hem, using strands of her own hair as thread. This charming old custom ensured their own early marriages, so with Jane on her wedding day would go the romantic hopes of all her young female friends.

Jiddy examined each final stage, and commented in amusement as she observed the different coloured threads catching the hem. Her own black hair contrasted strongly with Damaris' corn gold, Abigail Pinkney's rich auburn, and the mousey brown of Annie Harrison.

Each evening the dress was concealed in Damaris' wardrobe, and she guarded its secret with her life. Not even Elizabeth was allowed to see.

One day, Jiddy arrived with a triumphant smile and a small parcel under her cloak. To Damaris alone did she reveal the secret of the length of exquisite Valenciennes lace which her persuasive influence had obtained from Stoney Fagg's latest run from the *Kent*. The lace had been run ashore personally by Reub, and Damaris handled it with mixed emotions. She dreamt of the day that Reuben would bring her such a present.

The precious lace delicately sewn in place, Jiddy finally declared the dress finished to her satisfaction. Such elegant and beautiful work would bring her even more orders. No-one could match her natural flair, and with the combined skills of her young protégés an undeniable masterpiece of elegance awaited the great day.

May Day dawned bright and sunny. From first light joyful birdsong filled the air, much to the relief of Jane's mother who firmly believed in the old country saying, 'Happy the bride who wakes to the singing of birds on her wedding day,' a sign that the couple will not quarrel and will remain faithful to each other.

Damaris and Annie had been up before dawn to gather the May morning's dew, and wash their faces in the magical liquid as hopeful maidens had done for generations before them. Damaris collected a small amount in a little glass bottle and secreted it in her pocket. Later she would ask Jennet to make it into one of her love potions. She knew the old woman would be at the wedding. Invited or not, Jennet always turned up at any event, especially where there would be good food. She'd have to keep it secret, though. Liz would not approve.

Damaris and Annie gathered a large bunch of the rainbow-hued spring flowers which covered the meadow where their bare feet made visible tracks, weaving back and forth over the dew-covered grass. It was cold, but it felt very good, and the girls sensed the special magic of this early Mayday morning as they picked the flowers for Jane's head-dress and bouquet.

The pearl grey of the dawn sky glowed at first the palest pink, then gradually turned to molten gold as the rays of the rising sun slowly fingered their way across the dew-laden grass. The pasture sparkled with a million jewels. Each dew-tipped blade of grass refracted the soft light of the daybreak into myriad fairy rainbows, gilding the early-morning meadow with the extraordinary freshness which only a rising sun can produce. Fine cobwebs shimmered with a lacy delicacy, the spinners of nature unrivalled by any human hand.

The girls settled down on Annie's outspread cloak to weave the delicate blossoms into a coronet fit for a fairy princess. Jane had insisted on wearing wild flowers, for even with her proud delight in the exquisite gown, she was a simple country girl at heart. Trimmed with cascading ribbons which would flutter gently in the May breeze, the wedding coronet was a thing of breathtaking loveliness. Damaris and Annie held it aloft and turned it this way and that, the pure morning sun enhancing its fairytale beauty. Satisfied at last that it was perfect, they laid it in a basket of damp moss and placed it in the cool shade under a clump of tall grasses. An early morning butterfly alighted to sun its wings on the petals of a primrose. The girls watched in delight, wishing that the elusive creature could stay and become part of the coronet. As it flew off, they turned their attention to the bouquet. This was easier to make, and Damaris held the central stems whilst Annie placed the carefully chosen flowers into a tight posy. A frill of delicate green fern leaves and Queen Anne's Lace framed the pale flowers, then the stems were bound tightly with lengths of cream and pink ribbon. Damaris tied some into a multi-looped bow with a tail of trailing ends, and with this carefully tied to the stems, the bouquet was finished and laid in its basket. After the wedding, Jane would toss it into the crowd of assembled well-wishers and the lucky catcher would surely marry within the year. Damaris and Annie wove the remaining flowers into small coronets for themselves, as Annie teasingly remarked, 'If you catch it, Dam, will you marry Reub?'

'Who knows? Who cares, anyway?' Damaris leapt up from the ground, shook out her long hair, grabbed Annie's hands, hauled her up and swept her into a last barefooted carefree gambol across the dew-fresh grass. 'Come, Annie! If we mess about any longer, we'll miss Jane's wedding and only get there in time for yours - to Richard Bedlington!'

Damaris gave her a friendly push and chased off across the meadow, a blushing Annie stumbling in hot pursuit. Halfway across, they stopped dead in their tracks. 'Annie! The baskets!' How could they have been so caught up with their own secret hopes that they had momentarily forgotten all about Jane's flowers? The baskets hastily retrieved, Annie and Damaris returned companionably homewards, arm in arm. The rising sun gathered strength, and began to burn off the early dew in delicate fronds of pale steam. The magic of the early morning meadow was no more.

The village was already alive with the bustling activity of daily routine. A tantalising smell of frying bacon and new baked bread wafting on the fair morning air banished all romantic thoughts, and the two girls settled down with healthy young appetites to the breakfast Liz laid on the table before them.

Annie delivered the baskets to Jane's house on her way home. Jiddy was in attendance already, mouth full of pins, tweaking and coaxing the dress into the absolute perfection on which she insisted. No crease or fold was permitted to remain. Jiddy was setting great store by the public showing of this her finest creation. Jane stood impatient, frustrated and blindfolded, until Jiddy decided all was completely perfect. Jane lost all sense of time, and sighed impatiently as she tried to convince Jiddy that her wedding would be over before she, the bride, even got there.

'If you'd just keep still a minute, Miss Fidgets, we'd have a better chance,' muttered Jiddy through her mouthful of pins. 'Nearly done.'

Jane had embroidered the bridal garter which, traditionally would be raced for as a prize by the young men as she emerged from the church door. 'Wonder who'll have the honour of removing this,' speculated Jiddy, as the delicate garter was slipped over Jane's slim leg. Jane blushed. It was a slightly embarrassing custom that the winner of the bridal race removed the garter from the bride's leg himself, and, depending on the winner, a varying degree of boisterous teasing made the new bride blush. Jane hoped it would not be Ben Rymer.

'Now, stop thinking about all your past young men. Today you are supposed to be forsaking all others for that handsome William! Eyes tight shut, now, whilst we brush your hair, and then you can look.' Jane's long golden hair burnished to a gloss that rivalled the sheen on her silken gown, Jiddy carefully lifted the delicate floral coronet and placed it on Jane's head. The long ribbons mingled with her hair as they cascaded down her back. Finally the bouquet was gently lifted from its bed of cool moss and placed in her hands, as with a warm and loving kiss on her cheek, Jiddy removed the blindfold and turned Jane to look in the mirror and see herself for the first time. 'All's ready, Jane. You may look now.'

Jiddy's face broadened in a beaming smile as she beheld Jane's expression of complete wonderment at the beauty of the vision that looked back at her from the long mirror. Jane turned this way and that, looking over her shoulder to see the full effect. 'Oh, Jiddy! I never believed it could be so lovely. How can I ever thank you? I'm so elegant, William won't know it's me. He'll think he's marrying some fine lady!'

'And so he is, my dear. So he is,' said Jiddy kindly and quite sincerely. 'As for thanks, my dear Jane, just look at the faces as you walk past. My order book will be full for years.'

'But you won't make anyone else a dress just like this, will you?' Jane enquired anxiously.

'Indeed, no. This was a labour of love for a very special person. Besides, silk and lace like this doesn't grow on trees, you know!' Jiddy winked, knowingly. 'Come, now, Jane. Let's show the world what we've done to you.' Jiddy flung wide the door and with a mockingly sweeping bow she ushered Jane down the stairs to the waiting world and her wedding.

William paused, clad in his best blue velvet coat, doeskin breeches and gleaming white cravat, at the gate into the country churchyard, high on the hillside overlooking the Bay.

The stone walls of the sturdy little church, from which within the hour William would proudly walk with Jane on his arm as his wife, glowed warmly in the May sunshine. His heart beating in a confusion of mixed emotions of anticipation, love, and a degree of nervousness, William ran his finger inside the edge of his tight cravat, took a deep breath of the fresh cool air, and looked across the wide sweeping landscape. From where he waited, he looked down across a row of windswept trees which leaned steeply inland, bent into submission by the relentless winter winds. It was a landscape that changed dramatically with the seasons, and William realised that whenever he looked, it was never exactly the same. Changing light and sweeping clouds coloured the fields in a thousand different shades of green and brown. Today, in the warm sun, the blue waters of the Bay spread wide between the two headlands, outstretched protecting hands that gathered all who lived within their compass. On the sparkling waters a few white and brown sails dotted the blue, but they were the only vessels visible. All the fishing cobles were laid up for the day, their crews already either in the church or gathered in companionable groups outside.

Far down below huddled the red roofs of the Baytown cottages, one of which had so recently sheltered his beloved Jane. Across the wide expanse of countryside, nestling right under the edge of the moor which in autumn glowed with the rich purple of the heather, lay the neat buildings of William's farm. Surrounded on three sides by carefully planted trees to give shelter from the worst of the prevailing winds, the farm house stood firm and square, the outbuildings and stables close by. It had been the home of the Barnards for generations, founded way back when the early settlers sought shelter on the hillside from the Viking raiders, and William was proud of its substantial proportions and security.

A wry little smile spread as he idly wondered if Jane, with her fair Scandinavian looks, was a descendant of that race, the sons of Thor and Odin, which had so disorganised his predecessors? One thing for sure, thought William, she had 'disorganised' him alright, for his life had never been the same since he had met and courted the lovely young woman who, at this very moment was approaching up the hill to greet him.

William and Jane had carefully chosen this Wednesday for their wedding. Old rhymes and superstitions influenced many country events, and from their childhood both had been familiar with the old rhyme:- 'Monday for health, Tuesday for wealth, Wednesday the best day of all. Thursday for losses, Friday for crosses, Saturday for no luck at all.'

William heard the wedding procession long before it came into his impatient view. The strains of the village fiddler, preceding the party, playing a merry marching tune, eased the toil up the long hill from the village to the little church on top.

Jane, surrounded by her young friends all clad in their very best and bedecked with flowers, led the large group of merrymaking villagers. William hoped that the ones straggling in the rear would not arrive drunk and spoil the beautiful ceremony which was to bind him and Jane together for life, a solemn and intimate occasion, not to be sullied by intemperate villagers who had mainly come for the free flowing drink. Time enough for that, afterwards. The traditional serving of 'hot-pot,' warm spiced wine, at several resting places on the route from the village to the church, was a mixed blessing. It certainly encouraged the walkers onwards and upwards, but those who partook too liberally were definitely merry by the time they reached the churchyard gate, and it was not unknown for the minister to instruct the ushers to bar the merrymakers from the ceremony within. William chuckled at the recollection of one village wedding, where the groom had led the party up the hill one sweltering August day, slaking his thirst at every resting place and on arrival at the church was so loudly joyous at the prospect of his wedding, that the minister barred him until he had sobered up.

A little way behind the main party but keeping up a gallant pace, came a solitary figure accompanied by a strolling, one-eyed black cat. 'Aye,' she muttered, toothless jaws champing discontentedly. 'All very well, but you know what they say: Marry in May and rue the day. Should have gotten married yestiddy whilst it was still April.'

The old stone church which this day was to witness the happiness of the young couple so shortly to be joined in matrimony before its simple altar, had stood guard over the people of Fylingdales for generations. It had absorbed mixed emotions of joy and sorrow, thanksgiving and supplication, and the atmosphere within emitted a strong sense of understanding, quiet comfort, and great peace. Every Sunday its congregation praised and thanked their God for the week past, prayed for future guidance and strength to bear the worries of daily life, and commended absent loved ones into His keeping. Each week, the Reverend Charles Hepworth entered into the quaint three-decker pulpit, using the lower level for prayers, rising to the second to read the familiar words of the Bible, and climbing to the third to preach to his congregation, guiding their way through life and filling them with spiritual assurance of the great love God had for each and every one of them. Charles Hepworth regarded his congregation as his 'flock,' and with his gentle and caring attitude, they looked on him as their very own 'good shepherd.'

This bright and joyful morning, he waited with William with a shine in his warm brown eyes and an instinctive feeling that this was going to be a good marriage. With his long years of experience amongst this community - and he had known them for almost thirty years - he was rarely proved wrong. A quiet, kindly man, he readily perceived the needs of his people. He understood their financial need to be involved deeply in the running of contraband and although as a Churchman he could not openly condone it, it was rumoured that he was not averse to accepting the occasional keg of brandy, purely for medicinal purposes, he assured. Today he sensed William's mingled joy and anxious nervousness as the strains of the fiddler were now loud, therefore the arrival of his bride very close.

William's face shone with pleasure and pride as he regarded Jane, radiant with love, and clad in her magnificent bridal finery, the simple countryside flowers crowning her youthful beauty.

The Minister turned and offered his outstretched hands in welcome. He had no real need to ask if either were willing to take the other as man and wife, though in the ceremony shortly to follow he must ask, and they must answer firmly before their friends and before God. 'Come, my children,' he invited kindly. William took Jane's hand in his and led her along the uneven stone-flagged path between the nodding golden daffodils which carpeted the churchyard at this time of year. Jane's attention fell on the weathered inscription of a crumbling old tombstone: -

'By storms at sea two sons I lost
Which sore distresses me,
Because I cannot have their bones
To anchor here with me.'

She experienced a wave of compassionate understanding for that unknown mother whose sorrow lingered even now, and was thankful that she was marrying a farmer. Although her life ahead would not always be easy and she would have her fair share of sorrow, she knew that her sons would follow William behind the plough and the Barnard farmstead would continue into the hands of a new generation.

Jane turned to William with a smile of unsurpassable happiness. Together they entered into the church, deliberately placing right foot first as custom demanded to ensure a happy marriage, and followed Charles Hepworth between their assembled friends to the altar where they made their vows. William placed his gold ring on her finger, and they promised they would be faithful together till death did them part. Their assembled friends, witnessing such obvious happiness, prayed fervently that this parting would be many, many years ahead.

Up in the west gallery the church band struck up a joyful hymn tune. Jack the village fiddler had left the head of the procession and taken his place as leader of the assorted group of local musicians. Fiddles, clarinets and flutes scraped, warbled and chirped cheerfully. Old Amos had struggled in with his ancient 'cello and sat astride it with the natural, permanently bow-legged posture of a lifelong horse- man, and Seth the shepherd boomed out the bass notes on his battered old serpent, which Amos rudely complained sounded like a drainpipe with indigestion. Seth retaliated by chaffing Amos that he was only scraping the guts of a cat with the hairs from the tail of his old horse. Musical hostility was good-natured and would be eased later with harmony restored over mugs of brimming ale.

The old church was cool and dim; the sky clouded over momentarily as the wind blew the last of the April shower clouds from the Mayday sky, but the sun burst forth as the young couple emerged. 'Blessed is the bride that the sun shines on' quoth the old saying, and Jane was certainly blessed with happiness as William paused in traditional fashion on the threshold of the church porch, dipped deep into his pocket and cast a handful of shining copper coins spinning into the assembled crowd, symbolically spreading generosity so that he and his bride would not want in the future. Their good luck was sealed by the appearance of Jennet's old black cat which strolled up with casual nonchalance between the assembled guests and with arched back and battered tail held high, sinuously twined itself ingratiatingly around Jane's legs, purring noisily. Jane concealed a sensation of distaste and annoyance as its dusty fur left a faint mark on the pristine newness of her beautiful gown.

At the church gate the local lads were assembled, ready for the traditional race for the bride's garter. Usually the race ended at the bride's own home, where at the reception the winner would be rewarded by being permitted to remove his prize from the bride's leg himself. But on this occasion the race was a long one, out to Barnards farm, and the winning would sort out the fastest and fittest without a doubt. Jane's cottage home being small and the guests so many, it was an obvious decision to hold the celebrations at William's home where the large barn would hold all invited.

Meanwhile, the local maidens all jostled in a more decorous manner, keeping an eye on Jane, arms ready to reach up and catch the wedding bouquet when the bride decided the moment was right to cast away her flowers to her waiting friends. In her own mind she had already decided to tease them a little by pretending to throw, laughing as their upstretched hands eagerly grasped the empty air.

Together, Jane and William went arm in arm, back down the stone flagged path between the wild daffodils to the church gate, where Rosie the white cart horse stood, patient and resplendent, between the shafts of the decorated farm wagon. Rosie had not been without company during the ceremony, for the minister's horse, sheltered in the small stone stable by the church gate, had hung its shaggy brown head over the half door. Nuzzling noses companionably, the two horses spent a pleasant half hour in equine conversation. Their horsey talk was curtailed as firm hands grasped Rosie's harness, and urged her onward. Straining forward, powerful muscles rippling under her gleaming white coat, the cart wheels grated on the rough stony track. Shaking her head in a proud gesture of farewell to her erstwhile companion, Rosie set her harness jingling merrily as she moved forward up to the gate to carry Jane and William to their celebrations.

Jane still carried her flowers as she was handed up into the ribbon-bedecked cart. High above the crowd she paused in a graceful gesture before finally launching the bouquet in a colourful parabola, cream and pink ribbons streaming behind, into the hands of the impatiently waiting girls who jostled, eyes a-shine in bright faces, eager arms outstretched. An expression of delighted surprise, suffused by a spreading blush, transformed the normally rather plain, freckled face of Annie Harrison, the envied catcher. Damaris, standing close by, felt not envy, but the pleasure of genuine friendship as she now witnessed Annie's blushing transformation. Damaris glanced sideways. She was not alone in observing the new and attractive Annie. For some reason best known to himself, Richard Bedlington had not raced away to Barnards farm hoping to win Jane's garter. He, too, was looking at Annie with new eyes.

William took the reins, and urged Rosie onward, as the joyful procession slowly trundled forwards. Jane laughed delightedly, as Reuben Granger took his position at the head with the traditional squawking cockerel, only silencing it when the onlookers paid 'bride money' into his outstretched hat. The indignant bird was clearly recognizable as Abigail Pinkney's best proud cock bird, borrowed for the occasion, bright feathers fluttering and angry expression in its beady black eyes. Its loud squawks rivalled the merry tones of Jack's fiddle in unharmonious cacophony as the cheerful procession made its joyous way to the farm and the wedding feast.

Benjamin Rymer stumbled, panting and sweating with exertion, across the stable yard to where the doors of the great barn stood wide in welcome. Fine motes of dust danced merrily in the shafts of sunlight which penetrated its cool dim interior where the last touches were being put to the feast. Benjamin's flushed, triumphal arrival announced the imminent approach of William and Jane and signalled a final burst of activity within. Benjamin rapidly downed the proffered tankard of frothing ale in great, refreshing gulps, wiped his sleeve across his mouth and grinningly held out the empty tankard for more.

'Ho'd on now there, Ben,' admonished Isobel the serving maid, wagging a warning finger playfully before his streaming eyes. 'Thi hands must be steady to remove thi prize, otherwise if tha's all of a tremble, whatever'll Jane think of 'ee?'

'She can think what she danged well likes!' retorted Ben arrogantly with a suggestive leer.

'Nah then, be'ave thissen,' scolded Isobel.

'What about that drink, then?' reminded Ben.

'Oh go on, then, but that's thi last for a while,' warned Isobel as she filled a second tankard brim full and Ben supped, a little more moderately, winking at Isobel over its frothy capping. Ben was a right lad for the lasses, thought

Isobel, as she observed him out of her eye corner. He was a real good looker, strong and fit, too, as he had just proved. His rivals in the bridal race were only just now staggering in varying stages of exhaustion across the stable yard, gasping for ale as they collapsed, heaving, against the massive oak door-frames before slumping to the ground, legs outstretched, whipping off spotted neckerchiefs to mop their profusely sweating faces.

Once news got round that Ben had won the garter, speculation would be rife as to which lucky maiden he would favour with his fickle affections that day. 'Many shall be called but few chosen' quoted Isobel irreverently to herself, as she quelled the stirring of an uncomfortable attraction for Ben. A small seed of envy for the girl he would choose took root in her emotions. She would not let it grow, she admonished herself. Her cap was set at Christopher Fairfax, older and more staid than the flamboyant Benjamin to be sure, but a potentially reliable husband who would give her a good, steady life, if rather a comparatively dull one. Isobel was a level-headed lass, with the good sense to look to the future. Convincing herself that anyone else was welcome to the feckless Ben, she devoted her attention to consoling the runners up.

Rosie's highly polished hooves clopped on the stone paved stable yard, her new iron shoes ringing firmly on the hard level surface. The shiny yellow wheels of the cart turned like great golden suns, radiating flashing rays as the bright May daylight played on the gleaming new paintwork, grinding to a halt as William heaved on the reins with a final 'Whoa, Rosie!' The proud mare shook her great head and set her harness jingling, snickering loudly through her great soft nostrils. Eager hands gathered to assist Jane down from the bower of greenery atop the cart. As she raised her skirt to step forward, her glance caught the speculative eye of Ben Rymer, leaning in studied nonchalance against the barn door. She desperately wished it had been anyone but Ben who had won the race. She had long ago had her share of Ben's passing attentions, before settling for her dear William. On this day of all days, she wanted no reminder of any past affections, no matter how trivial. She knew that Ben would make some teasing and coarse remark that would embarrass both herself and her new husband. William had never known just how far Jane's relationship with Ben had nearly gone, and taking a deep breath to steady her nerves, she leaned forward into the strong arms, which guided her safely to the ground, their eyes meeting in silent knowledge as they passed.

All the younger guests had managed to make their way on foot, following with dancing steps the merry tunes of the fiddler as he played them along the long journey from his perch at the back of the wedding cart. Unrivalled for the latter part by Abigail's cockerel which had squawked valiantly if reluctantly, collecting Jane a goodly sum of bride money on the way, Jack the fiddler now ruled the roost, sensing great magical power in his bow as he played the happy crowd forward. Their feet bewitched by his merry music and eased on by frequent tots of hot-pot along the route, it was indeed a noisily cheerful band which crowded into the barn yard ready to do justice to the ample feast. Farm carts and drays had been thoughtfully sent out to carry the less nimble, and now these trundled in procession into the yard until it seemed that the whole of Yorkshire must be assembled. Mrs. Barnard anxiously hoped she'd prepared enough food. They looked a mighty hungry lot!

At the back of the last cart sat Jennet, old black bonnet nodding, beady eyes surveying all and missing nothing. The cat perched arrogantly beside her, its one green eye staring inscrutably at these strange surroundings.

By the barn door stood Isobel with the traditional plate of a small cake which she offered first to Jane, who broke and ate a small piece, then threw the rest over her head in the hope that she would always have plenty and some to spare. She then passed the plate to William who must throw it over his head so that it broke. He threw it hard; the guests cheered as it shattered into dozens of tiny fragments, assuring that the couple would have much good luck.

Entry to the feast was now traditionally barred by the winner of the bridal race. Jane forced a small smile as, face to face with the arrogant and uncouth Benjamin, she decorously lifted her skirt as he sank to one knee in the doorway, placed one foot on his proffered thigh and looked away as she felt his fingers touching her leg much higher and more lingeringly than was necessary for the discreet removal of the garter. Jane's impish humour returned and as Ben triumphantly held his prize aloft with a loud and raucous guffaw, Jane gave a firm push with her foot, sending him sprawling backwards into the barn.

Hungry guests surged forward to take their places at the laden tables, and Ben scrambled in an undignified and slightly drunken stumble away from under the trampling feet. Angrily, he straightened his cravat, and swore vengeance. No one assaulted Ben Rymer's dignity and made him a laughing stock, not even in good-humoured foolery. Nobody. But nobody.

Jane would regret her action.

Barnard hospitality was a byword in all Fylingdales and far beyond. The great stone barn had hosted countless country celebrations in its long life. Mell suppers at which the Harvest Home was celebrated in grand style, Yuletide festivities and New Year gatherings, Barn Dances in which generations of dancing boots had pounded the dusty floor, and today, yet another important family wedding. Jane and William, at the head of the table, presided over their bridal feast as their predecessors had done since medieval times. They both sensed the feeling of continuity and Jane was proud and happy to be part of this great family. Mrs. Barnard, senior, looked back on her own wedding many years ago and understood precisely what Jane was experiencing. They got on well together and Sarah approved completely of her son's choice of wife. She also observed with satisfied pride the results of her competent housekeeping, as the kitchen staff replenished the tables with a never ending flow of pies, hams, roasts of beef, pork, mutton, chicken, pheasant, turkey, rabbit and hare, and great steaming tureens of soups and home grown vegetables. All the guests had healthy Yorkshire appetites and with the blunt forthrightness of country people, would have gossiped disparagingly if supplies had run out.

Damaris and Matthew ate heartily along with the rest of the young folk. Rarely was a proffered dish refused, but Damaris did decline the serving of roast hare. Glancing around, she could not see Jennet, tucked away in a corner. The dish smelt mouth-wateringly of aromatic herbs and tasty gravy, but one could not be too careful where that strange old woman's peculiar habits were concerned.

Folk had eaten their fill for the time being at least, later on would come the procession of sweetmeats; fruit pies, custards and 'syllabubs under the cow.' Tables were cleared and trestles moved back to the walls, a rough platform set up for the musicians, who with a natural versatility could turn from hymn tune to folk dance at the turn of a page, and so long as liquid refreshment flowed, would play reels and jigs and hornpipes until the cows came home. Young men eagerly took their partners' arms and led them forth. At the head of the set, William bowed courteously to Jane, offered his hand, and amid cheers and clapping away they went, down the set and back again, raising the dust to the merry tune of 'Sir Roger de Coverley.' Behind William and Jane, Damaris blushingly accepted the invitation of Reuben Granger, Annie Harrison shyly took the hand of Richard Bedlington, and Isobel stepped out with the portly Christopher Fairfax, while the older folk looked on with amused approval. So long as there were lads as handsome and girls as pretty as these, future wedding jollifications were assured.

Dancing would continue well into the evening, though many couples drifted away into the privacy of the quiet moonlight. The older folk, whose dancing days were past, settled down in friendly groups to gossip and exchange news from the further reaches of the lonely dales. In a far corner, Jennet and her old crony Dorcas, the farm laundress, nodded companionably over their mugs of ale, reminiscing in the recognised manner of the elderly, memories gradually gently blurring in the solace of the home-made liquor.

Weddings were occasions for playing practical jokes. Ben Rymer, at the centre of a group of noisy young men, planned his revenge.

As midnight approached Jane left the celebrations with Jiddy to help her out of her wedding dress and into her night attire. So engaged were they in reliving the events of the lovely day that they did not hear stealthy footsteps approaching up the stairs, nor the quiet click of the lock as the key turned in the bedroom door.

In the barn, William raised a last glass and called for silence, to thank all his friends for making this day such a memorable one. He was unaware of the raucous snigger from the lads as he wished all good night and God speed on their journeys back home.

Mounting the stairs to join his new wife, William was surprised to be confronted with the locked door. Knowing Jane's impish humour and sense of fun, he assumed that this was her doing. Jane and Jiddy were equally surprised, and it was some time before Jiddy finally convinced William that Jane really did not have the key.

Always resourceful, Jiddy called through the locked door that William should go and find a ladder, and that she would open the window and help him through.

Embarrassed to be observed in undignified retreat, William vainly hoped that the farm-yard would be in deserted darkness, and most of his friends either homeward bound or in the barn partaking of 'one for the road.'

But Ben and the lads were waiting for him.

'Now then, William! Not abed yet?' they mocked. 'Fancy a walk in the moonlight with us instead?' they guffawed coarsely as they nudged him in the ribs.

Reluctant to reveal his discomfiture, William pushed them off, straightened his shoulders, walked firmly alone to the barn and returned with a ladder.

Placing it against the window where from above, two pale female faces peered anxiously, William began to climb. Hand over hand he went, looking ever upward into the eyes of

Jane and ignoring the antics of his boisterous friends below. Almost at the top he reached out to grasp the window sill, when Ben heaved his great strong body under the ladder, and the top with William clinging tightly, arched away from the sill, the outstretched hands of Jane and Jiddy just too distant to grasp him.

Ben and the lads had only intended to sway the ladder back and forth until William was sick with dizziness, but William's unexpectedly wild struggling sent the ladder out of control. It lurched dangerously backwards, past the point of no return, and William went hurtling heavily through the air. Jane and Jiddy screamed as he hit the ground with a sickening thud.

Damaris and Annie heard the noisy commotion and arrived just in time to help him up and brush him down. Miraculously he had fallen partly on a heap of hay, but even so, limped painfully away on a badly sprained ankle.

Moonlight glinted on the shaft of the metal key as Ben threw it insolently to land at William's feet. 'Don't know as though you'll be wanting that,' he jeered, as it clinked onto the hard ground.

Reuben and Richard were furious.

'Thoo gurt stupid fool, thoo might 'a' killed 'im!'

Ben swaggered away with an arrogant shrug. He hadn't intended his prank to go so far, only enough to frighten Jane as revenge for his earlier discomfiture, and he left the scene in an attitude of embarrassed stubbornness. The prank had turned badly against him, and he lost face with his mates for the second time that day.

Above the departing guests the stars shone, twinkling diamonds set on the black velvet of the night sky. A full moon shone brightly to light their way home over field and moor. Farmer Barnard put his arm round his wife's plump shoulders and heaved a satisfied sigh at the success of the day. Jennet dozed comfortably in the warm hay-loft where she had retired, unseen, for the night, whilst the cat silently stalked the barn for unsuspecting mice holding their own feast off the wedding crumbs.

William and Jane paused in the moonlit window, arms around each other, looking out on their future home with new eyes, the eyes of love, towards a lifetime of togetherness, and were extraordinarily happy.

Jennet stirred uneasily in her ale-induced sleep in the deep soft comfort of the hay-loft, where she had crept unnoticed whilst the commotion was going on in the barnyard. Dorcas would have found her room in the house, but there were times that Jennet preferred to feel closer to nature. A troublesome wisp of hay tickled her nose, making her sneeze. In her dreamlike state the fragrant smell of the dry hay gradually changed itself into that of the long, sweet smelling, fresh-growing grass of a summer meadow. She tossed restlessly, unable to find a comfortable position, yet the more she moved around in the hay the more restless she became. The ale she had consumed during the evening gave her a very light-headed feeling as if she was becoming detached from her body.

Mysteriously, Jennet felt herself becoming lighter and lighter, until she dreamed her spirit was floating high above her material body. Her eyes grew accustomed to the strange darkness and gradually she felt a sensation of twitching in her legs. She groaned and turned over again in the hay, but still the feeling persisted, growing stronger and stronger until she could no longer control the spirit that struggled for freedom.

Ben Rymer could not sleep that night, either. The events of the past day preyed on his mind. He hated being made a laughing stock. Twice that day his friends had witnessed his discomfiture and the ensuing loss of face would be embarrassing to live up to. He had plenty of enemies who would delight in sniggering at his humiliation.

He tossed hotly in his bed. The pellucid moon shone in through the window and hurt his eyes. Throwing back the covers, he rose and went to the casement. It was a beautiful evening, just right for a spot of poaching. He drew on his heavy corduroy trousers, took his gun from its hook above the fireplace, and let himself out into the night.

He paused momentarily, breathing deeply of the cool night air, letting his eyes become accustomed to the moonlight and his ears to the soft sounds of the night world, then creeping stealthily down the wood side he paused, as a rustling in the bushes drew his attention. In the bright moonlight he observed the form of a white hare, peacefully grazing on the sweet, dew fresh grass. Raising its head it stared with greeny-gold eyes, sensing the disturbing presence of human flesh. Warily at first it lolloped towards the stream that ran through the wood, thinking to cross the water and escape into the dense undergrowth on the other side. Strangely, it could not cross the stream, try though it would, and in panic raced in short bursts up and down the short length of the bank side. Ben kept it in the sight of his gun and when the moment was right, took aim and fired.

The hare leapt into the air with an animal scream of pain and panic, a scream that had a chilling uncannily human sound. Blood stained its beautiful white fur as it limped for cover to nurse its wound.

Ben trembled when he saw the strange look in the animal's eyes. He had seen those eyes somewhere else. As realisation dawned, fear grew as he recalled the way the hare could not cross the stream. Immediately to his mind came the old belief that witches could not cross running water. What had he done?

Jennet's freed spirit had rejoiced in the cool freshness of the night. She revelled in the dew damp grass and felt her legs stretching in the urge to leap and bound over the springy tussocks. Pausing a moment to savour the sweet grass, she sensed the smell of humanity. Fear seized her and her heart thumped as she bounded towards the swift flowing stream that wound through the wood. She must escape, cross that water to safety, but racing back and forth in short bursts of panicked activity, she could find no way across.

Suddenly a stabbing pain seared through her thigh and she limped away, screaming in agony.

Ben broke out in a cold sweat. All he could see, larger than life, was that pair of strange greeny-gold eyes that seemed to bore through his very soul. Wherever he looked, those eyes were fixed on him. There was no escape from their persistent scrutiny. Dropping the gun, he clapped his hands over his ears to shut out that dreadful scream. It rang round and round in his head. Ben started to run. Like the hare that he had just shot, he raced frantically backwards and forwards. There was no escape from his fear.

The hayloft echoed with Jennet's cry of agony in her dream. Her night cramps had never been as bad as this. Gritting her teeth, and easing her leg down the bed, she put down her hand to her thigh to massage and relieve the gripping pain of the tensed muscle. When she withdrew the hand, it was warm and sticky and covered with blood.

Part Three

Early one summer morning Damaris rose eagerly. Bright rays from the rising sun pierced through a chink in her curtains, streamed onto her face and probed her closed eyes with their brilliance until she awoke. Flinging back the drapes, Damaris looked again on her own special view of the world. She had witnessed it cold grey and white in winter, soft green and yellow in spring, and now, this hot summer morning, it was shimmering blue and molten gold. Vessels on the horizon quivered unrealistically in the heat haze. Damaris was sure she recognised the familiar tall masts of the schooner *Kent* as she headed back across the North Sea to Holland, confirming her dreamy recollections that the night hours had been disturbed by various noises. She strongly suspected that Zack was even now in their cellar, re-arranging its ever-changing contents.

The sparkling blue sea beckoned irresistibly. Damaris dressed quickly and tiptoed down the wooden stairs, counting carefully, stepping over the one that habitually creaked. That tell-tale fourth treader had led to her discovery more than once. It was loose for a very good reason, for it was hollow underneath and concealed a small, dark, very useful space.

The ebbing tide had receded from the slipway leaving a brand new, smooth sandy shore on which no person had yet set foot. Damaris stepped forth onto its early morning newness, stretched her arms upwards and breathed deeply of the sweet summer morning. The atmosphere at that time of day still held a touch of the magic of the new dawn. Although the sun was fully up, there still remained in the sky the last faint traces of the moon, a delicate white crescent against the blue sky; a moon which, the previous night had shone over illicit activity on this very shore.

Kicking off her boots and tying the laces into a carrying loop, Damaris ran lightly to where the tiny wavelets swept over the new sand with a final rush, before receding a little further, to gradually expose a whole brand new stretch of golden beach. Her bare feet left only light indentations which filled with water as she passed. The touch of the sea was icy cold and Damaris' small toes turned a delicate pink as she ran, tentatively at first, then more courageously as her feet became accustomed to the chill of the refreshing water. Tossing up showers of sparkling spray, she twirled and danced, a solitary figure in the morning sunlight, this smuggler's child, fully aware in her youthful maturity of the dangerous environment in which she lived, exhilarated by her blossoming love for Reuben, but on this midsummer morning also still possessed of a gloriously carefree innocence.

She ran along the shore until the Mill Beck, restrained between close banks as it fell from the high moorland, now spread itself in luxurious abandon across the unconfined stretches of the sand to mingle with the salty tang of the ocean. A group of gulls noisily bathed in the fresh water before it reached the sea, splashing and squawking in sheer delight of the cleansing sensation on their feathers.

Beyond Mill Beck, the cliffs towered steep and threatening. No escape here for unwary travellers caught by the incoming tide. Damaris and Matt only normally passed this point if the tide was on the ebb, or the incoming tide was slack. A fast, in-flowing sea could trap and pin its victim close under the dark cliff, pounding the body and rising in slow torture until it enveloped all in the eternal darkness of extinction. Even on such a glorious golden morning this stretch of beach exuded a feeling of menace. Damaris shaded her eyes against the bright sky as she paused a moment to gaze at the chittering kittiwakes as they fed and guarded their young chicks on the most precarious of nesting sites, tiny ledges on the dizzy heights of the sheer cliff face. The clever sharp-pointed oval shape of their eggs prevented many rolling off the edge, but the young chicks had no such natural protection, simply an instinct to stay put. Once they plucked up courage to take their first flight, though, there was no turning back, and many an inexperienced fledgling would meet an untimely death as it plummeted too soon from its nesting place.

Close to the edge of the lapping tide flocks of wading birds ran and dipped and searched, rising in alarm as she approached, only to settle a few yards further on and resume their urgent seeking for sustenance. The smart oyster catcher in his striking black and white plumage, scarlet beak probing, dipped deep, his reflection in the wet sand bobbing up and down. Twinkle-toed ringed plovers rushed busily back and forth, the flock moving as one, chasing the tiny wavelets as they receded, each bird eager for the small crustacea left by every new wave. Gulls wheeled and screamed joyously overhead, outstretched wings filtering the brilliant light of the summer morning as they drifted lazily on the rising thermals, circling slowly upwards and heavenwards. Damaris, earth-bound maiden, envied them their aerial freedom.

She had a whole morning ahead of her before she needed to return home to help Liz. This was unusual, for normally her day's work started early. Recently, she had been working especially hard with the early summer cleaning, and Liz, understanding the need for a little space of one's own from time to time, had given her the morning off. This time, therefore, was precious, to be enjoyed to the full.

After a while, she wandered to the edge of the rocky scaur which reached out into the sea, and finding a flat place, sat down to appreciate the beauty of the morning. The silence was almost tangible; there was no wind, the sea was flat calm, and even the birds had ceased there intermittent calling. At rare moments like this, it is possible, if one is attuned to nature, to actually hear the magic moment when the tide turns. The air stands still, the sea pauses for a split second, then, where the edge has been gently ebbing, it slowly begins moving forward. Damaris sat until the newly flowing water reached her ankles, enjoyed the refreshing coolness for a while, then rose to continue her journey along the shore. Now that the tide had turned, she kept a wary eye on its approach, but experience had told her the instant she should start to return home before the incoming tide trapped her. It had only just turned, so she had some time of safety left.

By Stoupe Beck, where the landscape eased a little as the high cliffs gave way to gentler slopes, a rough trackway led down the shore. Damaris stopped suddenly and gazed at the sand below her feet. Above the high tide level the soft, loose sand had been trampled by many small hooves and the ground was littered with the tell-tale currant droppings of sheep. The gentle incoming tide had not obliterated completely the disturbed marks which led from the trackway and disappeared into the edge of the sea. Damaris shielded her eyes and looked toward the horizon where now only the tops of the masts of the *Kent* still broke the skyline. Very puzzled, she turned her footsteps homewards, where discreet investigations would no doubt divulge a solution to this mysterious discovery.

If Damaris had turned towards Stoupe Brow instead of homeward to the distant village she could have discovered the answer very quickly. Over a laden breakfast table Samuel Barnard and William were regaling Sarah and Jane with the hilarious tale of the previous night's events.

As anticipated by Zack, the *Kent* had arrived in the Bay late in the evening. Samuel, a key figure in the run, had mistaken the date, not expecting her for another week. William's wedding had, he said, got him all flustered. He had to blame somebody! He winked and smiled at Jane in fatherly fashion. Perhaps what he did not realise was that his error could have had very serious repercussions indeed. It was vital that everybody concerned played their part efficiently. Mistakes were not taken lightly by the organizers of the runs. Samuel could have been in line for a severe reprimanding, the physical results of which could scar him for life. He would not be given any more chances. His carelessness also put others in jeopardy, the final effects of which would not be known for some time, but due to his thoughtlessness, many lives would be changed.

'Owlers' or 'woolers,' as the smugglers of wool were known, were in especial danger. Wool had been a valuable source of national income for centuries, and its disappearance from the coasts in large quantities was depriving the government of a great deal of useful revenue. As a deterrent, the punishment was severe. At the end of a jail sentence the culprit was taken to a public place where his right hand was chopped off, the stump wrapped in wool, and the severed hand nailed upon a tall post as a warning to others. Without a right hand a man's future in manual work was bleak.

The first part of the run of goods into the village had gone well. Too well. Stoney Fagg was uneasy when things went so smoothly. It generally meant trouble later on. He felt it in his bones as he paced the deck of the *Kent*, anchored a safe distance off-shore, scanning the beach for signs of Samuel Barnard and his men.

Stoney had run his contraband safely ashore. Even at this moment so soon after its landing, not a trace of barrel or keg, package or parcel, box or basket, was visible anywhere in the village. With the run successfully completed, Stoney had fully expected to load up his return cargo of sheep's wool and be away and over the horizon well before daybreak, and could not conceal his annoyance that the fleeces were not ready, shorn from the sheep, and tied into neat, light bundles. He angrily pounded his clenched fists against the ship's rail. Where the hell was Samuel? Every moment wasted brought the risk of discovery closer. Stoney called impatiently to be rowed ashore, to find Reuben and Zack. At least they could be relied on, he swore.

After a hurried and irate discussion, Reuben was despatched on a dangerous moonlight ride out to Sam Barnard's farm, to demand what the devil was going on? Samuel blissfully unaware of his gigantic blunder, slept soundly and woke in alarm at the urgent hammering at his door below. Rubbing the sleep from his eyes, he gaped down in bemusement at the enraged Reuben astride a sweating horse.

'Stoney says he'll have *thy* fleece, nivver mind the sheep's if he gets caught,' reported Reuben. 'So, Sam, what's tha goin' to do abaht it?'

Samuel's tousled head, now fully awake but empty of ideas, retreated through the open window, and he went next door to rouse William. Reuben dismounted from his horse and stamped around impatiently for what seemed hours, but could only have been minutes, until the sounds of the heavy bolts being withdrawn heralded the opening of the great oak door which admitted him into the presence of the two hastily dressed farmers. William limped slightly as he entered the kitchen still fastening his breeches. The three of them concocted a hasty plan. Reuben leapt to his horse to return at a gallop with the message and organize the Bay team whilst Sam and William headed for the cottage of the shepherd.

Seth, too, had to be dragged from the depths of deep, contented slumber. Sam and William now experienced first hand some of the restless anxiety passed on from Reuben. After an interminable time lanterns were lit and the three men headed for the field in which the sheep, brought down from the high moorland in readiness for their shearing, dozed under the pale crescent moon, the faint cold light silvering their soft and valuable fleece. Gently, the shepherd whistled to his dog, Tip, and together, man and dog roused the slumbering sheep and, backed by William and Sam, drove the dozy flock down the steep track to the shore.

Zack and Reub, meanwhile, had organised the local men, ready with boats, to ferry the reluctant four-footed passengers on board the *Kent* for their unexpected trip to the continent. With much scuffling the protesting sheep were bundled unceremoniously into the cobles and hauled on winches aboard the lugger. Stoney Fagg kept a wary eye open for the appearance of the Preventive men. Reuben had the presence of mind to alert Jiddy Vardy to their dilemma, and she was even then diverting the attention of Peter Maxwell in ways best known only to herself. The hastily made plans had miraculously worked, and the Barnard flock finally set sail on the last moments of the ebbing tide.

Groups of exhausted men made their thankful ways homewards, the difficult mission finally accomplished undiscovered, hoping and praying for their tracks to be covered by the newly turned tide. Zack was not to know that just after daybreak his own daughter would be first on the scene, to discover the tell-tale traces of the night's activities in the sand, and that Reub had been spotted by a jealous enemy.

Thomas Duke stood, legs astride, hands firmly thrust into his pockets, reading the notice nailed roughly to the door of the Fisherman's Arms.

Strolling down to his boat to prepare for the day's work, his attention had been caught by two magic words. 'REWARD. £500.' Lazy by nature, Thomas greedily grasped any chance of 'owt for nowt'in true Yorkshire fashion. He fingered the few coins at the bottom of his pocket speculatively. Five hundred pounds! It was a lifetime's fortune to someone like him. If he had that kind of money he would never have to manhandle his heavy boat down the slipway and go fishing ever again. He could … buy all the things he had ever wanted; he could … be clean and smart and well dressed and wealthy and attractive; he could … leave this dismal place and sail across the world to a whole new glamorous life. He realised he would have to leave, whether he preferred to or not, for if he claimed that reward, life would hold no pleasures for him here. Likely there would be no life once his treachery became known.

Even to be caught reading the offending notice would cause ill-feeling and suspicion. He glanced anxiously over his shoulder to ensure he was unobserved.

Quickly absorbing the remaining details of the tempting poster, nailed up by the village Constable after the episode of the *Kent* and the disappearance of Samuel Barnard's flock, Thomas Duke wandered casually away to his boat, deep in thought.

The tale of the vanishing sheep spread round the village in the usual exaggerated fashion. But those closely involved kept straight faces and tight lips and knew 'nowt'about it.

Away out on the distant farm Samuel and William relaxed once the expected visit from Constable Clarke had extracted no information from them. They, along with Seth the shepherd, had rehearsed their tales well. Each had individually given a carefully corroborated version to the Constable that none of them had heard a thing and when they went to the field in the morning, the flock had simply vanished. Yes, they *had* gone and searched, and no, the fences were *not* broken nor the gate left open.

'It were a reet queer goin's on, all tigether,' agreed old Seth with a remarkable degree of composure.

Sam and William congratulated Seth on his ability as an actor, though at one point they feared his grief over the loss of his sheep was being a little overdone, considering the payment he would receive in compensation. 'Eh, Seth! Thoo should be on t'stage in Lunnon in them fancy plays!' Sam slapped his shepherd heartily on the shoulder as Constable Clarke retreated, ambling back across the field, shaking his head in bewilderment.

Sam breathed a sigh of relief. He had carried a heavy worry in his mind since the whole episode began. At the time events happened so quickly that he didn't have time to think, but now, with hindsight, the foolhardiness of his action dawned sharp and clear.

By law any farmer living near the coast must register accurately the number of his flock. After shearing, he must also keep account of the number of fleeces sold and to whom. Customs and Excise officials examined his records meticulously, noting any discrepancies. Of course, the occasional sheep died, or got lost in the wild moorland bogs, but to 'lose' a whole flock would take some accounting for. So Sam and William acted their parts, scratching their heads, appearing suitably nonplussed, and gazing directly into Constable Clarke's eyes with admirable coolness.

Three weeks later, Seth leaned over the field gate, contentedly puffing a pipe of good tobacco. 'Yan, tan, tethera, nethera, pimp, sethera, lethera, hovera, dovera, dick. Yan-a-dick, tan-a-dick…..' He removed the pipe from his mouth and pointed the stem at the new sheep grazing contentedly on Samuel's lush meadow.

'Stand still, dang 'ee! Yan. Tan. Tethera.' He began counting, slowly and deliberately. When he got to fifteen, he exclaimed triumphantly 'Bumfit!' Then his eye caught another sheep grazing on its own in a corner by the hedge. It raised its black head and looked at him through yellow eyes. 'Yan-a bumfit?' he queried. 'That ain't reet. Tha's yan ti mony!'

Phlegmatically he scratched his head and counted again. The final tally was definitely one extra.

When he reported this to Samuel, Sam kept a straight face and said, 'Noo then Seth. Tha's getting old. Tha's miscounted'

'Nay, maister, ther's yan-a-bumfit alreet.'

'Ah, weel. Ah suppose tha's reet. Tha's been at t'job lang enough.' Sam permitted himself a small smile as he tapped the side of his nose and gave Seth a knowing wink. 'Reckon that un'll give t'missus a bit mair wool, then it'll mek us all a reet grand Christmas roast. Meat'll be real sweet in more ways than yan. Tha'll coom ti thi dinner wi' us as usual, Seth?' he invited.

'That Ah will and reet gladly! Thank'ee, maister.' Seth tugged his forelock respectfully, and with a twinkle, replaced his pipe, called his dog, and set off back to his cottage chuckling.

Sam was a very relieved man, to have got away with it this time. Next time, he would be more careful, as this escapade would be noted, and a keener 'sniv' start putting two and two together, as Sam's farm was already under surveillance after an embarrassing episode the previous year.

Sam and William had been taking an evening stroll along the cliff path, chatting over the forthcoming wedding plans. Bouncing along on the incoming tide was a single barrel, evidently having broken loose from a previously sowed 'crop.' The two farmers scrambled down the cliff, waded into the sea, quickly retrieved it and carried it up to the farmhouse. If, as they suspected, it contained a quantity of fine brandy, that would come in 'reet handy for t'weddin' feast.'

Unbeknown to Sam and William, some distance behind them, Peter Maxwell and James Herbert were also taking an evening stroll, patrolling the cliff, and talking over recent events. They also saw the barrel floating shorewards. Whipping out his telescope, Peter immediately identified Sam Barnard.

Sam and William had a good head start, being close to the track which led homewards. Peter and James made haste towards the Barnard farm.

In the farmhouse kitchen, all hands got to work. The barrel was unbunged, and the contents speedily transferred to milk churns, feeding buckets, and any containers which came to hand. These mysteriously disappeared into the stables. Meanwhile, Sarah filled up the barrel with fresh water, carefully replaced the bung, and set the barrel on the table. Sam and William came back in just as she was tidying the wisps of hair which had escaped from her mob cap during the frenzied activity. Sam had had a gut feeling that they had been spotted, so was relieved to find Sarah looking so calm and unflustered. He and William hastily mopped their sweating faces and had a cool drink of water just as Peter and James burst in without ceremony.

'Now then, Sam! What's tha got there?' James sauntered up and sniffed the barrel. 'Drop o' good stuff in there, I'll bet! Think the chaps in Whitby will enjoy this! Come on, Peter!' He hoisted the heavy barrel onto his shoulder, and cocking his head and winking at the disgruntled Sam, marched out of the kitchen.

It was a good six miles walk over rough trackways, and it was a very warm and muggy evening. He'd certainly be sweating when he reached the Preventive's headquarters. Sam, William and Sarah expressed appropriate distress, which soon turned to laughter, as they imagined the faces of the officers when they discovered the keg's true contents.

They had no evidence that Sam had tampered with the barrel - they did not believe he would have had time to empty it, for they did not know that Sam suspected they were in the vicinity. Sam had scratched his head and looked so genuinely puzzled that they were completely hoodwinked. On opening the keg, they were embarrassed to have been so easily duped and on this occasion simply forgot to report the incident. But suspicion was still there, and Sam's activities would be more carefully observed in future.

Thomas Duke's mind was not on his work at all that morning, his thoughts winging world wide in fanciful flights to exotic destinations. The small coins in his pocket grew heavy, transformed in his imagination into golden guineas which would open the door to riches and excitement, a life of ease, and, no more cold and smelly fishing!

Thomas leant against the stern of his boat, arms folded, deep in thought, his small, greedy eyes half closed as he glanced contemptuously at the other fishermen. Stupid, ignorant fools! he thought disparagingly. Condemned to a lifetime of discomfort, danger and ill reward. Not for him any more! But, how to go about it? He pondered and cast his mind back to the night in question.

He had been fast asleep when he had been woken by the sound of a galloping horse. Unusual in the steep streets of Baytown. Curiosity had roused him from his bed and he had peered from his high window to observe a tall figure hurtling toward the slipway. He thought it was Reuben Granger, and now, glancing slyly to where that young man was engaged in deep conversation with Zack Storm, whom Thomas had long disliked, the doubt in his mind disappeared. That same distinctive red kerchief had been clearly visible round the neck of the flying horseman in the moonlight.

Thomas Duke jabbed his thumb on a sharp fish hook. Damn! He sucked his bleeding hand. That did it! *No more!*

Angrily throwing down his line, Thomas turned away from his boat for the last time. Zack and Reuben glanced up as Thomas swore loudly.

Reuben did not like the calculating look in his eyes and a cold fear swept over him as Thomas headed away up Tyson's Steps in the direction of Constable Clarke's house.

Rebecca was lovingly polishing her best china teacups and putting the final touches to her tea table as Damaris entered the low doorway. The dark, low-beamed cottage parlour had been her grandmother's 'best'room in the home she had shared with Isaac since their marriage some fifty years ago. A homely room, it exuded a feeling of peace and quiet security and reflected Rebecca's own tastes and skills over many years. The snowy white table cloth with the lacy crochet edge, comfortable, plump embroidered cushions, hand made lace on the fall of the window curtains, all paid tribute to Rebecca's domestic pride in her more agile days, when her less arthritic hands plied delicate lace bobbins and crochet hooks and her undimmed eyes threaded the finest of needles.

The dark panelled walls carried pictures of sailing ships and strange souvenirs of far away exotic places, sent home by her sons before their tragically early deaths.

Every ordinary day, they lived in the comfortable kitchen with its big black cooking range and sturdy square table round which her young family had sat for their meals and pored over their studies. Here every Sunday evening, Isaac had opened the big family Bible and read to Rebecca and his three sons in just the same way that Zack now carried on the tradition in his own home. Rebecca had a fleeting but vivid memory of the three dark heads of her sons bowed in prayer and brushed away a glistening tear that escaped unbidden as memories of Christopher and Matthew flooded back. She and Isaac had drawn closer together in their great sorrow over the drowning of their two elder sons, but, always positive, rejoiced in the ebullient life of their younger son Zack, and his two lovely children. Zack's own son, Matthew, was already so like the dead uncle for whom he was named that Rebecca's heart frequently gave a lurch of emotion when, waking from a fireside doze and daydreams of the old days, her grandson stood before her and her mind leapt back a generation to the happy days when her own sons were young and fit and noisy.

There was no time for reminiscing now, she reminded herself, though Christopher and Matthew were always with her in spirit. Damaris had come with the news that Mr. Wesley would be with Rebecca for tea around four o'clock that afternoon.

Rebecca loved and admired the small, now grey-haired wiry man who spoke with such fervent conviction. Never was there a preacher who could fire the souls of his followers as John Wesley did. Standing on a small rising by the slipway amongst the boats he gathered a great crowd of listeners. Over the years he had grown very fond of the people of Baytown, though at times he rebuked them on their stubborn attitude, perhaps not realising that this was a natural inborn trait of all true Yorkshiremen. Being born and brought up in the gentler, flat landscape of distant

Lincolnshire John Wesley found that the northern coast was a wild and rugged place, and that his followers here had natures to match their tough environment. His first impressions of the place were graphically described in his carefully written journal:-

'Tuesday, 8 May, 1753; I rode to Robin Hood's Bay, near Whitby. The town is very remarkably situated; it stands close to the sea, and is in great part built on craggy and steep rocks, some of which rise perpendicular from the water; and yet the land both on the north, south and west is fruitful and well cultivated. I stood on a little rising near the quay, in a warm, still evening, and exhorted a multitude of people from all parts to "seek the Lord while He may be found." They were all attention, and most of them met me again at half an hour after four in the morning. I could gladly have spent some days here.'

It had become John Wesley's custom each year when the cold winter weather turned into mild spring sunshine to set out on a long and arduous journey, on horseback, to visit and preach to new congregations countrywide. Each year he selected a different itinerary and visited Robin Hood's Bay no less than eleven times in the thirty-one years he rode forth.

Rebecca had fallen under the spell of this great man on his first visit some twenty years ago. Although several years had passed since the drownings of Christopher and Matthew, Rebecca's heart still ached at their loss. She clearly remembered the warm, still summer evening when, wandering sadly down to the shore alone, she had been gathered in to the crowd listening to the compelling words of a small, brown-haired man. Rebecca paused on the edge of the group, and the perceptive eyes of the preacher held hers fast in a grasp of deep understanding. Rebecca knew that this extraordinary man was looking right into her very soul and reading her deep-set sorrow, a weight she had then felt would never leave her. 'Seek the Lord while He may be found,' Mr. Wesley exhorted his congregation and Rebecca felt the words of comfort were spoken to her alone. The lump in her heart eased and slowly, joy and a firm belief in the love of God entered her soul. A warm glow enveloped her sad spirit and from that day she never felt alone again. Her sons may be gone from her in body but she, and they, were safe in the keeping of a loving God.

Rebecca had drifted away deep in thought, and next day she was up with the lark to join the congregation that met him again at half past four in the morning. Dawn had scarcely lightened the sky as the preacher's voice had echoed across the silence of the cool morning. It was a moment Rebecca would remember all her life when John Wesley sought her out from the crowd and spoke to her privately. He had sensed her great need of comfort the day before and was glad she had returned that early morning. She had felt some degree of shame at the intensity of her depression when he told her some years later of the stoical acceptance of a much greater sorrow than hers. 'I visited a poor woman in Whitby, one who was ill in bed, and, having buried seven of her family in six months, had just heard that the eighth, her beloved husband, was cast away at sea. I asked "Do you not fret at any of those things?" She said, with a lovely smile on her pale cheek, "Oh, no! How can I fret at anything which is the will of God? Let Him take all besides; He has given me Himself. I love, I praise Him every moment." Let any that doubts of Christian perfection look on such a spectacle as this! One in such circumstances rejoicing evermore, and continually giving thanks.' He glanced at

Rebecca. 'So, you see, my dear Rebecca, no matter how bad your own circumstances, there are always some worse off than yourself.'

Now some twenty years on, Rebecca had several times entertained the man who had lightened her sorrowing heart. He professed a liking for her excellent turf-cakes so she was grateful for Damaris bringing her the time of arrival so that her baking would be done to perfection for this very special guest. Damaris vaguely remembered seeing the famous preacher, kind eyes twinkling above his tea cup, elegantly wiping the butter from his fingers on a napkin provided for the purpose. The young child had naively asked him why he did not lick them like her grandfather did? It seemed an awful waste of the good runny butter! She had received a rebuking prod from Rebecca who had been trying to present a picture of some refinement in her humble cottage home. Mr. Wesley had been greatly amused, yet tactfully explained that the thoughtful Rebecca had obviously not wished his greasy fingers to make sticky marks on his precious Bible.

It was three years since John Wesley had visited Baytown and Rebecca was avid for his news. Damaris could just remember his appearance but Rebecca had kept his memory alive by recounting stories surrounding his earlier visits. Her imagination was fired by the tale of the time he had been preaching by the slipway when, to quote John Wesley's own words in his Journal, 'a large cat, frightened out of a chamber, had leaped upon a woman's head, and ran over the heads and shoulders of many more, but none of them moved or cried out any more than if it had been a butterfly.' How Mr. Wesley must have smiled as he had written these words that evening and how pleased at the uninterrupted attention of his congregation, to be so undisturbed by the alarming event.

Damaris winced at the thought of a cat the size of Jennet's landing on her head. She had felt the impact of its sharp and cruel claws on her hands more than once and was sure she would have screamed with the pain. Damaris, understanding Rebecca's desire to spend as much time in Mr. Wesley's company as possible, suggested that she should remain and serve the tea, so that her grandmother could sit at the table undisturbed.

Just after four o'clock, as promised, Damaris answered a gentle knock at the door and beamed up into the stern yet kindly face, confiding that her grandmother had been so looking forward to this day.

'My dear Rebecca.' The two old friends embraced. 'How well you look. The Lord has been good to you after all,' he exclaimed. 'Well...' demurred Rebecca doubtfully. 'He's sent me a right bad old back ache. Some days I can scarce move from yon chair.'

'Ah, but He's sent you a charming granddaughter to brighten your old age,' he smiled at Damaris.

'If you will be seated, Mr. Wesley, I will bring your tea,' declared the 'charming granddaughter' politely. Ushering the two friends to the immaculate tea table she carefully placed the tea-pot before Rebecca and a plate of golden turf cakes before the preacher. With an impish smile she opened out the snowy linen napkin and elegantly laid it on his knee. 'For wiping your greasy fingers, Mr. Wesley,' she said with a gentle chuckle; they both recalled the amusing incident from her youth. Leaving the two friends in peace, she returned to the kitchen fire and her own plate of turf-cakes, and licked her buttery fingers with noisy appreciation.

'Damaris, my dear,' called Rebecca from the parlour. 'Put us another flaught on the fire, will you?'

Damaris took the long tongs, lifted the slab of turf, and carefully placed it on the fragile arched 'cave' left by the remaining glowing embers. The delicate structure of the burned peats collapsed under the weight of the newly placed turf in a shower of sparks which rushed, spiralling, up the chimney.

The action caused John Wesley's comfortably relaxed mind to jerk back to his childhood, evoking dramatic memories that would never leave him until his life's end, for he might very easily not be alive and here in Rebecca's parlour at all.

'Sit with us awhile, Damaris, and I will tell you a story.'

Damaris took the low fireside stool and sat, elbows on knees, chin resting on her cupped hands, gazing into the weather-beaten face of the preacher. Mr. Wesley's eyes held hers with the extraordinary compunction that drew all mankind within their gaze; warm, kindly eyes, but eyes that also held the fire of his deep conviction, which could flash with impassioned intensity; eyes which held a lifetime of joy and sorrow, love and hatred, for the John Wesley so loved by Rebecca was not so dear to all his hearers. His life was frequently threatened by those who felt his preaching disruptive. Houses where he had stayed had been torn down by angry mobs, and he himself physically attacked. Damaris knew that he was not always popular, and was glad that he found a safe refuge in the peace of her grandmother's warm and homely parlour.

John Wesley wiped his buttery fingers on the snowy napkin, leaned back in his chair and smiled contentedly.

'My dear Rebecca, no one in the whole of England provides a more enjoyable repast,' he complimented the kind old face opposite him. Rebecca, guilty of the sin of pride, glowed warmly under his praise. He was quite right, though, she admitted to herself. Her turf cakes took some bettering! 'And like Saint Francis, we should praise God for our servant, fire, who has baked us those excellent cakes. And, Damaris, taught me a very special lesson, that God needed me.

'My father, as you may know, was Rector of the Parish of Epworth in Lincolnshire. Like me, he was not always popular. People do not take kindly to harsh words of criticism, even though they know it is only for their own good, and to turn them from wrongdoing.' He cast a brief, worried look at Rebecca. She knew he wanted to speak to her of Zack's illegal activities, but not in front of his young daughter. 'Later, Mr. Wesley,' whispered Rebecca.

'Well now. One man hated my father so much that he set fire to our Rectory one night, with us all inside it!'

Damaris gasped, disbelieving that anyone could be so spiteful. Instinctively she reached out a consoling hand and gazed at him with her blue eyes full of compassion.

'I remember it so well, even though I was only five years old at the time. I had been asleep and when I was awakened by all the noise my room was ablaze and everyone running about outside, shouting. I ran to the window, anxious not only for my own safety, but for my brothers and sisters. I could hear them crying and my mother, Susannah, screaming "Where's John? Where's John?" My appearance at the window must have been quite dramatic,' he smiled, recalling the scene. 'Standing there, such a small, defenceless figure silhouetted against the background of the roaring flames! I remember panic setting in as I realised it was a long way to the ground. I thought no one had seen me. The room behind was getting very hot and sparks from our old thatched roof were dropping through my ceiling onto the floor all around me. Suddenly, a calm within my young mind reassured me. "Fear not, for I am with you," said a silent voice and at the same moment, a cry went up, "There he is! There's John!" and up came a ladder to my window. Strong hands hauled me roughly out. Just in time, Damaris, for as I fled the fire, the whole roof caved in, as your fire did when you placed on the new turf.'

The comparison made the horrific scene live all too vividly in Damaris' imagination.

'My mother grasped me in her arms, holding me high above the excited crowd, which had by this time gathered most of Epworth round our blazing home. "Is not this a brand snatched from the burning?" she cried, and ever since then, I knew that I had been saved at that last dramatic moment because I was needed and loved. It was not until much later in my life that I knew what I must do, but I never forgot that experience.'

He slid his chair back from the table and rose to his feet. Hands clasped and head bowed, John Wesley gave thanks for his life, his excellent meal, his valued friendship with Rebecca, and his ability to have brought comfort into the grieving soul of the sad young woman she had been when they first met so many years ago.

'You have been very dear to me over the years, Rebecca. You have suffered enough sorrow over your two elder sons and it pains me to learn that Zack is still involved in the smuggling trade. The penalties are severe and the risks great; he has the responsibility of those two dear children, apart from the moral fact that smuggling is wrong. As I told my congregation up in Sunderland only recently, none can stop with us unless he part with all sin, and particularly robbing the King, selling or buying run goods, which I can no more suffer than robbery on the highway. This I enforced on every Member the next day. A few would not promise to refrain, so these I was forced to cut off.'

'That may well be in Sunderland, Mr. Wesley, but you cannot so counsel them here,' advised Rebecca. 'Why, every one of them is in the trade and if you speak out against them, you will lose them all. I know these men. They are not evil; the money they earn from smuggling helps them to make better homes for their children. You say they are robbing the King? They would say he could very well afford to help their poor, hard lives a little. They will not give up, Mr. Wesley. I can promise you that. If I may be so bold as to suggest; speak not against them publicly. Advise them in private, if you so wish, but you have many good souls here who will carry your words to the ends of the earth, when those who sail away from here on long sea voyages will take your influence with them.'

Reluctantly, John Wesley acknowledged deep down that Rebecca was probably right. He was glad he had listened to her wise words, realising that he must accept these men for what they were, fallible human beings, and work with them, not against them. In that way some may turn away from their wrong doing.

Rebecca smiled as she said farewell to her old friend. It had been quite a serious afternoon's conversation. Her irrepressible good humour re-surfaced as she recalled her own involvement with free trading and hoped that he would never learn of her wicked ways. He would be sadly disillusioned, poor man, she chuckled. The rosy faced gentle old lady was not all she outwardly appeared.

A sudden thundering roar of cannon fire reverberated across the quiet stillness of the Bay, shattering the golden peace of the hot and sultry July afternoon. Flakes of sun-dried shale showered down from the northern cliffs, scuttering to the shore below in clouds of fine grey dust. Windows shook, china rattled on cupboard shelves, dislodged soot dumped down chimneys, sparking and flaring on the embers, messing clean hearths and spotting newly aired laundry.

Startled villagers rushed in curiosity to the vantage point on the high cliffs, leaving cottage doors hanging agape and wiping floury hands on aprons as they ran, abandoning their baking without a backward thought. Fishermen left their lines where they fell, and the clang of iron-shod boots on cobblestones echoed through the rapidly emptying village.

Out on the calm blueness of the Bay, shimmering in the heat haze, floated the familiar outline of the *Kent*, shrouded in clouds of delicate blue gun-smoke. It had been one of those extraordinarily hot, oppressive summer afternoons, where the horizon blended with the sky, blurring the line where the sea ended and the heavens began. Ships floated ethereally in the sky above the false horizon in a smudge of indefinable colour-tone. A great calm and peace had earlier hung over the village, necessary everyday tasks being carried on with a feeling of desultory lethargy. It had been too, too hot, the pall of quietness uncanny and uneasy, the sky heavy and humid. The shot which blasted the village into wakeful urgency was totally and shockingly unexpected.

The muggy July breeze sluggishly wafted aside the smoky trails, revealing to the watchers on the cliffs a scene of intense marine activity.

The *Kent* with her seventy-seven foot mainmast towered above the fleet of local fishing cobles which from the distance appeared to skim the surface like busy water-beetles, frantically spinning and scattering in all directions. Protruding oars jerked like panic-stricken legs in a frenzied, unco-ordinated effort to escape the danger area.

Zack Storm raised his brass telescope to his clear blue eyes and focussed on the scene. Scanning the horizon, his circular field of vision drew in two more familiar vessels in the Bay, the Revenue cutters *Swallow* and *Eagle*. Captains Whitehead and Mitchell had ineffectually harried the *Kent* in her illicit trading activities for years, and a long-standing animosity existed alongside a sense of frustration. Both Captains had frequently tailed the *Kent* and observed the blatant manner in which she sailed arrogantly among the local fishing vessels, dealing out contraband with unchallenged impunity. Heavily armed, and vastly superior in size, Stoney Fagg regarded the small cutters as no more than a trivial annoyance, and they frequently slunk away with the *Kent's* gunfire deafening their ears, spray from uncomfortably close cannon balls splashing their decks.

This hot July day, however, Captain Whitehead had signalled to Mitchell aboard the *Swallow* that help was at hand. Both Revenue Captains had warned their crews that before nightfall the presently peaceful Bay could witness a long and bloody battle. Impatiently they waited, circling the *Kent* at a safe distance to intercept her escape, until from the north, the two large Excise cruisers *Prince of Wales* and *Royal George* hove into sight. Captains Lewis Gillie and John Ogilvie had been informed that the *Kent* was once again trading off the east coast, and received orders to sail from their stations off Edinburgh until they intercepted her.

Zack's mariner's heart beat with strange elation as he focussed his glass on the two racy cruisers. Built for speedy and effective Revenue work, their elegant lines, fine cut bows, rakish masts and spread of snowy sail could not but raise the admiration of any true sailor. The gazelles of the ocean, these splendid cutters were, nevertheless, enemies to Zack and his companions.

Zack raised his telescope once more as the *Royal George* now approached within hailing distance of the *Kent*. Too far away on the cliff top, he could not hear Captain Ogilvie's shouted command through his loud-hailer 'Heave to, or we fire into you!' nor Stoney Fagg's arrogant retort, 'Then fire away, you buggers and be damned to you!'

Stoney had great confidence in the superior size of his ship, his ruthlessly fearless crew and his heavy armament. The *Royal George* and *Prince of Wales* were built for speedy chases not heavy bombardment, and as for the ineffective Eagle and Swallow, skittering around out of gunshot like frightened rabbits… Stoney Fagg spat derisively into the water and discounted them altogether. One good blast from a well-aimed cannon ball would scare them off the scene for good.

The faint echo of Stoney's ship's drums beating the *Kent's* crew to action stations, borne on the soft summer breeze, reached the keen ears of the excited watchers on the cliffs.

A brilliant yellow flash, a puff of blue smoke billowing from the bulwarks of the *Kent*, followed by the delayed sound of cannon shot. Battle had seriously been joined.

Captains Ogilvie and Gillie had planned their attack well, manoeuvering the Prince of Wales to starboard and the *Royal George* to port, thus effectively sandwiching the smuggler between their broadside guns. Stoney Fagg put up a brave fight. The *Kent* with her forty-strong crew, armed with blunderbusses and muskets, her sixteen four-pounder carriage-mounted cannon and twenty swivel guns, was a formidable opponent, well prepared with deadly chain-shot which at close range tore into the cruisers with devastating effect. The Revenue vessels replied with solid shot, hull-penetrating, mast-shattering, and lethal. Stoney Fagg's desperate crew cheered as they shot away the bowsprit of the *Prince of Wales* and she limped away, rigging damaged, sails flapping idly.

The *Kent's* crew, smuggling desperadoes as they undoubtedly were, showed themselves also to be fine seamen, as in the heart of the battle they hoisted full sail and drifted out of range of the guns of the *Royal George*. Stoney gestured rudely with two fingers towards the crippled *Prince of Wales*, and bared his tobacco-stained teeth at the *Royal George*, cannon still thundering away, but most of the shot now spiralling ineffectually into the increasing distance of sea between the two drifting vessels.

The watchers on the cliffs cheered wildly as the Excise cruisers flapped and floundered helplessly on the swelling tide.

Zack's face paled. He felt as if the blood had all drained from his being as his powerful telescope picked out his own fishing coble in the confusion of swirling gun-smoke and spouting spray. Rowing slowly out of the scene of devastation was a solitary oarsman. Reuben.

Zack lowered his glass and glanced across at Liz, bright eyed and animated in the midst of the excited women gathered to watch the naval drama.

He would not voice his fears until he was sure; until he could check with Reub whether or not Matt had been with him when he set out that morning.

Since proving himself to his father and Reuben after his involvement in the recapture of the brandy kegs, Matthew had been accepted into certain of the less hazardous activities of running goods. As Reuben so rightly said to Zack, 'He'll have to join us sooner or later,' and Matt, although still only twelve years old, had proved himself without a shadow of a doubt, both strong, trustworthy, and full of initiative.

Matt had doggedly persisted until Reub had finally agreed to take him off that morning to the *Kent* for a routine run ashore. Nothing exceptional. The Preventives were absent; even Maxwell and Herbert were patrolling across the other side of the moor, so Reuben, assessing the calm weather, gave Matt a manly slap on the shoulders and bade him make ready for sea.

'Better tell Liz tha's off wi' me,' advised Reuben, but when Matt had run up home and called out, the cottage was empty; neither Liz nor Zack were to be found.

'Oh well, Ah tried to tell 'em. Ah'll be back afore they miss me,' thought Matt hopefully as he scrambled back to the waiting boat on the slipway.

Reuben and Matthew had joined the fleet of local cobles heading out to the *Kent* anchored in the calm blue bay. Matt pulled manfully at his oar, ignoring the stickily oozing blisters that pained his sweating hands. Keen to prove to Reub that he was tough, Matt whistled snatches of a sea-shanty in between rhythmic sweeps of his oar. Astern, Reub smiled fondly at the stocky little figure. 'Now then, Matt. Wonder what Stoney's got for us today?'

'We'll -- soon -- find -- out -- Reub. We're -- nearly -- there!' Matt puffed breathlessly, between strokes of the oar.

Easing off, resting aching arms and backs, Reub and Matt leaned forward on the oars, letting the coble drift until they slipped silently under the stern of the *Kent* and made fast to the trailing ropes. Within minutes, the smuggling vessel was surrounded by dozens of small cobles, all fussing round like chicks round a mother hen. From the decks above, weather-beaten hands lowered away kegs and boxes for the waiting crews to stow under piles of nets and canvas. So busy were they, that, sheltered under the lee of the towering schooner, they did not observe the stealthy approach of *Swallow* and *Eagle*, nor were they ready for the sudden cannon shot that winged across their bows.

Startled out of his wits, Matt leaned forward to grab the oar which slipped from the rowlocks, a falling keg hit the bottom of Reub's coble with a heavy thud, the boat tipped with a sickening lurch. Matt was gone.

Cannon fire, deafening at short range, shattered the busy scene. Stoney Fagg cast off his mooring ropes, yelling to the coblemen to get clear.

'Matt!' shouted Reub in panic. '*Matt!!*'

'Get clear, Reub! *Now!*' stormed Stoney, 'or tha'll damn well get blasted out of the water!'

'But the boy!' yelled Reub. 'Where's Matt?'

'There he is!' shouted one of the *Kent's* crew as Matt rose to the surface choking, flailing the water in a terrified surge of panic. Sea water filled his boots and their weight began to drag him down. 'Throw 'im a rope! Ah'll get 'im!'

The previously calm sea erupted in a boiling foam of plunging cannon balls. Reub had no choice but to obey Stoney and get clear. The last he saw of Matt was the boy's white face above his soaking gansey as Stoney Fagg's man hauled him roughly aboard the *Kent*.

Zack focussed again. Was Reuben ashen faced? Was he rowing an empty boat with an attitude of despair and despondency, and was cold fear rooting itself in Zack's guts unnecessarily?

Only time would tell.

Elizabeth stood in the kitchen, white faced, tight lipped and rigid with icy gut-gripping panic.

Where *was* Matthew?

The instinctive bond between mother and son told her something was wrong. Very wrong.

It was two days now; two long days and endlessly dragging nights since Matt had gone out in the boat with Reuben; Reuben who now sat by the Storm family fireside, arms around Damaris, who sobbed inconsolably on his shoulder.

Reuben faced the situation with mixed emotions. Anxiety and deep regret for his responsibility for the unknown whereabouts of young Matt, mingled with a strangely homely feeling which surfaced in his thoughts in his close proximity with Damaris in her moment of despair. He had known her since her carefree childhood and watched with a brotherly amusement as she grew gracefully into young womanhood. He was aware that she pretended to ignore him, yet covertly watched him through lowered eyelids, hastily averting her gaze and blushing if she caught him looking in her direction. Now, with her in the close warm circle of his arms, scenting the sweet youthfulness of her body, feeling the silky smoothness of her skin and hair against his rough cheek, in that moment Reuben knew that Damaris and none other would be his wife in future years.

He placed a work-roughened finger gently under her chin and raised her tear-wet face from his shoulder. 'Come on now, Dam; tha's wettin' me gansey!' he teased softly. 'Go and dry thi eyes, tidy thi hair, and we'll gan tigether and see if any news has come in.'

'You gan along tiv Isaac and Rebecca, Liz,' he advised, looking up at her over Damaris' blonde head. 'Ah'll tek Damaris and see if we can meet up wi' Zack. We'll come to thi the moment we hear owt.'

Elizabeth accepted that this was good counsel. Rebecca with her deep and strong faith was always a comfort; but yet, if anyone could really know what had happened to Matt, surely that would be Jennet with her strange powers of foresight. Liz made up her mind. For once in her life, it would be Jennet to whom she turned in her hour of need. Snatching her shawl from the peg, she swung it over her head and ran out into the long, late afternoon shadows. Ignoring the speculative knots of fisherfolk who gathered on every street corner, falling silent with sympathetic anxiety as she approached, Elizabeth passed them without recognition, turned up the eerie path through Little Wood and out to the fields where lay Jennet's dilapidated cottage.

Reuben took Damaris by the hand and gently led her to the cliff top path by which Zack would return with news of good or ill report.

The weather had changed with uncanny rapidity. The sky darkened into the sulphurous yellow-grey that ominously preceded a summer storm. A cool wind tugged at Damaris' long hair and teased it from under her head shawl. Reuben gently fingered it away from her face and with surprisingly tender hands smoothed it back from her worried brow. Seeking a hollow which afforded privacy and shelter, yet also a clear view of the path, the two young people sat cuddled together, sharing the warmth of their new-found relationship. They both inwardly regretted that it was under such circumstances that they had finally been drawn together, but both also knew that their lives ahead would hold many anxious and worrying hours. Comfort in adversity was a sound beginning to the future of a fisherman and his wife, besides, the clouds would not always be grey.

'See, Damaris, t'sun breks oot even in the dark skies!' From their cliff top viewpoint they watched as the grey skies parted and a pale shaft of light beamed down on the surface of the iron-dark sea. Reuben smiled and hugged her close to his firm, masculine body, and that was how Zack found them as he approached home with some small ray of hope for the safety of Matthew.

Liz frantically battled her way through the clawing, clutching branches of Little Wood, anxiety banishing the moments of fear she always experienced on this eerie and lonely path. Emerging into the open fields at the top, she broke into a desperate, panic-stricken stumbling run, tripping over tussocks of rough grass which lay, deliberately it seemed, in her path to hamper her progress. As the smoke from Jennet's cottage became visible, drifting vertically in stark white swirls against the thundery black sky, Liz picked up her long skirts and ran frantically across the last remaining fields as the first heavy drops of rain began to fall. Her distressed body drove her onwards unthinkingly, at a time when her more rational mind would have made her pause for thought, but by the time she realised why she had come to Jennet instead of Rebecca it was too late to return. Jennet had heard her hurried approach, and was already opening the door as Liz raised her hand to knock and virtually fell exhausted into Jennet's surprised arms.

'My dear Elizabeth! To what do I owe the honour of this somewhat hasty visit?' queried Jennet with faint sarcasm. Then, observing the signs of distress on Liz's tearstained face, banished all traces of mockery and drew her gently indoors, settling her down and stroking her brow with healing hands. Leaving her step-daughter to calm her heaving body, Jennet hobbled painfully to her cupboard and poured a small quantity of an unsavoury looking liquid into a dusty, dark coloured glass. The mysterious wound in her thigh still suppurated and troubled her, refusing to heal, no matter what salves and potions she treated herself with.

'Drink this, my dear. It will make you feel better and clear your mind. Then we can talk about your troubles.' Jennet knew Liz well enough to know that something must be very wrong to have driven her here to the cottage in this semi-hysterical state. Liz, the calm, practical and unflappable, must be in deep distress to have come seeking consolation from Jennet, when usually as Jennet disappointedly accepted, she turned straight to Rebecca.

Jennet had sensed something was amiss that afternoon, for even up in her cottage, distant from the sea, the faint boom of gunfire had reached her ears though behind the closed door of the cottage, she had naturally mistaken it for a distant summer storm. Her cat, with its keen hearing and feline dislike of thunder, had retreated to her bedroom where it had burrowed under her grubby quilt and remained for the rest of the afternoon.

Jennet's powers of second sight were not so acute that she could foretell the future with ease. She needed some object in her hand or a clue to focus on before her powers became active. To be the true possessor of 'second sight'one had to be born the seventh child of a seventh child, and although Jennet's mother had been the last of seven children, Jennet herself had only been the sixth, and last born. She often thought, somewhat regretfully, that she always just managed to miss out on life.

However, her past relationship with the step-daughter now sitting by her fireside, considerably calmer and in a fit state to reason sensibly, thanks to the carefully administered tranquillizing drug, gave her enough foresight to see that Liz was certainly very distressed, and needed all the help and love she could give.

Gradually, the soothing potion took effect and Jennet listened attentively whilst Liz voiced her fears for Matthew's safety.

After a while Jennet rose and, lifting the black velvet cloth which covered her precious crystal ball, gazed into its mysterious depths. At first, all she could see was a swirling mist but slowly her mind focussed on the small, dark speck that appeared to float in a fathomless void; a lost soul, or at least someone in great trouble or danger. Now that Jennet knew that the person she sought was none other than Matthew, she concentrated with an intensity that brought stabbing pains to her eyes. Willing with all the strength of power in mind and fingers for the floating speck to take shape, Jennet closed her eyes and raised her head in deep concentration. The tendons in her scraggy neck stretched almost to breaking point. Liz watched, fascinated, as the pulse in her neck throbbed visibly, and rich colour suffused her veins. When she opened her eyes and peered closely into the ball, the formless speck had settled on a shape which, to a vivid imagination, could be a boat. The speck became a small boy who had his feet firmly on the deck. Jennet could see no more, but her crystal ball had told her that Matthew was alive and on board a large ship, but where she could not tell.

The picture faded, and the interior of the ball reverted to a swirling grey mist. Jennet leaned back in her chair with a sigh, and rested her eyes for a moment.

'I must be losing my powers in my old age,' she remarked regretfully to Liz. 'However, I can assure you that at this moment Matthew is alive, yet I could not tell where he is, except that he is on a boat. A large one. But he is not out of danger. The story is not yet ended, Liz. I sense further trouble. In a moment I will try again.'

Placing her scrawny, gnarled old hands over the crystal for a second time, Jennet closed her eyes and rocked slowly backwards and forwards, summoning up her powers as strongly as she could. Even in her distress, the fastidious Elizabeth could not help but wince inwardly at the state of Jennet's hands; dirty and stained, the overlong, unkempt fingernails black-rimmed with grime. Liz felt a pang of conscience that she did not visit and care for the old lady. The comparison with the plump pink and white, spotlessly clean and shining Rebecca was disturbing, and Liz determined that from now on she would really try to take Jennet in hand. In spite of everything, they had a long-standing relationship. She had known Jennet much longer than her mother-in-law Rebecca. But, she reasoned, to ease her sense of guilty shame, Jennet was set in her ways and would not welcome what she would regard not as help, but interference. Perhaps best let things lie as they were, and just make more regular visits and keep a wary eye on her general well-being.

At last, Jennet's greeny gold eyes opened in a fixed stare. She leaned forward, hands clawing the crystal ball, her bony forehead beaded in perspiration with the intensity of her effort to foretell the fate of Matthew. Liz could almost experience the desperate exertion the old woman was forcing from her mind.

Thunder rumbled ominously overhead, charging an already tense situation with an elemental drama.

'I see him! He is surrounded by many rough men and much confusion – there is smoke – and fire.' A red mist suddenly and painfully blinded her eyes...... 'and *blood!*' she cried.

A blinding flash illumined her face with an eerie, greenish light. Simultaneously a vicious thunderclap right overhead made them both jump. Jennet gave a high pitched moan and crashed forward onto the table, one side of her face hideously distorted, the dribbling mouth drawn down in an evil sneer, the eyes rolling wildly. Her head caught the side of the crystal ball and sent it spinning to the ground where it shattered into shimmering, tinkling fragments on the hard stone floor. Liz leapt to her feet, hands over her mouth in horror, and rushed to Jennet's aid, her boots crushing the sharp shards of splintered glass into powder. Lifting Jennet from her chair and laying her on the long couch by the window, Liz bathed the bruised forehead and waited for her to revive. Jennet's eyes opened in confusion. She raised herself slowly, looking around the room with a glazed and stunned expression. Observing the shattered glass on the floor, she reached out her hands, gave a great cry and fell back on the couch, unconscious.

Poor Elizabeth just did not know what to do next. Half of her told her that she was needed here - the half of conscience and compassion. The other, stronger half of motherhood, instinctively pulled her back to Zack and

Damaris and the unknown plight of Matthew. Torn between the two, she hesitated only a moment longer. Making sure Jennet was comfortable and safe, Liz raced back to the village, heedless of the storm raging round her, the torrential rain plastering her flying hair and soaking clothes, her wet skirts hampering her speed.

Above her the black sky split with a blinding flash. The devil's fork mercilessly stabbed the metallic surface of the sea with great prongs of angry lightning. The air reverberated with the rumbling thunder and the earth shook with the fury of Thor, the great god of her ancestors.

Alone on the deserted hilltop high above the raging sea whose white capped waves glowed with an eerie luminescence, Liz had never felt so lonely or so terribly afraid.

Somewhere, out in that elemental hell, was her young son.

Zack, Reuben and Damaris sat round the kitchen table, treating themselves to a pot of contraband tea, looking and feeling much calmer now that Zack had brought home some reasonably reassuring news. They were unaware of the fearful experience Liz had undergone, fully believing that she was with Rebecca.

Shut away from the thunderstorm, the atmosphere in the small cottage was almost cosy, as Zack, in between gulps of the hot soothing tea, shared his information.

Zack's concern for his son had overpowered his fear of the Preventives. He had gone straight to the Customs House in Scarborough to learn the true facts about the *Kent*. From Reub's information, Zack was almost certain that Matt would be on board, but where the stricken vessel was, once she had limped out of sight, he had no idea. The Customs

Officers were naturally reluctant to give any information at all to one whom they recognised as one of Baytown's most notorious smugglers, but believed his unlikely story, understanding his paternal anxiety for his young son, and also secretly admiring his bravery in confronting them. After all, smugglers were also men with normal human feelings. Well, some of them were, thought the officer who gave Zack the news that the *Kent* was still afloat, though badly damaged, and being towed by two boats manned by the ship's crew, rowing the drifting vessel with the ebbing tide towards the Dutch coast. A long haul, indeed.

Messages had been passed to the Royal Naval frigate *Pelican* to intercept her and complete the capture but that would take some hours. No, the Customs chief did not think there would be much resistance, considering the state of the vessel, he assured the anxious father. But Zack knew Stoney Fagg of old. He would not give up without a bitter fight to the death.

So, with mixed feelings, Zack had mounted Reuben's horse and returned to the cliff path which would lead him home.

A white faced, breathless, dishevelled and soaking wet Liz burst into the kitchen, flinging open the door and launching herself sobbing into the arms of Zack, who caught her just before she knocked over the entire table.

'Hey, steady on, lass!' Reub leapt from his chair and Damaris instinctively grabbed the precious teapot and held it high above her head for safety.

Any bystander would have viewed the chaos in the normally calm household with amusement had it not been for the serious nature of all the threads of circumstance which now knotted themselves together in this one small cottage room.

Time was rushing by. Strange how the speed of time could vary so, mused Reub philosophically. Up on the cliffs, with Damaris in his arms, time had stood still. Now it was hastening as if there was no tomorrow.

Zack managed to calm Liz sufficiently to tell her that the news of Matthew was hopeful at present but there was nothing they could do except wait for further developments. The priority now being Jennet, Zack and Reub called on Silas Biddick and Sandy Kellock to come and give them a hand to bring Jennet down to the Baytown cottage.

'What? Help that old witch?' was Silas's first unconsidered comment. Sandy gave him a sharp kick on the shins.

'Hey! Remember them potions tha used to ask her for when tha had thi eye on Jiddy?' asked Sandy with a sly wink.

Silas had the grace to blush. 'Whaa! They did no good.'

'Nah! Jiddy had too much nouse to get hersen mixed up with an old rogue like thee!'

'Gerron with 'ee. Give ovver foolin.' We've got work ti deah,' interrupted Reuben impatiently, and the four men set off in companionable rivalry up the woodland path to the distant cottage.

Damaris calmed Liz with the last of the tea in the pot, then together they prepared a bed in the parlour ready for the return of the invalid.

Matthew leaned over the bow of the *Kent* watching the oarsmen as they laboriously towed the stricken vessel slowly towards the Dutch coast. Her sharp, elegant bow which had sliced through the water like a pirate's cutlass when she was in full sail, arrogantly hurling spray aside, now merely parted the smooth oily water with hardly a displacement. On deck Stoney Fagg reviewed the situation, issuing orders that would clean up both his ship and crew as best they could. Proud of his ship and his men, Stoney was noted for keeping a tidy vessel, maintaining that an orderly ship was an efficient ship, a fact which had been proved without doubt in his many years of dangerous illicit trading. Even though he knew that this was, inevitably, his last voyage in the *Kent*, true seaman that he was, he would not give her up in a state of chaos. Cutting away the fallen mast and rigging which trailed over the side, acting as a sea anchor and hampering the progress of the oarsmen, Stoney watched with gloomy despondency as the topmast and topgallant of the great seventy-seven foot mainmast, which had so proudly raked the skies, fell away and drifted astern. With it went Stoney's heart.

Down on the orlop deck the ship's surgeon busied himself patching up the injured crew, whilst up on the main deck the more able swept and swabbed. Gun crews cleaned and tidied up the cannon, carefully returning any unused powder and shot to the magazine, where the thick felt curtains, continuously hosed down with sea water, kept away any spark which, in a split second's carelessness, would ignite the ammunition and blow them sky high.

Matthew felt uncomfortably idle and spare. He turned from his place in the bows. 'Cap'n Fagg,' he called. 'Can tha find me a job, sir?'

'Why, sure, me hearty; Ah need all t'spare hands Ah can muster, though Ah fear all's up wi' the poor ol' *Kent*. Still, we're not dead yet, lad! How's thi head fer heights? Tha's the lightest man on board, an' wi' t'state o' yon foremast, Ah need a lightweight look-out. Daren't send Big Jake up aloft - he'd bring t'lot down! Wi mainmast gone, we can't spare anither! So, up tha goes. Keep a good look out for sail on t'horizon!'

Matt squared his shoulders proudly. Stoney Fagg, of all people, had called him 'man,' and for ever after Stoney became a hero in young Matt's eyes. 'Aye, Aye, Cap'n! Up aloft it is!' repeated Matt in true naval fashion. He knew that orders were always repeated to ensure they had been correctly heard, and wanted to impress his new champion. Swallowing his nervousness, Matt began his long climb, hand over hand up the ratlines to the crosstrees atop the remaining creaking mast.

'Don't look down,' Matt told himself as he became   sick-eningly aware of the increasing distance between himself and the deck below.

'Good man! Keep goin'!' encouraged Stoney Fagg in a voice that appeared unnaturally faint and distant to Matt, now in the dizzying heights nearing the topmost shrouds. 'Nearly made it,' said Matt to himself, heaving his thin lithe body through the cross trees which led to the final climb to the crow's nest atop the swaying mast. 'Wouldn't fancy bein' up 'ere in a gale,' he thought as the high top described dizzy circles as the ship dipped and yawed even in the gentle swell.

'Keep your eyes fixed on the horizon when you feel sick,' was always Reuben's good advice whenever Matt felt queasy out in the coble.

Sheer determination to impress Stoney and dogged will-power somehow kept Matt's stomach in its rightful place. After a while he began to enjoy his new world, up with the birds, above the unreality which unfolded below.

From his high perch the two boats towing the *Kent* looked like large insects, long oars the legs which swept in orderly rhythm to keep them afloat and moving.

Matt began to feel hungry. With all the activity on deck, Stoney Fagg had probably forgotten all about him.

In the fading light of the early evening, storm clouds were gathering over the land - now a mere faint line behind him, and Matthew felt his first twinges of homesickness and concern for those at home. He wished fervently he had not gone with Reuben without finding Liz, early that morning, a lifetime ago.

Over towards the Dutch coast the sky was still clear and Matt could now make out the masts of a tall vessel breaking the horizon.

'Ho! Deck below! Sail ho!' Matt cupped his hands to his mouth and bellowed as loud as he could.

'*Kents*! Action stations!' roared Stoney. There was a flurry of activity as the crew prepared for their last fight, for Stoney Fagg had recognised the approaching vessel as the Royal Navy frigate *Pelican*.

Matthew, ordered down from the foretop, scrambled to the deck. The *Kent's* remaining guns fired defiantly as the *Pelican* approached, ignoring her Captain's demands to surrender. Stoney had never given in to anyone on all his sea going career and he wasn't going to capitulate easily now. He would go down fighting to the bitter end.

So Matthew found himself in the midst of the confusion of battle, the smoke and noise and blood which Jennet had seen so clearly in her crystal ball. At close quarters the noise and smell of battle was terrifying. Matt watched with awe as a bar shot from the *Pelican* smashed into the base of the foremast, and his recent perch crashed across the deck, a mangled heap of torn sail, splintered wood and tangled rigging.

160

Totally dismasted now, the once proud *Kent*, which for years had struck terror all along the coast, was little more than a sinking hulk. Many of the brave crew lay dead. The arrogant and defiant Stoney bled profusely from a head wound. Captain and ship finally surrendered to the boarding party from the *Pelican*. The Royal Navy Captain, contrastingly smart in his gleaming brass-buttoned blue coat and white doeskin breeches, read the warrant of capture to the remaining crew of the *Kent*, Matthew among them, informing them that they were now prisoners of His Majesty King George and would be treated as such. The remains of the *Kent* would be towed south to the Humber where in the King's warehouse the remaining cargo would be stored.

The Captain of the *Pelican* spotted Matt amongst the ruffian crew of the *Kent* and commented that he seemed somewhat youthful to be engaged in such reckless and dangerous activities. 'You should be at home with your mother, sonny,' he remarked sarcastically. 'Get your gear, come with me, and I'll hear your story later.' He swung away with an arrogant swagger, unaware of the cheeky grimaces on the faces of the smugglers. Even in this desperate situation they kept their impudent pride.

And so it was that Matthew found himself in the neat after-cabin of the *Pelican*, the last of the evening sun's rays slanting through the stern lights across the charts on the Captain's table. Reflections from the sea flickered on the immaculately painted woodwork. The hanging lantern swayed rhythmically in time with the gentle swell of the waves. After the turmoil of the recent battle, the quiet peace was almost unnerving.

The contrast with the rough and ready conditions aboard the *Kent* was daunting. Matt experienced a feeling of misplaced loyalty as he realised how life could be on board a decent ship. From tales about the Press Gang, he was aware that life below decks for the ordinary seaman could be grim, but if he worked hard at his studies, who knew that perhaps one day he, Matthew Storm, would be in command of his own splendid vessel. In his imagination he was already sitting at the other side of that polished mahogany desk, dressed in immaculate uniform, plotting his charted voyages to all parts of the world.

The Captain coughed, and drew Matt's wandering thoughts back to his present situation. Matt's loyalties were, however, still with the Baytown men and Stoney, and he found himself relating with careful thought, as much of his own story as he could without implicating his friends, and thus securing the Captain's assurance that once they docked in Hull, messages would be relayed and he would be returned in due course to his anxious parents.

'Thank you, Sir.' What a tale he would have to tell to the boys of Baytown after Chapel on Sunday. He wondered if they would really believe him.

The 'Reverend' Jocelyn Whyteacre sat astride his fine horse and viewed the sweeping landscape that greeted him as he crested the long ascent from the Whitby road. Panning out before him in the rays of a glorious sunrise lay the broad sweep of the Bay, stretching from headland to imposing headland. The view was magnificent and his artistic soul revelled in the beauty of the scene. In the brilliant glare of sun on water, it was difficult for him to accustom his eyes but gradually he focussed on the small silhouette of the sailing ship to which his colleague in the smuggling syndicate,

Squire John Farsyde, had summoned him. On board lay the supposedly dying sailor, needing the 'reverend's' comfort. Or was he as ill as rumour would have him believe?

Jocelyn felt somewhat apprehensive. He had never conducted a funeral in his life, although he had attended many. Too many, he contemplated sadly. Could he play the part convincingly, he wondered? He could but do his best. He'd always fancied himself as a bit of an actor and enjoyed taking part in the Christmas charades at the manor house where he lived in modest affluence. Now was his chance to prove it.

Having absorbed the stage of his prospective drama Jocelyn gently urged his horse onward, leaning well back in the saddle as Firecracker cautiously, hoof by hoof, descended the steep hill track. The early morning mist was beginning to burn off from the dew-damp heather, emitting a sharp exhilarating odour as it swirled round his horse's hooves.

So far, he had met no one, only viewed the early morning activities of the distant holdings with diminutive figures and animals beginning to move in the fresh occupations of a new day, far off and make-believe as his small son's toy farm. Jocelyn spared a fleeting thought for baby Simon, cradled in the arms of his beautiful young wife. After today, he decided, he really should seriously consider taking a less conspicuous part in running 'free trade' goods. He was not often so openly involved, and usually in his own moorland village some miles inland, where he was well known and amongst friends. This being his first foray into unknown country, he experienced some uneasy feelings.

'Mornin' Squire! A fine mornin' to be oot on a grand 'orse! Tha's got a reet good 'un theer! Ridden far?' A broad Yorkshire voice suddenly roused Jocelyn from his pleasant reverie as he ambled round the corner and found himself face to face with a farmer on a beautiful white horse. He paled as he remembered the local story of a gruesome ghost, that a phantom man on a white horse would be seen riding up and down on this stretch of road on the night a run was due, to scare off any inquisitive onlookers. This was the only stretch of publicly used road linking two lonely pannier tracks, and therefore it was wise to keep it clear on certain occasions. Meeting with the ghost was supposed to bring extreme bad luck, and many local people strongly believed it.

Jocelyn smiled faintly and recovered his composure. The horse may have been white but the farmer certainly looked too ruddy and substantial to be at all ghostly without the white sheet he donned on his night-time patrols.

'Yes, good morning, my man,' Jocelyn put on his finest accent. 'It is indeed a splendid morning. And that is a remarkably decent bit of horseflesh you have there, too, if I may say so! Come, Firecracker!' Jocelyn put heels to his horse's side and trotted briskly off before any further conversation could ensue. The farmer sat his white horse and scratched his head, staring after Jocelyn with a puzzled expression. Who was he, and what was a fine fellow like him doing in the likes of this place? He made up his mind to follow at a discreet distance and chuckled knowingly when Jocelyn turned in to the imposing gateway of Thorpe Hall. Ah! So it was true that something was afoot. The farmer was wise and experienced enough not to trouble himself further with what did not directly concern him. The stranger would be no threat if he was a friend of John Farsyde's.

'Well, now, John. What is this all about?' asked Jocelyn, settling himself into a comfortable armchair in front of the blazing logs in the impressive stone fireplace.

Squire Farsyde poured two glasses of Madeira from an elegant cut-glass decanter and handed one to his friend. The rich ruby liquid glowed in the light of the fire, and Jocelyn held his glass up to appreciate the delicate faceting of the design. 'Your good health, John!' he toasted. 'And mine!' he added apprehensively to himself as he sipped the fine wine. He had time to absorb the atmosphere of the dark oak panelled parlour with its fine paintings, rich Turkey carpet, and deep upholstered furniture, whilst John fiddled with a carved biscuit barrel and arranged some of its contents on a silver salver. Tall stone-mullioned windows with leaded lights gave onto a long garden of great tranquillity and beauty. In the far distance, the narrow line of the sea sparkled in the sun through the delicate branches of the fine beech trees. His friend certainly lived in some style, and Jocelyn knew exactly how he managed financially to enjoy this standard of living. At the side of the substantial Elizabethan house, hidden by the trees, ran the upper reaches of a moorland stream that wound its way through dense woodland straight into Baytown itself. A lonely and wet link with his smuggling colleagues in the village, but a very convenient and private one which led close to the special cavity in his front lawn, where frequently he would find kegs of brandy, bales of silk and lace, and packages of tea and tobacco for his own use. John's eyes followed Jocelyn's glance to the stone flagged area on the lawn on which stood an elegant statue. They lifted their glasses to each other, and winked. 'Drink up, Jocelyn. Plenty more where that came from!'

His glass topped up, Jocelyn settled down more easily to listen to the Squire's plans for him that day. Over the fireplace, two portraits of Farsyde ancestors looked knowingly down.

Delicately nibbling the expensive biscuit that perfectly complemented the Madeira wine, and carefully flicking any crumbs from his lace cravat, John Farsyde outlined the arrangements.

A colleague of Stoney Fagg's, David 'Smoker' Browning, had been unable to land his cargo of contraband owing to the increased activity of the Revenue Cutters following the demise of the *Kent*. Flushed with success, the Preventives were intent on making a clean sweep of the area, so further landings had to be made discreetly, cunningly, and in small, manageable quantities. Smoker's vessel, a small lugger of a common design, was less well known in the Bay. It was thus a simple matter to hoist a few different house flags and slip a change of name board over the bows and stern. Today, in the guise of *Girl Sally*, she was tacking about the Bay, having sent a crew member ashore with a story of a dying sailor who needed a priest to give him the last sacrament before passing to the life beyond.

The local minister was conveniently at the other side of the county for a few days, sick-visiting a distant relative. News of Smoker's problem had reached John Farsyde some days previously, Smoker's vessel being part of his own ship-owning syndicate. A clever plan had soon formed in John's mind. He sent word back to the ship that a friend of his, a vicar from a nearby parish, would be visiting him the next day, and he would arrange for him to be taken to comfort the 'dying' sailor. Jocelyn, the amateur actor, was therefore summoned to appear, soberly clad, to take on the role of visiting clergyman, one that appealed to his ego but worried him slightly in case he could not carry it off convincingly. Much, therefore, depended on his acting ability.

Down by the slipway a group of sympathetic fishermen and wives gathered round the seaman from the *Girl Sally*, waiting to take the reverend gentleman out to the ship. 'Oh, aye, t'poor feller is real bad, dean't reckon he'll last t'neet oot.' The mariner blew his nose loudly on a grubby neckerchief. He, too, was a natural actor. He had to be, as the success of the plan of action fell heavily on his ability to carry it off realistically. A respectful silence fell as John and Jocelyn quietly walked into the group of sorrowing folk. Jocelyn was introduced, and with a deferential tug at his forelock the seaman assisted the 'clergyman' into the boat and began the long row out to *Girl Sally*.

By the time he was returned in the same manner, Jocelyn was enjoying himself hugely. Soberly he stepped from the dinghy, and in full hearing of the waiting crowd, spoke in his best far-carrying stage whisper. 'Poor fellow, he can't live more than an hour or so. So sad. And away from all his loved ones, too. Such a shame.' He shook his head sympathetically. 'I suspect it may be yellow fever...' he added for good measure, gratified at the horrified gasp from the onlookers. 'So, we must bury him immediately. Leave the arrangements with me, my good man, and I will meet you here at dawn. Make sure the ship's carpenter makes a good tight job of the coffin. We want no infection to escape here.' Nor any tell-tale drops of brandy, he added to himself, silently.

With a sad nod in the direction of the waiting group, Jocelyn walked alone back up the road to Thorpe Hall to report to John the success of the venture so far. The first part had gone splendidly, and the two men enjoyed a pleasant evening of friendship, good wine, and an excellent game of cards.

During the early hours of the morning two of the Farsyde gardeners assisted the local sexton to dig a deep hole in an unused corner of the old churchyard. The sailor had, as planned, 'died' during the night and a heavy coffin, followed by a few sorrowing crew members and a number of local fisherfolk paying their respects, toiled up the hill with it on a creaking fisherman's cart. Being from 'foreign parts' the sailor had no bereft relatives to follow and mourn him, in fact, if they had known what was happening, they would probably have been having a good chuckle. Waiting at the churchyard gate, borrowed Farsyde family prayer book in hand, Jocelyn marvelled at the natural quality of the acting of the group of sailors who now approached close with their heavy burden. No trace of a flicker of amusement passed any eye, neither did they overdo their supposed grief for a lost mate. Jocelyn was impressed.

'Good morning,' he greeted them quietly, then solemnly led the procession down the flagged path to the gaping hole. 'I am the resurrection and the life....' he began, and felt the first pangs of conscience as he spoke these solemn words under false pretences.

The crewmen lifted the coffin with as much care and respect as if it had contained the body of their lost mate. Ropes were placed round it and the men took the strain as the heavy box was slowly lowered into the earth, making sure it remained level. Fortunately the contents had been well packed, for any dislodgement would give the game away fast. The coffin reached the bottom of the grave. The ropes were not removed, but carefully coiled and laid on top of the lid.

The traditional clod of earth thudded hollowly, as Jocelyn intoned 'ashes to ashes, dust to dust'- and the sorrowing group filed silently away, each shaking Jocelyn's hand as they departed to return to their ship, leaving the gardeners to fill in the hole.

This was not done with the usual care for one good reason. Within a few hours they would have to dig it up again and retrieve the contents of the well-made box which contained, not the poor sad corpse of a dead mariner, but a full load of small tubs of brandy, the spaces in between packed tightly with yards of expensive Valenciennes lace and Lyons silk. Smoker had got his cargo ashore in fine style.

Just before midnight a faint scratching was heard on the window of the panelled parlour at Thorpe Hall. John Farsyde raised his head from his doze to glimpse the soft gleam of a shaded candle. A third tapping signalled that he should open the door. Outside stood the seaman who had conducted Jocelyn to the *Girl Sally*. Tugging his forelock, he respectfully removed his red woollen cap.

'Evenin,' Squire. With Cap'n Browning's compliments, Sur, 'ere's a little nip o' brandy for t'parson!' he said with a broad wink, as he deposited two half anker tubs inside the hall door with a satisfying clunk.

Within the hour, the moon shone on the departing sails of *Girl Sally*, now most likely under yet another false name, on her next trip across to Holland.

The sun was well up, warming Jocelyn's back comfortably as he rode Firecracker up the rough track down which he had come, it seemed, half a lifetime ago. His progress was slowed owing to the weight of the two oak tubs of best French brandy slung across the saddle bow. After a good night's sleep he was feeling particularly pleased with himself, and confidently broke into song. The words that came readily and appropriately to mind were those of a folk song, 'The Poor Smuggler's Boy,' a sad tale of a boy whose father, a smuggler, had drowned at sea leaving his young son to carry on the trade. So carried away was he with the rousing chorus *'for the keg of good brandy,'* that he did not observe two formidably recognisable figures riding towards him only a short distance away as he rounded a blind corner.

He knew Riding Officers Peter Maxwell and James Herbert well enough by sight. Unfortunately they also knew him but as far as he could recollect, they would not recognise his horse, his previous mount being a grey, and Firecracker a relatively new addition to the Whyteacre stable.

The words of Jocelyn's song died on his lips, and he began to make speedy plans for his evasion. If he was caught now, the whole game would be up. No way could he escape with his skin *and* his brandy. One or both would have to be sacrificed. The bright rays of the low lying sun fortuitously shone directly into the eyes of the Preventives, dazzling and disguising the identity of the rider approaching them. Whilst his luck still held, Jocelyn bent forward on his horse's neck and quietly slipped from the saddle. Head down, his body shielded by the bulk of the horse, he stealthily crept into the densely wooded valley and crouched low under a thick bush.

Firecracker stood, shifting his hooves, uncertain what to do. By nature he was a docile horse, regarding most humans as friendly beings with sugar or apples in their pockets. Shielding their eyes, Maxwell and Herbert slowly rode up to the waiting animal. No rider was in sight. Searching the wooded valley would be like looking for a needle in a haystack. Besides, the contraband was there for the taking. Being experienced riders, they knew better than to gallop up and startle him, and so lose their quarry. Whilst still some distance away, Peter Maxwell slid to the ground and gave his reins to his fellow officer. Reaching in his pocket for the apple he had reserved as a treat for his own mount, he slowly approached Firecracker, hand outstretched, apple balanced temptingly on his flat palm.

'Now then, my beauty! Where have you been this lovely morning? You're a very fine fellow, aren't you?' Firecracker responded to the flattery of the quiet, friendly voice in the only way he knew how - a gentle whicker and flaring of the nostrils. One eye on Peter Maxwell, the other on the tempting fruit, he drew back his soft lips and gently nuzzled the outstretched hand, taking the proffered apple between strong teeth. Juice ran down his hairy chin as he munched, and Peter stroked his forehead and scratched between his ears in the favourite spot of most horses. From there it was no problem for Peter to reach and grasp the bridle, and begin slowly to lead the unresisting animal back to his waiting colleague.

'Well, well! What have we here?' Herbert queried unnecessarily, prodding the two kegs slung either side of the saddle. 'I think we'd better look after these. You never know whose hands they might fall into. There are some strange folk around these parts!' he chuckled. Such an easy and unexpected capture was a bonus to their day's activities. 'That horse will fetch a bob or two, as well. Wonder who he belongs to. I don't recognise him from around here. Maybe someone else will know him. We've got the vital evidence, anyway. Some poor chap will be missing out on his tot of brandy for a bit!'

Jocelyn peered out cautiously from under his bush with a sense of dismay and unbelief, as he watched Firecracker heading off in the opposite direction, tail swishing, chestnut rump swinging contentedly, seemingly quite happy with his new 'friends.' 'Fickle beast,' grunted the annoyed Jocelyn discontentedly. Unless he was to give himself up and ruin all the previous days work as well as incriminating himself, the only thing he could do would be to head off home on foot, and then decide how to get Firecracker back again.

A couple of weeks after this unfortunate event, it was the time for the annual horse fair in Jocelyn's nearby village. Word reached him that a fine animal, remarkably resembling Firecracker, was coming up for sale. Undecided whether to go and bid himself, or send one of the village men in his place, Jocelyn pondered the dilemma. Finally he reasoned that a mere villager buying such a fine horse would cause surprise and questions, whereas in his own position of respected status, it would appear normal enough. Besides, he considered that if he went about it openly, and was seen to be bidding and buying, even at a high price, no one would ever dream that he was purchasing his own horse for which he had already paid good money. If suspicions were lurking in his direction, his open actions would surely take attention away from him.

Jocelyn had been wise in his decision, for on the day of the auction, prominently among the crowd but in civilian clothes, were Maxwell and Herbert, showing a particular interest in Firecracker.

'Well! Good morning, Mr. Maxwell!' Jocelyn greeted him with an open smile and the outstretched hand of friendship. 'Some good horses for sale today, eh what? You after anything special yourself?'

'I could be doing with a younger horse, certainly. I like the look of that chestnut over there.' He glanced sideways at Jocelyn as he nodded in Firecracker's direction. 'Maybe he's a bit fine in the leg for my kind of work. Need something a bit sturdier. But I really wouldn't mind him for my own stable!' Peter Maxwell's well-bred background came to the fore on such occasions, and he anticipated the looks of admiration from his friends if he turned out for the hunt on such a fine mount.

Jocelyn began to feel apprehensive. Supposing Maxwell really was serious, it was on the cards that he could lose Firecracker altogether.

'Mmm. I rather fancy him myself,' said Jocelyn casually, bending down and running his hand expertly down Firecracker's fetlock. 'Want him for hunting, would you?' he enquired of Maxwell.

'Yes, that and a bit of cross country racing. He looks as if he could be fast on an open gallop'

'I wouldn't advise that,' lied Jocelyn. 'Here, feel this weak tendon. No good at all for going over the sticks. Could snap any time, and give you a bad fall as well as breaking his own leg. No, it could be very nasty and a great pity. He's such a nice horse.' Jocelyn's ability as an actor came to his rescue yet again, there being nothing at all wrong with Firecracker's legs. 'All I need is a nice quiet horse for a gentle hacking around. My wife would love him, and he would be ideal for my baby son to grow up with. He seems very docile.' Jocelyn looked Firecracker direct in the eyes and gently blew in his nostrils in his old familiar way of greeting. Firecracker whinnied in recognition. 'Think I'll have a word with the auctioneer and put in a bid. If I can get him cheap because of that leg, I think I'll risk him. He'll have a nice easy life with Philippa.'

Jocelyn sauntered off, hands in pockets, more casually than he felt, to speak to the auctioneer, who happened to know him well. Unless there were other bidders, the chances of buying him back cheaply were good, with a discreet word in the auctioneer's ear.

Maxwell and Herbert looked at each other, shaking their heads. No suspicions there, that was for sure.

'Any further bids for this fine horse?' cried the auctioneer. 'Are you done, gentlemen? Going, going, gone!' The gavel banged down on the table with a reassuring crash. 'Sold to you, Sir!' and Jocelyn rode back home on Firecracker, chuckling with anticipation at the tales he would share with Philippa.

It was a pity about the brandy, but you can't win them all, he thought. At least he was returning safely himself, and best of all, he'd got Firecracker back.

Damaris' world stood still, poised between the last glorious days of St Martin's summer and on the brink of a long, cold, irksome winter. Hidden in a sheltered grassy hollow on the cliff top, cradled in the crook of Reuben's arm, smelling the saltiness of his skin, and the strong oily odour of his gansey, she experienced an unexplainable and confusing mixture of wonderful tranquility tinged with a frightening foreboding.

She did not deserve such happiness, and feared deep down that she may lose it. It was so precious yet vulnerable a feeling. Her euphoric contentment lay in the fact that her early, long standing affection for Reub was growing into the very best kind of relationship - that of lover, future husband, and most important of all, true companion. She had often smiled at young married women who declared that their husbands were also their best friends, but now she began to realise the wisdom of that, for a true and long lasting marriage was built on far firmer foundations than sensual feeling alone.

She began to understand the glances that passed between her parents, glances that needed no words to express the emotions behind them, and how they laughed when after a long period of silence they would suddenly voice the selfsame thoughts. They lived in each others' minds, and that, thought Damaris, was just how two people should be.

Glancing across to Brow Side, she observed with the receptive eye of an artist - another recently acquired understanding growing out of her new mature being - that the corn had all been harvested on William's farm, the remaining stubble glowing golden in the slanting rays of the sinking evening sun. The corn had given of all its vitality, growing vigorously young and green in spring, burgeoning heavily with a full crop of grain in the summer months, and now lay, shorn of all energy in the autumn of its days. Just like human life, mused Damaris. She was still in the green springtime of youth and longed with natural stirrings deep within, for the time when she should bear her fruit to Reuben.

Autumn heather glowed royal purple on the edge of the hill-side where it met the hot blueness of the sky in an almost garish clash of colour.

Red Admiral butterflies, drunk on the strong nectar of a clump of Michaelmas daisies reverted to the wild from a nearby cottage garden, hovered and dipped and folded their wings as they partook of nature's late bounty with long, curling, probing sensuous tongues. Fat, furry yellow and black striped bumble bees lumbered with noisy, lazy wings, in amongst the flowers, filling the air with a soporific drone.

House martins and swifts scythed through the air above, frantically feeding on the rich harvest of flies, before leaving for warmer climes. It seemed to Damaris that they almost played with a wild hysteria, as they swooped, screaming, in wide circles round the rooftops, under whose eaves they had laboured to bring off yet another brood. All nature seemed to have achieved its summer purpose of breeding and rearing young, to ensure the continuance of the species.

Reaching out, Reuben picked a seeded dandelion head and held it softly against Damaris' mouth. Blowing gently, she wafted the delicate seeds into the spreading wind. 'This year; next year; sometime….' Reub's finger silenced her lips before she could utter the word 'never.'

Far below them, the sea swelled gently in a multitude of shades of blue and grey picked out with white tipped waves where the offshore wind caught the peaks and scattered them into delicate foam patterns.

All nature had its rhythms, she mused, even the ever-changing moods of the water.

Her sweet voice softly hummed a lilting folksong, as they rocked together in the rhythm of the earth and sea. Reuben's fingers idly twisted and plaited a single long stem of grass into a small circle which he slipped over Damaris' finger, cupping her soft hands within his own. He closed his eyes against the rush of protective love that charged through his whole being.

Reuben had never wanted anything in his whole life as much as he now wanted to make love to Damaris in that glorious late summer evening, with the long grasses whispering in the gentle breeze behind his head.

Damaris fingered the firm column of his throat, feeling the strong pulse of his life flowing through his veins. She laid her head against his chest and listened to the steady beating of his heart.

Reub gently unfastened the buttons of her blouse and slid the garment down to reveal the creamy skin beneath. The warm setting sun glowed richly on her soft young breasts, and Reub lowered his mouth to arouse her with the gentlest of kisses.

Beneath his weather-beaten tan, he flushed with emotion. Damaris was so very beautiful, and he knew she loved him. He also knew that he would be the first to love her in the complete way in which he wanted, now, in this glorious summer evening. He wanted it to be wonderful for her, too; slow and smooth and beautiful, the most perfect union of a first and tender love. A slow tear of sheer happiness squeezed from her blue eyes, and she raised her mouth slowly to his. Warmth flooded her whole body as he enfolded her gently within his protecting arms. There was a great sense of rightness about it, and when she moved away from him her eyes were shining.

Part Four

Raging seas pounded against the cliff with a thunderous roar. White spray hurtled upwards in great spiralling spouts, the wild October gale slamming it against the attic window with frightening violence.

Damaris woke with a startled jump, heart thumping and eyes bewildered by the sudden awakening. Rough fingers of wind fumbled with the catch on her window, rattling and tugging to gain entry, roaring and shaking with angry frustration.

In her disturbed dreams, the great sleeping lion-shaped headland that protected the Bay had woken from his stony slumber and rampaged across the sea in a fit of primordial temper, kicking up great waves and hurling them against the high cliffs, flinging stones and sending shreds of seaweed streaming down her high window. Through the thin cotton curtains, stirring in the penetrating draughts, the bright moon shone fitfully against the racing clouds.

Revelling in a deep set primitive fear, Damaris felt exhilarated by the furious unleashing of the elements. She stood, wrapped in her warm quilt, gazing transfixed at the untamed power of the sea, from the safety of her little room. Tonight the unstoppable waves crashed over the paws of her sleeping guardian, the imaginary lion of Raven Hill, the same yet not the same great headland she had observed in the cold still moonlight at the dawning of the year. This night her lion roared in anger as, captive, he was powerless against the fury of the relentless waves. Damaris wished he could free himself, as in her dream.

It was an awe-inspiring sight. Damaris felt an instinctive understanding, inborn in generations of seafarers, of the respect her father showed for this terrifying environment in which he must live. So different from the shimmering, baby-blue waves she had delighted in on the golden summer mornings. Those gentle babies had grown into roaring, death-defying beasts. Damaris shivered, and went back to bed.

Pulling the quilt tight round her head for warmth and to shut out the noise of the storm-monster hammering at her window, Damaris tried to return to sleep. But sleep did not come easily when pounding seas sent thudding shock waves deep through the cliff and the whole house shook with the impact.

Not for the first time was Damaris thankful to be safe in a warm bed and not at the mercy of that fear-inspiring source of power, the sea.

In the next room within the safe confines of his bunk Matt lay awake, revelling in the excitement of potential danger. The salty blood of his ancestors stirred him with restlessness and desire for the freedom of the open ocean. This night's storm exhilarated him as never before. After his adventure, the latent passion that had been dormant since his birth had grown stronger, every changing mood of the sea affecting him more deeply. Liz noticed the signs with the intuition of a mother of generations of sea-faring folk long before Matt himself understood the cause of his turbulent feelings. In their big bed, Liz's thoughts reached out into her son's wakeful mind, and she turned closer to Zack, curving her soft body into the manly strength of his back, thankful to have his comforting presence still with her. Her maternal intuition generated cold pangs of fear that nothing would prevent Matt going to sea. She was only one of such mothers in countless families, facing the inevitability of years of anxiety, danger, and the distinct possibility of the death of her only son, but like all before her, those of her own generation, and mothers yet to be, Liz knew that she had no choice but to accept her son's own decision. 'God grant me the serenity to accept what I cannot change,' she prayed, 'and keep all sailors safe this terrible night,' she added, knowing deep down that it could not be so.

The gale had sprung up during the early morning hours with an unsuspected suddenness. All had been calm enough when Damaris had retired to bed though Jennet's ancient cat, its dull and rough fur now beginning to gloss with the milk of human kindness, had sat with its back to the fire all evening, a sure prediction of a coming storm. Being a wise-woman's cat, it should know.

However, the storm had taken not only herself by surprise.

Across on Fisherhead at the other side of the dark village, candles burned low late into the night in the home of Big Isaac McGraw. Together with Silas Biddick he sat by the fireside, fidgeting edgily with his unlit pipe, anxiously awaiting news of Sandy Kellock, their partner in the smuggling trade. Sandy was not the happiest of men at the moment. Earlier in the year he had achieved a long-held ambition to own his own vessel. He had bought an almost new three-master from a Dutchman and had gone into the coal carrying business with a little discreet smuggling on the side. Fate had not smiled kindly on Sandy Kellock and what she had given with one hand snatched away with the other, as his pride and joy, the *Grey Dove,* was wrecked on her first voyage. Sandy had lost all in that ill-starred venture and was in the mood for revenge for the once-proud vessel that now lay shattered on the shore of the treacherous Bay.

The flames in the fire flared brightly, a down-draught of smoke belched chokingly into the room as the door opened and admitted the darkly attractive figure of Jiddy Vardy. Swinging off her long cloak with a graceful gesture, and hanging it on a nail behind the door, Jiddy joined the two men by the fireside.

'Seen Sandy anywhere?' asked Isaac, anxiously.

'No, but summat's afoot,' reported Jiddy. 'Ah've just left Zack Storm saddling Reuben's horse, and he told me he's off for a little moonlight ride!'

Jiddy rubbed her cold hands and held them out to the fire. The glow from the flames flickered on her dark hair and dusky skin. The rough smugglers eyed her appreciatively as she reached for a tankard of ale that stood on the mantel and continued her report. 'Zack said he'd spotted Gobbit riding hell-for-leather off on the road towards Scarborough, so he's gannin' after to see what he's up to!' she added with a wide smile and a broad, knowing wink of her sloe-dark eyes.

'Gobbit'was not to be trusted as far as you could throw him, agreed Big Isaac and Biddy. Nicknamed because of his big mouth which blabbed information to the Preventive Men, it was strongly suspected that he was a spy. Not a Bay man by birth but a 'foreigner,' Gobbit had never been accepted by the community, and sorely resented his exclusion. A natural suspicion of all outsiders was an inborn trait of all the Bay folk. Sometimes it was as well to be tight lipped, as in the case of Gobbit, but it was hard for newcomers to become accepted. Gobbit was an eager tale-bearer against the unfriendly fisher folk, but his gullibility made him easy game for carrying false information.

Earlier in the day Jiddy had been conversing with Reub, well in earshot of Gobbit, and had deliberately indiscreetly spoken loudly that a Dutch smuggler was due in to land cargo off Raven Hill that night. Gobbit's sharp ears had pricked at the news and in pretence of baiting his hooks he bent diligently over his lines, all senses alert. As soon as Jiddy had gone, Gobbit was off, riding away to Scarborough to the Preventive men and the Dragoons.

The front door banged again, wafting another cloud of smoke into the room as Sandy Kellock finally arrived. 'Poof! Isaac!' Sandy beat at the smoke with his cap. 'Time thi got that swept! Ah's danged near chokin! Wait until t'fire's oot, then Ah'll bring thi one o' me old hens and drop her doon t'chimbley. That'll fettle it for thi!'

'Nivver mind aboot a bit o' smoke, Sandy. Hearken to this!' and Jiddy had to tell her tale yet again while Sandy warmed his feet and downed his ale. He dumped the empty tankard on the table, folded his arms and declared 'Ah can smell a storm comin'. Ah'm just wonderin' whether t'snivs'll tek t'bait and sail roond in this weather. They'll prob'ly risk it, as it seems Gobbit got a reet good tale to tell 'em, thanks to Jiddy 'ere!' He gave Jiddy a wink that was half way to a lecherous leer. 'They'll likely be 'ere afore daylight if they're comin'. Ah think it's worth sayin' they'll tek t'risk. Let's go!' He grabbed his cap and rose energetically to his feet. He was in a reckless mood. Revenge for the loss of his own ship and a good few glasses of ale had brought out the ruthless streak in him. Any way of getting at the 'snivs' was fair game to Sandy Kellock.

'Hang on, Sandy. We need more men.' Jiddy, with her sharp foresight, realized that Isaac, Silas and Sandy would need at least another pair of hands to take over the Revenue boat. They would need Reuben. 'And,' said Jiddy, 'we need a signaller from Raven Hill. What aboot young Matt? He's small and wick enough ti get inti t'signalling chamber. 'Ee's grown up a lot lately. Can we trust 'im?'

'Ah reckon Zack would'ny be too pleased ti hear thi doot 'is lad,' retorted Isaac. 'Go get 'im, Jiddy, an' mek sure 'e's got a good lanthorn. Reet, then, off we go!'

Jiddy swung her cloak round her slim shoulders and headed off to find Reub. As luck would have it, Matt was also by his fireside, being fed up with womens' chatter, and anxious about his father, knowing that he had ridden off like the devil on Reub's horse.

She burst into the cottage unannounced, gave brief orders to Reub, found a lantern, candles and a tinder box, and turned to Matt. 'Get a warm jacket – that one of Reub's will do fine, and come along of me. Quick, lad!' as Matt hesitated and began to ask questions. She dragged him by the arm, and they set off up the cliff path.

Down by the slipway two small boats were prepared for launching. Sandy and Isaac climbed into the first and made ready for sea, closely followed by Reub and Silas.

A dim figure leant in the shadowed doorway of the Fisherman's Arms, watching slyly as Reuben Granger manhandled the second boat into the choppy waters. Thomas Duke had not yet given up his plans for a rosy future. Constable Clarke had noted his previous information against Reub after the disappearance of Samuel Barnard's flock, but had informed Duke that he'd need stronger evidence before he could make an arrest. A red kerchief round the neck of a galloping horseman in the dark could have belonged to anybody. Thomas had left disgruntled, but even more determined to collect the evidence that would open the door to his own future.

Reuben was unaware of the sinister figure as he and Silas pulled away from the shore towards the rendezvous under Raven Hill.

Jiddy Vardy and young Matt Storm toiled up the steep pathway up the treacherous slopes of Raven Hill. Lanterns were little use on this dangerous path, and theirs were shaded so as to shed the faintest of lights, for safety's sake. Along the shore small groups of men trudged towards the meeting place. They all hoped it would be worth the effort. It was the sort of night all sensible folks would be in the inns, enjoying the companionship of a few pints, and they felt a twinge of envy for their friends left behind. It was a wise policy that only small groups left the village at any one time. A mass exodus would certainly alert the sharp wits of Maxwell and Herbert.

A second group of smugglers reached the pre-arranged meeting place along the path down which Zack would return from his jaunt to Scarborough. Darkness had fallen early, but Zack knew the road well and Reuben's horse was sturdy and sure-footed. He had waited, sheltering with the horse under the ruins of Scarborough castle, high on the headland that had guarded the town for centuries past. He watched as the unmistakable silhouette of the Revenue sloop slunk out of the harbour, ploughing through heavy seas, and headed north. It was enough for Zack, who urged Reuben's patient animal back on the homeward trail with a degree of excited urgency.

The sound of his muffled hooves brought the waiting men to a high pitch of alertness, with the news that the sloop was well on her way. Plans had been carefully laid and every man prepared for action. Lights and an old Dutch flag were attached to the listing masts of Sandy's lost lugger, *Grey Dove*. He and Isaac took Reub and Silas on board the small rowing boat, beaching Reub's boat for the use of the men making their way along the shore. They wrapped rags round the oars to muffle the tell-tale squeak of the thole-pins, leaned on the oars, and waited.

Up on Raven Hill, a faint light flashed from the secret signalling chamber, cut into the rock high above in the cliffs. Matt was crouched in the small aperture, waving his lantern as instructed. Jiddy hid in the bushes close by. 'She's coming!' whispered Matt as he waved the lantern back and forth. The Revenue boat was on her way, as anticipated, making heavy weather of the stormy conditions. Matt, with his great love of the sea and ships could not but admire the plucky little vessel as she plunged, nose down, into the steep waves. From this great height, and in the added drama of the darkness, she looked small and very vulnerable. In spite of himself, and though he had no love for the 'snivs' on board, Matt could not help hoping that the gallant little vessel would be safe.

He watched intently as the small Preventive sloop splashed her way in the choppy waters round the headland and dropped anchor in the Bay. Two boats lowered over the side and pulled away to the stranded 'bait'anticipating an easy, red-handed capture - if Gobbit's information had been correct.

Sandy and Reub took the strain on their silenced oars and headed noiselessly across the dark water to the anchored sloop, expecting some resistance. All realised that the silence of surprise was vital. Shipping their oars, they drew close under the stern.

For his size, Big Isaac was a nimble man, used to a lifetime of agile climbing amongst ropes and rigging. Heaving himself on board, he hurled his heavy body against the back of the unsuspecting watchman who fell to the deck with an unprotesting thud. A second crewman was similarly summarily overpowered, trussed and gagged with sailorly efficiency. The young boy deckhand fearfully cowering under the bulwarks gave no trouble. Within minutes the capture of the sloop was complete.

Isaac, Biddy, Sandy and Reub, all experienced seamen, rapidly slipped anchor and hoisted the sails, heading away into the freshening south-easterly breeze. About a mile from shore, the captives were unbound and set adrift in an open boat.

The shore team, using Reub's boat, cautiously approached the stranded *Grey Dove,* to spy on the Preventives. Wisely, they rowed silently back to the shore while the officers were searching for the contraband below decks. Fortunately they had not been required to take violent action, which could have resulted in the identification of Reub's boat, thus implicating him in the affair. It was enough to leave them stranded and chuckle over their discomfort when they emerged and found their sloop stolen.

Reuben had not time to realise that being involved in the capture of a Government vessel had turned him overnight from a smuggler into a pirate! He straightened his neckerchief and saluted Sandy with a wide grin. 'Aye, Aye, Cap'n Kellock!' he retorted smartly to Sandy's orders to take over the watch.

It had been mutually agreed to elect Sandy Kellock acting captain to recompense him for the loss of his own vessel. Fate had turned the wheel of fortune to favour Sandy once more, as the sale of the captured sloop to shipowners in Holland provided enough money for the purchase of a replacement vessel.

Ships were frequently held in joint ownership, and Sandy took Isaac, Biddy and Reub into a new partnership. The other men who had played active parts in the affair were promised payment from the sale of Sandy's first cargo. Sandy Kellock was a fair-minded man, and his friends were generously happy that his luck had turned.

The gale which had woken Damaris was now blowing with full fury and pounding the remains of Sandy's first loss to pieces on the rocks at the foot of the sleeping lion.

Preventive men and Dragoons spent a fruitless night searching for the non-existent 'Dutch crew' of Sandy's wrecked lugger. All they found were some very wet and disgruntled colleagues wading ashore, furious at having been so easily duped.

In the cabin of their vessel safe in the harbour of Flushing, the four partners toasted their future, trying to decide on a name for their new boat. It was considered unlucky to change a ship's name once she had been launched, but the Yorkshire sailors realised that their fellows would never pronounce the Dutch name *Veel Voorspoed* now painted on the bows. Enquiries revealed that a rough translation would read *Good Fortune*, and that, they all agreed, would do very nicely, under the circumstances!

Reuben mused on the rapid change in his status over the past twenty-four hours - from poor fisherman, to crafty smuggler, to desperate pirate, and now wealthy part ship-owner.

Zack returned with Reuben's horse, dried and fed and stabled him, and went home, a dripping wet, windblown figure. Liz welcomed him with a relieved hug and hung his salt-spray soaked jacket to dry by the fire, where Damaris found it the next morning.

On his return, Matt found it hard to explain where he had been. He already knew the importance of loyalty and secrecy, even within his own family. Fortunately, his mother was too wise to ask, when Jiddy pushed him, exhausted, through the door in the early hours.

Jennet crooned tunelessly to herself as she rhythmically rocked back and forth in Liz's chair, slippered feet on the shining brass fender, the firelight rosying her wrinkled face and reflecting red sparks in her mysterious, far-seeing eyes. The cat stretched luxuriously on her knee, flexed its claws, yawned, and squirmed onto its back, imploring Jennet to scratch its upturned belly. At its advanced age it appreciated its home comforts and was enjoying life in Liz's comfortable cottage, where it was warmer and better fed than at any time in its life. A gentle saunter down to the boats ensured an easy meal of fishy scraps in total contrast to the effort it expended catching the skinny mice that inhabited Jennet's kitchen back at the cottage across the fields. Occasionally a plump field mouse or an unfortunate scraggy bird found its way into the cat's diet, but on the whole, its hunting expeditions bore no exciting results. The cat was becoming fat and lazy, revelling in its new-found good fortune. Its black fur was now thick and glossy. Jennet reached out a bony finger and absently scratched under its chin, arousing deep-throated purrs of contentment and a satisfying stretching of its neck as its one green eye closed with rapture.

'You're getting idle, like me, old puss. If you live here much longer, you'll have forgotten what mice look like. As for me, I'll be losing my magic touch. Time we were thinking about going home, my feline friend.'

The cat responded by opening its pink mouth wide in a yawn of protest, showing off its sharp pointed teeth. It was quite happy where it was.

Jennet had recovered well under Liz's watchful care. Gradually her slurred speech cleared and movement returned to her paralysed limbs. She was beginning to long impatiently for her own home and her own set ways. Her old cottage had stood empty since her illness, though Damaris and Matthew had kept a watchful eye on it on their autumn rambles. Matt had tamed the wild garden, pruning and trimming the special herb bushes, while Damaris tidied the cupboard shelves full of Jennet's special medicines. She had found herself taking a keen interest in the contents, spending long hours learning the uses of herbal remedies from Jennet's wide experience, and her special books. Her particular favourite was also Jennet's own pride and joy, a beautifully illustrated version of Culpeper's Herbal, a book that dated back to the time of Elizabeth the First. Both grandmother and granddaughter had gained much from their new enforced companionship.

Matthew gathered the herbs to Jennet's instructions and Damaris tied them in bunches to dry in the autumn sun that filtered through the dusty windows of the lonely cottage. Liz planned to give the whole place a good cleaning and encourage Jennet to return to her former life. Late autumn was a good time as there would be plenty to occupy her with the drying and preserving of the herbs and the preparation of her winter potions. Before long the villagers would be in need of her cures for coughs and colds, the certain companions of winter.

Jennet's presence in his home was now causing Zack some irritation. From her seemingly permanent place in his wife's favourite chair by his fireside, she slyly watched his every movement and listened to every word of his conversation. Even when apparently asleep, Zack was aware that she still observed each and every word and action. To a man of the open sea, used to the sunny atmosphere of his happy home, her continual presence was becoming oppressive and tensions were beginning to mount. The cottage was too small to contain such a guest for too long. Jennet's eavesdropping curbed conversation, but all the same, Zack knew that she read his very thoughts, and plans unspoken even to Liz seemed uncomfortably open to Jennet's piercing mind. Zack did not trust her, especially now that news of a planned 'run,' a big one, was slowly filtering through to the landers concerned. At their centre were Zack and Reuben. Zack sensed that Jennet already knew more than was good for her - or him. He thus was spending more and more time away from his home and family in the safer company of Reuben, a young man to whom he was close and completely in trust.

Liz was also guiltily feeling regrets that Jennet was overstaying her welcome. Trouble was, she also felt aware that Jennet knew exactly what she and Zack were thinking. Jennet's was not a comfortable presence. There was no privacy even in one's innermost thoughts when Jennet was there, brooding and monotonously rocking. Several times Liz had almost brought herself to the point of suggesting that it was high time that Jennet was well enough to resume her own life. It was already the end of October and if she didn't move soon Liz feared that she'd be set in for the winter, and that neither of them could face.

Damaris and Matt were not so far out of their childhood that the old traditions of Hallowe'en were beyond their enjoyment. Matthew had come home the night before with a large muddy turnip which he dumped on the kitchen table, and had driven Liz to exasperation with the ensuing mess of hollowing it out with Zack's clasp knife, carving a spooky face from whose features the candle would glow fearsomely. Bits of turnip littered the entire room before Matt finally puffed out his cheeks with exhaustion and stood the grinning face on the mantelpiece. Liz had curbed her irritation as she had thoughtfully watched her son, tongue stuck out as he worked. Too soon he would leave her, that she knew. Hating waste, she gathered up the bits of the hacked out turnip, carefully washed them and threw them into the stewpot for the next day's hot soup.

Damaris and Annie, making their own preparations for this most magical evening of the year with girlish enjoyment, were a little uncertain of Jennet's reaction. How many Baytown cottages would be celebrating Hallowe'en with a real live witch, and her cat, by their firesides?

Like most young boys Matt was scornful of the fortune-telling games they played but he was sure to be around for all the traditional foods that Liz would prepare; turf cakes and toffee apples, jacket potatoes piled high with butter and cheese, pickles and parkin, and best of all the fluffy hot baked apples bulging with raisins, dates, and cream, and fragrant spiced mulled wine.

Darkness was falling early that Hallowe'en, and Liz entered the warm kitchen whose only light was the glow from the peat fire. Pausing in the doorway she observed Jennet's huddled figure outlined in the flickering firelight. The movement played on the motionless features, bringing them to an unnatural kind of life. The cat, ensconced on a cushioned chair by the fender, stretched out a long hind leg, and slowly and deliberately licked along its thigh, pausing to gaze at Liz with a defiantly nonchalant expression. Its long fur caught the firelight in a red halo. To her eyes as yet unaccustomed to the dim kitchen, the cat appeared as if on fire, its single eye glowed like a hot coal, and it turned its face to her with an evil grin. The dirty white fur on its belly became a red vest, it flexed its long claws, blood-scarlet in the fireglow, and twitched its tail, spitting angrily at the prospect of disturbance. Liz shuddered herself into sensibility. Jennet was most certainly outstaying her welcome if that cat was becoming boss in her kitchen. Liz determined she would tolerate the devil no longer, and bore down on the feline fiend with a vicious flick of her apron. The cat spat and thudded to the floor angrily, lashing out a sharp-clawed paw that caught the back of Liz's hand, leaving a fine stitching of blood. It stalked out of the room with as much dignity as it could muster, tail held defiantly erect, the merest tip twitching in annoyance. Liz was sure the long hair on the end of its tail had divided into a three-pronged fork!

With the exit of the cat the atmosphere was changed as Liz lit the oil lamp and a soft golden light flooded the kitchen. The Biblical quotation came into her mind: 'The light shone in the darkness and the darkness overcame it not.' Her light dispelled the gloom and fear of a few moments ago, and it was banished completely as Damaris and Annie burst in with the cheerfulness of youth and all came back to normal. Liz glanced at her rosy cheeked, bright eyed daughter gratefully. Even so, tonight was All Hallows Eve and the girls' innocent fun had portentous overtones.

On the table they dumped the apples freshly picked from Annie's own tree, and the hazel nuts straight from their own secret bush in the eerie Little Wood. During the days leading up to Hallowe'en they had somewhat self-consciously chosen a hazel bush, tied it round with a black ribbon to ensure it contained its secret and danced round it with nonsensical chants not knowingly learned from any human being, but dormant in their subconscious from the beginnings of time. The fruit of their chosen bush would then foretell their fortunes for the coming year, and the magic nuts now lay smooth and brown and glossy within their sheath of protective leaves.

Each laid their five chosen nuts in the shape of a cross, the best placed at the centre. The four surrounding kernels contained unspoken wishes, to be granted if the nuts exploded in the heat of the fire. The central nut symbolised their unnamed sweetheart, a name known only to the girl in question, but Damaris and Annie had been friends long enough to know exactly who was named in each of their innermost thoughts. If this one split in the fire, then surely true love would follow. Smiling blushingly at each other, they laid the formation on small squares of metal which would later be placed on the glowing peat for the primeval forces therein to determine the outcome.

Jennet's greeny gold eyes slid sideways under her lowered lids, cynically observing the girls, whilst pretending to be asleep. 'Hmph! What do they know of magic?' she scoffed, forgetting that to their young minds these were just amusing games. 'If she did but know what she has in store she would not be laughing now!' Jennet's pride rose with reminiscences of her past powers but felt a pang of regret and sorrow for the granddaughter she had come to know and love over the past few months of her illness.

The year was moving on relentlessly. Jennet knew that very soon, fear and grief would come to this young girl, not through any natural forces or disasters but through the greed and jealousy of man, and one man in particular.

Outside, a clatter of boots and chatter of voices heralded the arrival of Matt and his friends. On the table Liz had placed her large brown-glazed earthenware bread pancheon, full of water on which floated six of Annie's rosy apples. Matthew held his hands behind his back and dunked his face forward into the bowl, grunting with annoyance as the tempting fruit slipped tantalisingly away from his grasping teeth. Bobbing for apples was a game played for generations and Matt and his friends carried on the tradition, splashing water everywhere and laughing and spluttering far too much to have any success in capturing the elusive fruit. Annie and Damaris jostled the boys to join in.

There was so much youthful laughter and noise in the cottage that no-one noted the arrival of Zack, surprisingly accompanied by Reuben. After a while Reuben smiled and gently moved Matthew out of the way. Putting his finger to his lips and winking at Zack, he replaced Matt at the bowl. His larger jaw grasped a slippery apple with ease, and clamping it firmly in strong white teeth, raised it from the surface of the water. Damaris was so busy concentrating on grabbing her own apple that, face dripping wet and hair plastered over her eyes, she had not even noticed that Reub had replaced Matt as her opponent. Raising her eyes above the remaining bobbing fruits, cornflower blue met peat brown and her wet face suffused with a deep blush under the drops of water glistening on her fair skin in the soft glow of the firelight. Reub's eyes twinkled in a merry and loving smile. It was the only way he could express his appreciation of the attractive picture before him, his mouth being fully occupied by the prized apple.

Taking Damaris by the hands, he drew her to him, bending down to match her delicate height, wordlessly offering the apple to her. Fire swept through her body as she accepted his token of affection. Tentatively she bit into the apple, still firmly held in his teeth. Reuben held on tightly, as it would be an ill omen of rejection if the apple dropped before his chosen lady had taken her own bite. His strong eyes willed hers to look into them, and when she shyly raised her glance to his, Damaris saw an expression there that she had never dreamed could exist. She and Reub, in that crowded family gathering, were in a private world that no other could enter. He enfolded her gently in his strong fisherman's arms, and the apple, its red skin scarred white where the two bites had been taken, fell between them, trapped uncomfortably against Damaris' young breast. Holding her close against his rough, oily gansey, Reub affirmed that he never, ever, wanted to let her go.

Matt broke the spell by tugging at Reuben's jacket. 'Hey! Move ovver, Reub. Let a feller 'ave a go!' His thoughtless remark, deliberately misinterpreted, brought a friendly spank on the backside.

'Tha can't kiss thi sister!' retorted Reuben.

Matt hit him back. 'Ah didn't mean that, tha' daft 'ayporth. Ah want a go at them apples!'

As he bent over the bobbing fruit in the bowl, Reuben dunked his head firmly into the water and Matt came up spluttering, but with a juicy red apple lodged firmly in his teeth. The tension of the moment was over, but the realisation that Damaris' future had truly been revealed that evening, remained with them all for a long time to come.

Damaris had no real need of any more fortune telling games; she had known for some time where her destiny lay, and joined in the rest of the games with new found joy.

The younger boys had found the knack of grasping the apples by the stalks and were all happily munching away in a huddle in their own corner.

Annie and Damaris however, continued the game, peeling their fruit in one long paring, throwing it over their shoulders and reading the curling shape as it fell on the floor. It was supposed to fall in the initial of their sweetheart, but Annie, reading from all angles, could not determine whether hers had really formed an R or a B, but Damaris was quite certain that hers had landed in a very satisfying G.

Zack and his future son-in-law sat contentedly by the fire with tankards of Liz's excellent home brewed ale. Zack had noted with great satisfaction what had transpired between Reub and his daughter. He could wish for no better and determined to further the relationship. Lifting his glass to the younger man, Zack smiled his toast of approval.

Jennet and the cat watched the proceedings silently. She knew that troubled waters lay ahead, but in what form the danger would come was not clear as yet. She only had a strong sense of foreboding as two initials began to form in her mind's eye.

The evening progressed to the time for roasting the hazelnuts. Annie and Damaris each placed their trays on the glowing embers of the fragrant turf and, chins cupped on hands, expectantly awaited the splitting of the roasted skins. The order in which the nuts had been placed on the trays was all important, for as well as the unspoken wishes, they represented the old 'this year, next year, sometime, never' time charm predicting marriage. The central hazelnut, being the biggest, was supposed to remain intact to the last, but Dame Fortune, thinking that too much good luck had come Damaris' way that evening, took a hand and directed the forces of the fire in a way that shattered the rest of the good natured fun.

Suddenly, the central nut on Damaris' tray split apart, showering fragments of hard shell into the fire where they burned and crackled with a fierce intensity, spitting red-hot fragments onto the clippy mat before the hearth. A smell of scorching alerted Liz and she quickly stamped on the glowing embers. Jennet leaped from her chair, heaving the protesting cat unceremoniously onto the floor, and pointing a finger at Reuben, shrieked shrilly 'Beware the name Thomas! He will cause you much sorrow!' She spun towards Reuben, eyes wild. Her flailing arms caught Damaris and swirled her into Reuben's grasp. 'Beware, beware, beware....he is evil, evil, evil.......He will part you before the year is out!'

Damaris clapped her hands over her ears to shut out Jennet's frightening prophecy and fled tearfully from the warm cottage into the cold and dark, seeking oblivion in the warren of twisting alleyways. The heavily emotionally charged atmosphere of the evening had become too much for her to take.

Everyone stood transfixed, as if momentarily turned to stone, stunned by the sudden dramatic happening. Time stood still for the split second it took for realisation to dawn. Liz and Reuben made for the door to run after Damaris but Zack held out a restraining hand.

'Let her be. She needs to be alone for a while. Let's face it, privacy is a rare luxury round here these days,' he added, with a pointed glance in Jennet's direction. She sat, slumped back in her chair, rocking, rocking, rocking, eyes fixed in a distant and far-seeing blank stare.

Reub, somewhat shaken, paled under his weather-beaten tan, raised a faint smile and shrugged his shoulders, inclining his head with a sideways jerk and tapping his forehead, indicating his opinion that Jennet was crazy. Even though the warning had come as a shock, Reuben believed it was all nonsense. Just at that moment in time he could not think which of his acquaintances by the name of Thomas could be meaning him such harm and trouble. As yet he was unaware of the extent of the jealousy of Thomas Duke.

Zack put his hand on Reuben's shoulder. 'Come on, lad. Damaris'll be alreet. She just needs a bit o' space. It's time we was off. We'll be a bit late back, Liz. Don't wait up.' He gave Liz the usual cheek-pecking farewell, accompanied by the secret hug, three quick movements of his fingers on her waist, warning her that he was going out 'on business.'

'We're gannin ti meet a lady!' confirmed Reub in a conspiratorial whisper, this being the verbal confirmation frequently used in the village that a run was expected.

'Be careful. You especially,' Liz warned Reuben. A little of Jennet's influence had rubbed off on her these last few months. She, too, felt an unexplained pang of anxiety as far as Reuben was concerned.

'Keep *him* busy.' Zack's eyes silently sought out Matthew. 'We don't want 'im out toneet. Ah knowed 'e's bin wi' us before, but toneet it could be dangerous. Can't tek any risks of owt goin' amiss.'

'I understand,' she promised. 'Now then, Matt!' she spoke with false brightness. 'How about some gingerbread?' The young people's teeth were soon stickily engaged in piles of

Liz's Hallowe'en speciality in companionable silence. The recent drama soon forgotten and swept aside as an old woman's eccentric behaviour, they cheerfully munched and planned the rest of the evening's games.

Out in the dark warren of the streets of Baytown, Damaris blindly stumbled over the rough cobblestones until, exhausted, she reached the edge of the high cliff above the village and threw herself sobbing into the arms of mother earth. Tears of emotional shock flowed until they had washed her mind clear and as her breathing eased she slowly calmed in the peaceful and quiet darkness. Lying close to the earth she absorbed a strange clarity of thought. Gradually a plan began to form, seemingly of its own accord. In the depths of her subconscious mind Jennet was speaking to her. 'If you really want to know the truth, go at midnight to the old church, and wait, and watch. Only then will you discover whether Reuben will live.' 'Or die.........' whispered the wind, passing close by her ear. For at midnight on Hallowe'en, so it was firmly believed, a ghostly procession of those souls who would leave this life in the coming year would enter the church porch. A frightening spectacle that few dared witness, especially as it was rumoured that the watcher would be inexorably drawn to follow on.

Moved by an unseen force, Damaris rose refreshed from her spent tears, brushed the dead leaves from her skirt, and purposefully, yet as if in a trance, set out on the road leading from the village. That it was the self same road along which she had followed last spring in the joyful procession to Jane's wedding did not enter her thoughts. The familiar path became unfamiliar territory for her solitary excursion. Tonight she had one sole aim in view.

The way was dark. Only in the silent hedgerows where unseen birds and animals slept, the occasional rustle or faint squeak indicated that she was not entirely alone. Hidden lives still went on all around her and she drew comfort from their unobtrusive presence. Overhead an owl swooped so silently that she did not hear its passing, only felt the movement of the disturbed air and glimpsed a dim shape in the night sky.

The moon shone with a pale, watery lustre, clouds moving slowly across its face, constantly changing with the indecision of threatened rain. Damaris' eyes had become accustomed to the darkness and the faint light was sufficient to guide her on the right road. As she toiled upwards, the stocky silhouette of the old church rose over the hill top horizon. She hastened her footsteps in her anxiety to reach it before the hour of midnight, otherwise her journey would have been in vain, and she would return home none the wiser. She had no idea of the time, but instinct told her there was not much left.

At the entrance to the ancient churchyard the oak gate swung creakily on its hinges as she carefully pushed it open. Normally at this time of night she would have hesitated, fearful to step into the silent garden of the dead, reluctant to invade the privacy of their eternal sleep. During the hours of daylight it was different, a peaceful, gentle place, where the long grass swayed in the passing wind and sunshine and shadows played fitful silent games over the weathered tombstones. All was part of the Great Plan of life and death and Damaris had often sat quietly by the graves of her ancestors, placing flowers of remembrance in the warmth of the summer sun, not thinking of the mouldering bones in the chill earth only a short depth below.

But in the dark night it was a different place altogether. The moon's cold light was no substitute for the warm sun. Its pale beams played sinister tricks with the light, conjuring up shapes and shadows that chilled the imagination. Night breezes teased rattling noises from the tall dry grasses growing on neglected graves, spirits straining to break free of earth-binding bonds and soar into the element of infinite space above them.

Damaris broke out in a cold sweat as the first fears swept over her. Her heart beat loudly in her ears, a great boom - boom - boom echoing in the silence of her mind. Her stomach contracted in panic and her knees shook, bones that would have rattled without the muffling covering of her living flesh. Taking a grip on her rising terror, her love and anxiety for Reuben surpassing all else, Damaris slowly pushed open the gate and took her first fearful steps onto the path to the church, treading the very stones which would shortly feel the weightless feet of the spectral procession she had come to witness. Raising her eyes above the sinister shapes of the ground, the passing clouds granted her a glimpse of the small cross perched on the apex of the church roof, reminding her that this was the house of a loving and caring God, but what courage it required to reach it.

Step by step, glancing apprehensively around, she approached the church porch. Suddenly, with a rush, a small shape shot across her feet. Her hair stood on end as cold fur brushed her bare ankle. Panic won and she blindly dashed for the shelter of the porch as if all the hounds of hell were in pursuit. A small white tail whisked around the corner of a tombstone. Damaris raised a weak, shamed smile. Fancy being scared by a rabbit! How Matthew would snigger. The rabbit was probably peeping out at her, more scared than she was.

Settling herself on the seat within the shelter of the old church walls she had a clear view of the path to the porch, where the phantom procession would enter.

From this high viewpoint she turned her gaze to the horizon and observed the pale moonlight just silvering the sails of a tall schooner as she headed back out to sea.

From his hiding place behind a leaning gravestone, Thomas Duke also witnessed the departing vessel in the fitful moonlight, smiled inwardly, and settled down to wait, for the first part of the rumour he had picked up earlier in the day was evidently true. A lady *was* expected.

The passing minutes seemed endless to the two separate watchers in the dark churchyard, both totally unaware of each other's presence. Potential enemies though they were, both may have been glad enough to keep watch together, the only two living human souls in this dark kingdom.

The hands of the church clock high above them creaked regularly as each minute inexorably passed to the next. Time meant nothing to the dead, but to Damaris each minute seemed an eternity.

As midnight approached the soft ticking of the clock became joined by the tread of soft-soled boots and creak of muffled wheels of a cart, the horses' hooves wrapped in sacks, as the line of men toiling up the hill from the village drew to a silent halt by the church gate. Soft whispers no louder than the wind and the solid clunk of wood against wood as the kegs were lifted from the cart and hoisted onto strong shoulders. Outside the churchyard wall a procession gradually formed. The gate creaked open. Dark figures moved slowly forwards. Tonight of all nights the old church would be a completely safe place to store the evening's goods. With the fear of ghosts and the supernatural, no living soul would be brave or foolish enough to try and prove the old superstition of watching the midnight procession of the dead. The smugglers were almost certain of being undisturbed on Hallowe'en, but even so they acted in silence and with caution, for a passing reveller, coming late home, might just pass on the road nearby.

With measured tread, the dark line of men moved slowly onwards down the church path towards the two unseen watchers. Thomas Duke's keen ears picked up the first footfall as a boot kicked against an uneven flagstone. He eased himself round to get a clearer view.

Damaris, from her seat by the wall, saw a faint, flickering light by the gate. The hairs on the back of her neck rose in utter horror. Until this precise moment of realisation she had persuaded herself that the superstition was not really true and that after a little while longer she could safely get up and go home with the knowledge that Reuben was not under threat. But now, with the appearance of that lantern, it seemed that the old tale *was* true, for six dark figures silently approached the church porch. Frozen into immobility, the cold sweat beaded her forehead, the dark world of the graveyard spun round dizzily and Damaris fell to the ground, for the faint light from the horn lantern leading the procession had shone briefly upwards to dimly illuminate the shadowy but unmistakable features of Reuben - and Zack!

Thomas had seen enough. Fate, for once, had played right into his hands. If he acted fast he could have Constable Clarke informed, alerted, and ready out on the road awaiting the return of Reuben and Zack.

Slipping quietly from stone to stone, stumbling over the raised mounds of the uneven graves, Thomas reached the gate, took to his heels and fled down the steep road that led back to the village. The reward money jingled in the pockets of his imagination. This time he really would claim that £500 and be off to his ideal future.

As he reached the secretively huddled cottages, they seemed to close in on him, trapping him and slowing down the last part of his journey. Impatiently, he put out his hands and pushed against the walls of the narrow alleys. It was a peculiar sensation, brought about by the fact that Thomas was still running fast, and the contrast between the open road suddenly being replaced by the confines of the twisting alleyways of the old village impeded his efforts in his hurry to reach Constable Clarke's front door. Oblivious to the few curious eyes that saw him pass, Thomas stumbled up the wide steps that led to the Clarke's house on Fisherhead. Breathless with effort, he fell against the door, beating as hard as he could with his bunched knuckles.

After a seemingly endless time, the door opened a crack, letting out a flickering beam of light into the dark, and haloing the plump face of Mrs. Arabella Clarke, a large, ghostly figure in her white night attire, long grey plait falling over one shoulder.

'Who's there? Whatever do you want at this hour?'

Rudely, Thomas pushed past her and closed the door quickly behind him, leaning his bulky body against it. Arabella backed away from him with her candle and repeated her question. Recovering from the shock of being so roughly assaulted, she regained composure and dignity.

'Well, young man, who are you and what do you want? Answer me, or I shall call my husband. He is Constable of this place,' she added importantly.

'Ah knaw very well who 'e is,' snapped Thomas. 'That's why Ah'm 'ere, thoo stupid woman. Get 'im for me. Now!' he demanded, placing his hands on Arabella's shoulders and pushing her roughly towards the staircase. 'And hurry, damn you! It's urgent!' Thomas's angry impatience sent Arabella tripping over her long nightgown as she turned to mount the stairs. At the head of the staircase, a second candle flickered into light, shining on the long white nightshirt and tasselled cap of the Constable. Even in his insistent state Thomas had to smile, for the fat Constable in his night attire was really a very amusing sight.

'Constable Clarke!' he called up the stairs. 'It's Thomas Duke. Ah need to talk to thi. Urgent, like. Ah've gotten information thi must follow reet away. Theere's a big run on, and Ah knaw wheere it is and who's in on it. If we're quick, we can catch 'em on the way back.'

'Can't it wait until the morning?' yawned the Constable who was not enthusiastic about being disturbed from his sleep to turn out into the cold night on what might well prove to be yet another wild goose chase.

'No, it danged well can't!' Thomas stamped his booted foot in childish temper. 'Ah've gotten information to lay. Ah'm gannin ti dea it now, and thoo's comin' wi' me. Or else Ah'll mek a report to Whitby that thi's not doin' thi duty!' he threatened with purposeful quietness.

'Oh, very well then, if I must.' Jos Clarke smothered another yawn with a sense of annoyance. 'Wait down there and I'll be with you as soon as I'm dressed.'

The clock on the hall wall ticked loudly in the darkness, each measured click taking Thomas's dream of rich reward a second further from his greedy grasp.

For his size and weight, Josiah Clarke had dressed in breeches and boots remarkably quickly, pulling his coat round his shoulders as he stumbled down the stairs. He had taken Thomas's threat more seriously than he liked to admit. Arabella stood on the landing, candle in hand, still bewildered at the sudden rush of nocturnal activity. The candle flame wavered violently in the draught as Thomas hustled the Constable out into the night and slammed the door behind them.

'Now then, what's all this about?' enquired Josiah as he led the way down to the main street, Thomas impatiently hustling him from behind as his great bulk lumbered down the narrow stepped pathway.

At the junction with the street, Thomas turned the Constable and headed him in the direction of the steep hill which led out towards the country and down which Zack and Reuben must return home.

Josiah did not like Thomas Duke, but as village Constable he had a duty to perform. He realised full well that Thomas's earlier words were no empty threat. This young man had a gnawing resentment against life in general and the Storm family in particular. Jos reluctantly had no choice but to pursue his duty if he wished to keep his usually easy job, pleasantly comfortable home and position of respect in the community. After all these years he had become used to life in this odd village. At his advancing age he did not fancy an enforced change.

So he toiled up the hill, puffing and panting at its steepness, whilst Thomas impatiently slowed his young, fit footsteps to a matching pace and told his story.

At the old church, the last of the procession entered and quietly closed the solid oak door behind them. Zack and Reub had already reached the loose flagstone under the three-decker pulpit from which the Reverend Hepworth spoke guiding words to his congregation. Zack's dry sense of humour would indeed have been touched had he but known that next Sunday's sermon was already written on the subject of the ills of immoderate drinking. Directly underneath the respectable, white-cassocked figure of the minister, in its secure hiding place, would be a load of several ankers of the best geneva! Lantern light flickered on the whitewashed walls, casting long shadows between the old box pews. Any glimmering reflections on the tall windows, should they be glimpsed from outside, on this particular night would more than likely scare away any curious investigators, rather than attract unwelcome attention. All local people knew and respected the ancient midnight tradition. Few would ever be foolish enough to attempt to prove its veracity.

The strong oaken kegs were all gently lowered to their resting place and the flagstone carefully replaced. Satisfied that all was exactly as it should be, Zack straightened his aching back and shook hands with his team.

'A job well fettled, lads! Goodnight, me beauties.' He tapped the closed wooden panel behind which the heavy stone slab hid the treasure. 'Nice and cool doon theer. And in good company, too. Hope they don't drink too much of it!' he quipped, for the secret hiding place was indeed the family burial vault of one of the landed gentry, not that its present occupants were in any fit state to enjoy it. Reuben smiled at the thought of a skeletal binge, and chuckled at the macabre juxtaposition of a surfeit of drink unable to be enjoyed by those of the company it bore. How those old bones would stir at the pungent wafting of the alcoholic fumes!

'Gan along careful, now. It's gone well toneet so far. Now it's up to t'Squire,' said Zack. The next stage of the run would be the retrieval and transport of the goods by pack ponies, organised by Squire Farsyde and carried out by Farmer Barnard and William.

'Best go singly, or in pairs,' advised Zack, 'and if tha meets onybody, pretend tha's drunk. Toneet's a good neet fer havin' a bit o' fun, and wean't attract too much notice.'

In response, one of the younger fishermen lit up the turnip lantern he carried as a precaution and swung its grinning skull-like face in front of his companions. Reeling and hiccupping realistically, they practiced their foolish subterfuge with an enthusiasm that only a release of tension could effect, then realising they were still in the church they ceased with shamefaced grins.

Zack and Reuben, being the last to leave, made sure that no traces of the night's activities were evident. Reub took up the lantern and together the two men closed the church door. The lamp swung as they turned the corner and the swinging beam swept across the corner of the porch, illuminating a small, pale, round object. Reub touched Zack's arm. 'What's that?' he whispered, holding the lantern higher.

'Only one of the tonnips,' replied Zack. 'Hey, 'ang on a minute, though.' Silently they approached the huddled contour on the ground, now dimly visible; no vegetable form, but a human shape. Stooping down and turning the body over, Zack, forgetting the need for silence, uttered a loud cry. 'My God! Reub! It's Damaris!'

The obvious questions of how, what and why, tumbled unanswered from Reuben's lips.

'Nivver mind all that,' Zack retorted. 'She's badly. We

need help, and all t'men 'ave gone. Ah'll stay wi' her, and thoo run fer help and then gan on home and warn Liz to fix a hot drink and a warm bed.'

Zack gently lifted his moaning daughter and hugged her closely to him. Opening her eyes, she stared blankly into the familiar bearded face of her father. Regaining consciousness, she felt the blissful warmth of his solid living-fleshed reality, buried her face in the comforting, familiar smell of his gansey and wept hysterical tears of sheer relief.

Reuben ran as if borne aloft by the wind, skimming the rough road with the sureness of fleet-footed youth. The night air whistled round his ears, chilling his face, and his heart pounded with the exertion. The fickle moon, which had so far lighted his way, treacherously hid her face behind a cloud. In the sudden total darkness, Reuben reached the top of the hill leading down into the village, and ran full tilt into the solid arms of the Constable.

Liz closed the cottage door behind the last of Matt's friends, fondly smiling as the grotesque faces of the illuminated turnips grinned back at her from the darkness as they bobbed along the alleyways towards the boys' homes.

'Now then, Matt. Bed!' Somewhat to her surprise, Matt started up the narrow stairs without protest. Unbeknown to his mother he had plans of his own, for his keen ears had picked up Zack and Reuben's whispering and their sideways glance in his direction had not gone unnoticed. Matt was sharper than they realised. Liz, relieved to be spared the usual arguments about bedtime, turned to tidy the aftermath of the party. She was mentally tired after the drama of Jennet's outburst and would be glad to lay her head on the soft pillow, pull the warm quilt about her and close her eyes on the events of the evening, though she would not sleep until she felt the bed creak and the mattress sag as Zack safely returned in the early hours of the morning. Damaris, she was sure, would have gone to Rebecca as she always did when in trouble. She would come back home in the morning.

Jennet must also have exhausted herself and gone to bed already, thought Liz, for when she turned to wish the old woman good night, the rocking chair was empty. Even the cat, usually quick to leap onto the warm seat and curl up for the night, was missing.

Liz shrugged her shoulders, damped down the peat fire, blew out the lamp, took her night candlestick in hand, closed the kitchen door and wearily mounted the wooden stairs to her bedroom.

Matt lay down in his bunk fully dressed, and pulled the covers close round his chin just in case Liz poked her head round to wish him a final good night. This evening she was too weary and he heard the click of her bedroom door and lay for a few moments, ears straining until he heard the familiar creak of the big family bed as Liz climbed in.

All clear! Matt carefully left his bunk, picked up his boots and cautiously crept across the floor. He had purposely left the door slightly open so that its latch would not give him away with a tell tale click. He had even taken the earlier precaution of buttering the hinges so they wouldn't squeak, for the night-silence magnified any small sound. Like all old cottages, Matt's had its fair share of familiar grumbles and creaks as the building settled itself for the night, cooling off from the warmth of the day. But any strange new sound alerted keen ears. The moon shone through his window, lighting his way to the stairs. Feeling the handrope, he tentatively put one foot in front of the other, counting carefully to avoid the creaky fourth treader with its loose board. Entering the kitchen, Matt looked about him, tiptoed over to the mantelpiece, where the turnip still grinned challengingly at him. 'Come on, then!' he whispered to the bizarre object, quietly taking it down, igniting a paper taper from the embers of the fire and lighting the candle inside. The familiar kitchen took on a strange appearance as its walls reflected back the enlarged image of the turnip face. Matt smiled at the grotesque flickerings as he swung round towards the door. He paused, listening intently. All was reassuringly silent as he very slowly and deliberately turned the handle and let himself out into the dark street.

Tonight, he knew the unlocked door would not betray him, for he had overheard Zack's advice to Liz not to wait up as he would be late. Matt knew that Zack and Reuben were not just having a companionable drink at the Fisherman's Arms but were off somewhere on a great adventure. For once, Matt did not know where they planned to go. Usually his keen ears and observant eyes picked up information readily. Over the years he had come to interpret Zack's every nuance with the intuition of an only son, close to his father, but this night, Matt had no inkling of which direction to explore.

Taking his turnip lantern in hand, a wise precaution, for anyone he met would simply assume him to be returning late from a Hallowe'en party, Matt gingerly trod the steep street down to the Dock.

Here he had five choices of which way to take; down the slipway to the shore, up Covet Hill to the cliffs, through Marner Dale to Little Wood and the country, along the Main Street to the hill top and out to the open road, or back up his own steep street and past his home to the northern cliffs. He considered each alternative choice carefully. Noting the state of the moon, he calculated that the tide would be coming in fast, and being familiar with the moods and dangers of the shore he wisely decided against that direction. Having just left his home and come down the street there was little point in going up and past it again. It would be just his luck for Liz to twitch open the curtain and spot him. The main street would be too public with late revellers. That left two choices. The cliff path could be wet and slippery and treacherous in the dark, where a misplaced step could send him on a great plummeting fall to the shore below. The choice was made. Turning left down narrow Albion Street, Matthew walked into Marner Dale and the approaches to the sinister Little Wood.

It was a creepy place, even in daylight, and on Hallowe'en of all nights, Matt's vivid imagination began playing tricks and he almost wished he hadn't come. Even the companionable glow from his turnip lantern mocked him as it grinned grotesquely and the candle flickered in its hollow eyes.

Undeterred he plodded on, hopefully checking all the regular hiding places he had discovered over the years; overhanging tree roots by the stream, hollow trunks, thick bramble bushes, all empty tonight so the smugglers had not been this way.

Suddenly, with a scattering of dry leaves and cracking of broken twigs, something rushed out from the dense under-growth and shot past him. Bounding up the path ahead of him and out towards the country, faintly visible in the moonlight was the white hare that he and Damaris had followed to Jennet's cottage in the spring. Matt's heart pounded with fright then he smiled at his foolishness. Jennet was snug in bed at home. Or was she?

Matt had already decided that Marner Dale would reveal no smuggler's secrets this night so thankfully he turned and retraced his footsteps through the wood without losing face. To no one, not even himself, would he admit to being the slightest bit scared.

As the trees thinned and he emerged into the clearing near the village the moon shone across his path. Coming towards him, tail stiffly erect and fur bristling, came Jennet's cat.

'Hey, puss! What're you doing here?' Matt bent down to give the cat his greeting but instead of responding to his outstretched finger with its usual purr of pleasure and sinuous twisting round his leg, it spat, and with the tip of its tail flicking with annoyance, stalked unswervingly past and on into the wood.

'Now then, young man. Not so fast!' panted Jos Clarke, somewhat winded by Reuben's solid body hurtling itself full tilt into his rotund belly. 'Where are you going in such a hurry, at this time of night? Up to no good, I'll be bound!'

'For help!' retorted Reuben. 'Damaris has been tekken badly up at t'old church!'

'Now what would a sensible wench be doing up there, tonight of all nights?' deliberated the Constable, slowly scratching his chin.

'Nivver mind what she bin doin.' She's ill and needs help. I mun fetch t'other chaps quick.' As Reuben broke away to continue his flight down the steep hill to the village, Thomas Duke quickly extended his leather-booted foot and tripped him, pitching him headlong on the rough cobbled road.

'And what were *you* doin' up at t'old church?' glowered Thomas Duke, gripping Reub roughly by the collar and hauling him to his feet. He glared malevolently into his adversary's eyes. 'Oh, yes, I saw you, Reuben Granger, *and* Zachariah Storm.' Thomas spat on the cobblestones. 'I knows exactly what you was up to, and now so does Constable Clarke. Is that not right, Constable?' challenged the angry young man.

'Well, erm, so you say,' hedged Jos Clarke. 'But I have no definite proof, only your word and I shall need more than that.'

'Reet, then. Let *us* go to the rescue of the fair maiden oursens,' sneered Thomas Duke, 'and maybe we shall find other fish to fry. Who knows?'

It was therefore in an uneasy companionship that the three men returned up the dark and lonely road to the old church on the top of the hill.

Josiah Clarke's age and size restricted the party to a frustratingly slow pace. Thomas Duke, seething with impatience to have the evidence of his eyes solidly proved, thoughts of his reward money greedily in his mind, Reuben in a torment of anxiety about Damaris, and now the danger in which, by his sheer carelessness, he had placed the unsuspecting Zack.

'Ah'll gan on ahead,' blurted out Reuben in his desperation to warn Zack. 'We're tekkin' far too long gettin' theer.'

'Then Ah'll gan wi' thee. Ah dean't trust thee as far as Ah can see thee, and toneet that's not very far,' retorted Thomas sarcastically.

'Oh, no you don't. You both stay with me!' Constable Clarke reached out a pair of plump restraining hands and clamped them firmly, one on the shoulder of each of the impatient young men. 'We'll get there, don't ye fret.' He puffed and panted as the steepness of the narrow road took his breath.

The Constable's slow and deliberate pace tormented Thomas Duke to an almost unbearable pitch of frustrated impatience. He was an impetuous young man, who on his own would have rushed back to the church and begun his search single handed, but for the fact that he must have the Constable as first-hand witness when he discovered the goods.

Time was now on Reuben's side for the slow journey gave him opportunity to collect his wits and plan a campaign of action. Somehow he must alert Zack and Damaris that he had run into trouble. As the dark silhouette of the church appeared on the skyline, it became obvious to Reuben that he must act now, if Zack and Damaris were to be warned into any chance of escape. Turning his head away from his companions he drew a deep breath and, cupping his hands round his mouth, uttered the ear-splitting cry of a screech owl repeated three times, the secret signal that he and Zack used to warn each other when danger threatened. The third cry was cut short as Thomas realised what was happening and clamped his hand roughly over Reuben's mouth. But enough sound had escaped to reach the keen-eared Zack in the churchyard.

Alerted, Zack roughly pulled Damaris to him. 'Hear that, lass? Trouble! Quick, we must hide!' and grabbing the semi-conscious girl he bundled her quickly round the back of the church and behind the wooden hut where the gravedigger kept his macabre tools. Flinging her to the ground he snatched a sack from the open shed and, dropping to the earth beside his bewildered daughter, drew the rough hessian close round them both and lay still, his hand gently across her enquiring mouth. Complete silence and stillness was essential if they were to escape and avoid yet more trouble, for Zack's mind was in turmoil when he heard the cut-off cry of Reuben's warning. Loyalty persuaded him that he should assist his friend but common sense and duty to Liz, Damaris and Matthew prevailed and he lay silent and still as the dead that surrounded him in his eerie hideout. Reub was a young, single man, full of resourcefulness and cunning and Zack had no immediate fears for his ultimate safety.

But on this occasion Zack did not know that his enemy was the determined Thomas Duke and that Reub was already in the firm-handed presence of the law.

Up the church path the Constable plodded on heavy feet. 'Well, young Reuben, where's your damsel in distress? No fainting females here that I can see. I fear you've been imagining things, young man. You saw a ghost. Yes, that's what it was. It's Hallowe'en after all!'

Reub was about to protest vehemently when he noticed a faint wink in the Constable's beady eye and took the subtle warning to keep silent.

Thomas Duke seethed with impatience. 'Oh nivver mind all aboot silly lasses,' he grumbled. 'I tell thee there's newly run goods in t'church and this one knows where they are if anybody does.' He poked Reuben viciously in the ribs and roughly propelled him toward the stout oak door that closed the church porch. Turning the heavy iron handle, the latch clicked and the door creaked open for the three men to enter the dark and musty smelling gloom of the eerily silent church. Like its surroundings, the building took on an uncomfortable atmosphere in the darkness of the night hours. It seemed no longer a light and sunny and peaceful house of God, but an oppressive place, full of suppressed fear and latent malice. Even the hard-headed Thomas shrank at the chill atmosphere as he entered with only one thought in mind.

Constable Clarke lifted his candle lantern and swept its faint and flickering beam round the crumbling walls, examining with poking and probing fingers all the likely hiding places. The marble memorial tablets, covered in dust, had certainly not recently, if ever, been detached from their original fixings. Tapping a few wooden panels to ascertain whether any were newly loosened and shining his lamp on the large stone tomb slabs in the floor, searching for new chisel marks which would indicate fresh lifting, the Constable found nothing, nothing at all to betray the night's hiding place.

Then, with a fitful gleam, a scurrying cloud briefly exposed the face of the waning moon, and a sinister finger of cold light pointed straight at a shiny object on the stone floor. A faint glint of metal, then the traitorous cloud covered the face of the moon once more, but it was enough for Reuben to see that it was his knife.

As Thomas also saw and swooped triumphantly, Reuben attempted to stamp on Thomas's fingers, but he was not quick enough. Thomas grabbed the knife, examined it quickly, and thrust the object under the Constable's lantern. 'There!' he exclaimed in triumph. 'Tell me, who does *that* belong to?' For in his hand he held a fisherman's clasp knife with the initials 'R.G.' incriminatingly engraved on the handle. 'Now try to tell the Constable thou wasn't here toneet!' Having lost his temper and attacked Thomas, Reuben had condemned himself and proved his guilt.

Thomas resumed his search with renewed vigour and enthusiasm, and grabbed the lantern with a fanatical fervour to search every likely nook and cranny. Reuben's heart sank as Thomas approached the back of the pulpit, for he knew his eagle eyes would spot the disturbed panel. Sure enough, with the loud and raucous laugh of a madman, Thomas kicked and pulled frantically at the shattered timbers as his heavy boots began his work of investigative destruction.

'Now Thomas, that's enough!' bawled the Constable, 'or I'll arrest you for willful damage. Remember where you are!'

'*They* didn't care much where they put t'stuff,' snarled Thomas. 'I tell thee, Jos Clarke. Theer's run goods under theer, and that's one of 'em that put it theer.' The words bubbled out of his mouth in a spitting fury of frustration and angry eagerness, betraying the hint of insanity that many of the local fishermen had always feared was latent in the mind of Thomas Duke.

The last planks of the concealing wood split apart, and thrusting the lantern into the gaping vault, Thomas gasped in triumph and horror, for there, sure enough were the proceeds of the night's haul of brandy kegs, but in falling, one had shattered the rotting wood of an ancient coffin and its withered occupant stretched out a tattered lace-cuffed bony hand as if to reach the contents of the barrel within its skeletal grasp. Even beyond the realms of death, the gentry appreciated a tot of spirits, or so it would seem.

'Well, Reuben, I'm afraid it looks as if Thomas has laid strong evidence against you, especially as you were so careless as to leave this behind.' The Constable fingered the telltale knife with a mixture of satisfaction and reluctance. It was rare that he ever got around to making an actual arrest, a task he avoided whenever possible, keeping his main duties to upholding the law in a low key fashion, just efficiently enough to keep his position of authority. But with Thomas Duke watching him with the keenness of a hawk, and the threat of losing his job no idle one, he had no alternative but to clamp his heavy hand on Reub's shoulder and utter the dreaded formality of the words 'Reuben Granger, I arrest thee in the name of the law and his gracious majesty King George, on suspicion of unlawfully receiving and concealing contraband.'

Thomas smirked in thorough satisfaction. Tomorrow Reuben Granger would be on the way to York jail and he, Thomas Duke, close to the five hundred pounds that would open up his new life.

Crouched low against the cold earth under the rough sack, Damaris huddled close to her father, shivering as the damp penetrated through her thin clothing.

Zack could hear the noise Thomas Duke was creating in the church and realised that he must get Damaris to her feet and safely away whilst the commotion inside covered any sounds of their escape.

'Coom on, lass. We must mek a run for it. Tek my hands. Tha's quite safe wi' me.'

Zack heaved his still faint daughter over his shoulder. One pair of feet would make less noise should she have tripped and stumbled.

From where they cautiously crept from under cover, Zack could see the way to the rear entrance gate was clear. The old church had been built on a steep rise of a hill on a triangle where two roads joined at its top point. The path from gate to gate cut straight across the churchyard lower down the slope, affording a convenient short cut for anyone going across to the villages beyond, and it was to the gate on the far side that Zack made his way to freedom.

In her confused and shocked state Damaris did not realise what was happening in the church but Zack was well aware of the danger and led her quickly into the dark fields beyond, where they could stumble their way downhill to Baytown without fear of discovery.

It was well into the early hours of the next morning before their own cottage door closed welcoming and secure behind them. Zack gently placed Damaris in Liz's chair, poked the dampened fire to a lively glow, placed the heavy black iron kettle on the hot turf, then climbed wearily upstairs to rouse his wife.

Damaris, wet, bedraggled and muddy, too tired to explain, was soon comfortably asleep through sheer emotional exhaustion, blissfully unaware as yet of the tragedy of Reuben's arrest.

Next morning, when the news spread like wildfire throughout the village she was in a torment of remorse and self reproach that remained with her for many months.

'Oh, mother, if only I hadn't been so foolish, none of this would've happened. Losing Reub is all my fault!'

'Hush, lass. Dinna tek all the blame on thissen. For that matter, if that old trouble-maker had kept silent, we might all be better off,' replied Liz, glancing across at the empty chair so recently vacated by the sudden departure of Jennet.

'And remember, Reuben has not been sent for trial yet. He may not be found guilty.' Liz spoke the faintly optimistic words with more hope than she truly felt, simply to rouse Damaris from her depression. The likelihood, as she well knew, would be that Reub would be sentenced to a term of five years in the navy, a severe enough punishment, for His Majesty's ships were notorious death traps of danger and disease. But if he survived, and being young and strong and used to the ways of the sea and ships, unlike many inland smugglers, he had a fair chance of returning after his punishment. Better also, than if he had been sentenced for wool smuggling, for then the culprit would be maimed for life, with the public amputation of his right hand as a gruesome warning to others.

Liz had a sudden mental picture of Reuben cradling Damaris' golden head in that same threatened palm and shuddered with relief that at least he would not be deprived of caressing her daughter's corn gold hair when he became a free man once again.

As dawn broke the following morning three distant figures on horseback made their way up the steep Sledgates hill. Mist swirled in soft wraiths around the fetlocks of the three horses as they picked their way through the fading heather. The first pale rays of the rising wintry sun shafted delicately across the bleak countryside, seared with the first frost of winter, touching all with a faint warm rosy glow. The chill in the heart of the young man in the centre of the group would need more than the full strength of the November sun to disperse his despondent gloom.

Reuben Granger reined in his horse and turned in the saddle for one last look at the wide Bay spread out before him, looming ethereally through the wraps of the morning mist. A grey fog rolled in soft clouds at the foot of the cliff, hiding all but the red rooftops of his native village. Rising high above all, the imposing headland of Raven Hill dominated the landscape. Pausing to greedily feast his eyes on the picture and fix it in his mind, Reuben blinked back the tears that blurred his vision, their wetness sparkling the image, making his final farewell even more unreal. He had seen this view so many times before but never had it seemed so precious, so beautiful, and so meaningful. His growing love for Damaris had, he suddenly realised, exposed his senses to a tender awareness of the beauty of all around him. Physically strong and tough though the young fisherman was, he harboured a hitherto untapped streak of the artist and poet. The gentle touch of love was all it had needed to bring it to the fore.

Maxwell and Herbert slackened the reins of their own mounts, which, fresh from the stable, tossed their heads and pawed the ground in their impatience to start the long ride over the moors. The two Riding Officers shrugged their coat collars high round their necks and looked at each other with a degree of real sympathy and regret. They had known and respected Reuben Granger for a long time during the years they had been stationed in Baytown and they carried out this escort duty with a great sense of reluctance.

Both felt that his arrest was a most unfair and unfortunate occurrence, a happening of sheer bad luck when they considered that just about the entire male population of the village was as deeply involved in the smuggling trade. Both of them knew that Thomas Duke had been jealously determined to bring Reuben down, that he had had his knife into the successful young fisherman for many months, and that he was envious of his love for the beautiful Damaris.

Peter Maxwell leaned from his saddle and put a gloved hand on Reuben's bridle. 'Come away, now Reub,' he urged, not unkindly. 'We must be off. The escort from York will be well on the way to meet us and Herbert and I have dispatches to collect at Saltergate on our way. Remember that the Bay will always be here,' he said gently. 'You're a young man, Reuben, and you will return. I know you will. We'll keep an eye on Damaris and the family, and before you know it, you will be riding up that hill to your wedding!'

Reuben turned and looked wistfully at the little square grey church poised on the distant hill top, the scene of his recent arrest. He gave Maxwell a wry smile, dashed the drops from his eyes with a quick sweep of his cuff, gathered his reins and urged the horse forward, breasting the brow of the hill and facing the broad expanse of heather-covered moorland that lay between the Bay of his childhood and the city of York where the Court would determine his immediate future and his punishment.

'Thomas Duke, do you swear to tell the truth, the whole truth and nothing but the truth, so help you God?' enquired the Court Usher as he solemnly handed the black leather bound copy of the Bible to the witness now taking the stand. The Judge, sitting in stern authority over the Assize Court at York, peered shortsightedly over his half rimmed spectacles at the rough-looking character standing before him.

Thomas glanced venomously across at Reuben, standing miserable but proud in the prisoner's dock. Thomas adjusted the kerchief round his stocky neck, cleared his throat, and answered distinctly and with noticeable emphasis, 'Aye, Sur.'

'Constable Josiah Clarke, you bring this man, Reuben Granger to trial at this Court. Will you please outline the case to my learned colleagues on the Bench?'

Jos Clarke rose plumply to his feet and shambled self-consciously over to the witness stand. Notebook in hand, thumbing through the grubby dog-eared pages, he related the feeble course of events in which Thomas Duke had laid evidence against Reuben. The Judge was obviously soon tiring of his trivial detail and beginning to wonder why he was wasting his time.

Thomas Duke fidgeted, impatiently waiting his turn to speak. In his mind's eye, the bag of gold coins gleamed temptingly close. In his pocket, his hot hand grasped the handle of Reuben's fisherman's clasp knife.

When his turn came to give evidence he spat out his story with a venomous contempt that was not lost on the Judge. Finally, reaching into his pocket, he handed out the knife with the engraved initials. 'There, me Lord. That's the knife I found on t'floor o' t'church. Yon Constable was with me at the time. Look at the initials. R.G.!' The Judge carefully examined the condemning exhibit.

'Is this yours?' he enquired of Reuben, peering over the tops of his spectacles.

'Yes, my Lord. I regret that it is,' admitted Reuben.

'It seems then, without doubt, that you were indeed one of that nefarious gang of smugglers - but knowing your kind, it is unlikely we shall learn from you who your compatriots are. I fear I have no alternative but to sentence you to five years in His Majesty's Navy, in the hope that it may also serve as a warning to those others who were involved with you. Smuggling is an offence against the law of this land, and indeed, a crime against His Majesty himself, depriving him and his Government of the necessary income to run this country....'

The Judge droned on, obviously launching into a colloquy that would occupy him for as long as the patient Court would stand for. One or two of his colleagues on the Bench shuffled uncomfortably. It was not unknown for them to have enjoyed the odd keg of brandy or box of tobacco as a gesture of gratitude for leniency shown to certain offenders who came before them. The Judge, unfortunately for Reuben, was a man of sterner character.

Reuben ceased to listen. His brain repeated the words 'five years in His Majesty's Navy' until the reality of the severity of his sentence finally dawned, although he had known all along that this would be the likely outcome. Hearing it from the lips of the Judge himself merely confirmed it without doubt.

Thomas Duke leapt up in his seat. 'My Lord! My reward!' The Judge cast him a contemptuous look that would have frozen a less sensitive man to the spot where he stood.

'See the Clerk of the Court,' snapped the Judge. 'Court rise!' and the dignified members of the legal profession left the Courtroom in single file.

Thomas lost no time in leaping over the rails of the witness stand. Grasping the bag of coins already laid on the Clerk's desk, he shook them in the face of Reuben with a triumphant smirk.

'Pleasant voyages, Reuben,' he spat sarcastically, and turning on his heel, strode out of the Court, turning his back on his past and heading for the future he had obtained at such cost.

Peter Maxwell rode slumped in his saddle, deep in thought, grateful for the need to ride single file along the narrow paved trod that led across the high moor.

Behind him, his fellow officer, James Herbert, also rode

wrapped in his own thoughts. The events of the past few days had told deeply on both of them. Although their jobs were to uphold the law and patrol the area, being billeted in such a close community as Baytown for any length of time made it hard not to become involved in the lives of the people to a considerable extent. For this reason, it was not usual for officers to remain in the same area for more than a few months, but the territory around the Bay and the moors was so dangerous and complex that experienced and knowledgeable men were essential if any control at all was to be successfully exercised.

Both Peter and James fully realised that Reuben had been used as a scapegoat and that the evidence laid by Thomas Duke was biased and deliberate. Perhaps now, things would settle down more peacefully. Reuben would most likely survive his sentence, but the other smugglers would certainly lie low for a while, being visibly stunned by the capture and sentencing of a close associate, one who had been betrayed by their own kind, at that. With Thomas Duke out of the way, the rest of the winter should be reasonably uneventful.

It was with these thoughts in mind that Maxwell and Herbert approached the distant light from the Saltergate Inn dimly shining through the mist. Set in a desolate landscape this ancient hostelry on the salt road from York to the coast, along which passed some of the main fish trade of the day, was a welcoming point at any time, but especially on a chill and foggy night such as was closing in on the two horsemen.

Sliding from their cold and tired horses, handing them over into the care of the ostler, the two officers swung their arms and stamped their feet to restore the circulation in their cramped limbs. Breath steamed from their mouths in wispy wraiths, as each offered the other the invitation to enter and partake of a warming glass or two of spiced mulled ale and toast their toes before the glowing peat fire.

The bar was almost empty that night. Only a few farmers belatedly returning from Pickering market still remained in the cosy room, reluctant to go out into the clammy cold to resume their journeys to distant farmsteads.

William Barnard and his father, Samuel, were two of the company, anxious to hear at first hand the news of Reuben. Sam paled visibly under his weather-beaten tan, and stared at the strong right hand that grasped his ale mug. It might so easily have been himself on trial, and for sheep smuggling as well. He remembered the penalty for that all too vividly.

In a darkened corner of the snug, sat a group of men whose countenances were vaguely familiar to the two officers. After a while, Peter Maxwell, who had a good memory for faces, realised that they had been sitting at the back of the courtroom. From their angry reaction to the sentence, he recalled that they were certainly no friends of Thomas Duke.

The glowing turf settled with a shower of sparks as the landlord piled on more fresh fuel. 'Must keep it going,' he stated. 'Do you know, this 'ere fire has been burning for as long as anyone can remember. If ever it goes out, it means bad luck for the Inn. They do say that a gruesome murder was done in the old days, and that the body is hidden right there under the hearthstone, with the curse of disaster should it ever be removed.' Satisfied that the peat was well alight, he shuffled off back to his kitchen. James and Peter looked at the hearthstone and shuddered.

Whatever the truth of the story, it ensured that travellers were assured of a warm welcome no matter what time of the day or night they arrived. It also provided a totally secure hiding place for any awkward contraband. No one in the know would dare to search under that hearth.

Samuel and William rose, paid their bill, and headed off into the cold night on their long way back to the farmstead in the hills above Baytown. Even though the hour would be very late, they agreed to ride down to the village on the way home and pass on the news of Reuben as they had heard it first hand from the Riding Officers. The men from the shady corner drew their hats down over their eyes and their coat collars tight around their necks. Also bidding the landlord farewell, they too set furtively off into the darkness.

Maxwell and Herbert having warmed their chilled bones, were in no hurry to return home, as neither had wives or families anxiously awaiting them. An appetising smell of roast beef assailed their nostrils, an odour that, after the long and distressing day, was completely irresistible. 'Landlord, you have wafted that heavenly aroma deliberately in our direction! Bring us, therefore, some of that excellent roast and some more ale whilst we are waiting.'

After a further flagon of the landlord's potent brew, and a comfortable and leisurely meal, Peter and James reluctantly began to make a move for home. The landlord, coming into the bar, wiping his hands on his ample apron, stood squarely before the two men.

'Well, gentlemen! Hast tha seen the fog? It's a reet pea-souper. Ah couldn't even see across t'roaad when Ah leuked oot jest now. Ah wouldn't give much fer thi chances of getten back ti Baytown toneet. One false step off that trod, and tha's in t'bog up to 'ere!' He indicated his stubbly chin and grinned, a mouthful of stained and broken yellow teeth giving him an unfairly sinister appearance, for he was by nature the most genial of men. 'Tha'd better bed down 'ere toneet, and mebbe this fog'll lift wi' daylight. Thi 'orses are warm and well fed; they wouldn't thank 'ee fer draggin' 'em oot o' my good stablin' toneet.'

The tempting thought of a clean bed and another warming pint or two convinced the officers that it would indeed be both pointless and foolish to attempt the journey back that night. Nothing untoward was likely to happen; not with the news of Reuben freshly buzzing around the smuggling fraternity. They noticed that the shifty looking customers in the corner had also gone, so they had the Inn to themselves.

'Your good sense and advice convinces us, landlord.' Peter Maxwell stretched his arms above his head and yawned lazily. 'Bring us another couple of tankards of your excellent ale and one of your wife's delicious pasties, and we'll be most happy to partake of your hospitality.'

If they had foreseen the macabre outcome of the receipt of the day's news, they might not have slept so soundly in their warm beds in the desolate moorland inn.

When the fog cleared in the morning, they returned to find the Baytown community agog with the gruesome news that a canvas bag containing five hundred golden sovereigns had been found by a passing traveller on the road from York to Whitby - and in the bag, along with the money, was a bloody, severed right hand.

The sun was rising beyond the horizon - a great scarlet burning ball, flooding the gently heaving sea with brilliant, scintillating colour, dispersing the last remnants of the heavy fog which had blanketed the coast for the past few days.

It was a magnificent morning, full of the promise of one of those rare late-autumn days when the sun was warm as summer and the sky gleamed a clear and cloudless blue. The air held a clean freshness, subtly tinged with the lingering scents of the fading year.

For Peter Maxwell, striding down the village street, still in its early-morning newness, the day held a peculiar poignancy. For himself, it felt great to be alive and free to walk wherever fancy took him. If he chose to divert his footsteps to the cliff path and wander among the late autumn bracken, glowing golden brown on this glorious morning, he was at liberty to do so; or if he chose to wander at leisure along the clean wave-swept sand at the water's edge, the whole world before him, he could do that too; or if his preference turned towards his own homely fireside, then no man would stop him. Never before had he reflected on the joys of freedom which he formerly had taken so much for granted.

All his philosophical thoughts this crisp autumn morning were, not surprisingly, influenced by the happenings of the past few days. Strong minded though he was, Peter Maxwell could not ignore the lump in his throat as he gazed across the calm beauty of this snug, red-roofed village, with thoughts of Reuben, that freedom-loving young man, now in handcuffs on his way to punishment. Trying to cheer his thoughts, Peter reflected that during his five years sentence in the Royal Navy, rough though the conditions on board the majority of ships were, at least Reub would have the freedom of sight of sky and sea, and not be immured in the dank darkness of a damp and rat-infested prison cell.

He smiled inwardly at the ironic news that Reuben's 'prison ship' was to be none other then the *Pelican*, the very vessel which had finally captured the *Kent* way back, it seemed an eternity ago, in the summer. The very vessel which had, in fact, rescued young Matthew. *Pelican's* Captain was known as a fair minded man, running a good ship, and Peter was sure that Reuben's skills as a seaman would soon be noticed and appreciated, a rare change from some that were ruthlessly press-ganged into naval service without having ever set foot on a deck in their lives, not knowing one rope from another. Some of these captives were more bother than they were worth.

Feeling in his greatcoat pocket to ensure that a certain envelope was still securely in its place, Peter collected his thoughts and headed down the winding street to the sea, then turned sharply up the steep cobbled alleyway to the Storms' cottage.

Before he even reached the door the appetising aroma of Liz's freshly baked bread assailed his appreciative nostrils, reminding him that on this bright morning he had not yet eaten any breakfast. Pangs of hunger rumbled noisily in his stomach.

Reaching the stout oak door which shut Zachariah and his family away from the dangers of the outer world, he raised his gloved fist and knocked hard. Zack's gruff voice called 'Who's there?' and the door opened just sufficiently to waft out the smell of frying ham.

'It's Peter Maxwell, Zack. I have news of Reuben for you and a package for Damaris. May I come in?'

With the resentment felt by all Baytown natives for any stranger, Zack reluctantly admitted the Riding Officer, but with traditional courtesy seated him at the table, offering food and, with a faintly whimsical smile, a mug of precious tea. 'All bought fair and square and above board, Mr. Maxwell!' assured Zack, with the distinct feeling that Maxwell did not altogether believe him.

'Never mind all that today, Zack,' he replied. 'I've just received the news early this morning that Reuben has been assigned to the *Pelican*, due to sail from Newcastle in three day's time. That means he should be sailing past within sight of the Bay some time on Friday. I thought you would like to know. Also, he sent this for Damaris.' Maxwell laid the small packet on the table. 'I don't know what's in it, only that he pressed it into my hands just as he was leaving, anxious that I should deliver it to her in person just as soon as I could.'

'Thank 'ee, Sur. That was kind. Ah appreciate tha thoughtfulness. Ah knaws thee did thi best for Reub. We shall not forget that.' A brief smile with a rare hint of friendliness flickered in Zack's eyes, but was almost instantly extinguished by the inbuilt resentment that existed between 'them' and 'us.'

'Damaris!' Zack shouted up the narrow stairway. 'Coom away down, lass, theer's summat for thee.' Red-eyed and tear-stained, her corn gold hair hanging untidily round her swollen face, Damaris reluctantly opened the stairs door and peered round into the kitchen.

His heart plummeting with sorrow for this young grief-stricken girl, Peter Maxwell raised his eyes in a deep sympathetic smile, and held out his hand, courteously inviting her to the empty chair at the table. 'Miss Storm,' he declared simply and with dignity, 'I brought you this from Reuben. He wanted you to have it as soon as ever possible.'

Damaris stared bleakly at the packet for long moments before slowly laying the contents open on the scrubbed pine table at which Reuben had eaten so many joyful meals in her company.

Before her now lay simply his distinctive red neckerchief on which he had roughly pencilled the words 'I love you, Dam. Wait for me. Reub.'

Damaris laid her head on the table and wept all the tears as yet unshed.

Zack reached out and placed his roughened, clumsy fisherman's hand gently on his daughter's heaving head. Peter Maxwell rose quietly from his chair, and without a word, let himself out into the street, now beginning to hum with the ordinary bustle of another day's work. For some, he reflected, life would never be the same again.

Early on the Friday morning a small, lonely figure watched with her father's telescope, waiting patiently until the majestic ship hove into sight. Sailing out of the rising sun, her sails aflame with pink and gold, her bows cutting the waves and throwing glittering spray in her wake, she was truly an awe-inspiring and magnificent sight. The sturdy hull rose and fell on the gently heaving swell. The square sails on all three masts bellied with the following wind as the *Pelican* made steady headway across the bay. As she drew level with the village, Damaris watched in admiration, and allowed her pride that her hero was aboard such a splendid ship, to some extent ease her sorrow at their parting. She was a true daughter of the sea, and proud to be so. Sailors' wives had to become used to separation, and at least Reub had not been press-ganged into a battleship, where his chances of survival would have been poor. She would bravely wait for as long as it took until he returned. As the ship sailed close in, she raised her slim arm high in the air and let fall the red kerchief which shook itself in the breeze and fluttered like the proud flag on the stern of the *Pelican*. Damaris could not be certain that Reuben saw her, but she hoped so very keenly that the single figure high in the rigging was Reuben and he was looking for her.

The second mate on board the *Pelican* had instantly recognised Reuben's seagoing skills, and learning the details of his unfortunate story, felt a slight and unusual degree of sympathy towards his latest enforced recruit. As they sailed into the Bay, he strolled up behind Reub hard at work on the rigging and brusquely ordered him up aloft. 'Take that with you and keep watch on the horizon.' Grasping the proffered powerful telescope and tucking it securely in his waistband, Reuben scrambled hand over hand up into the topmast rigging. As the ship drew level with the old village, tumbling, it seemed from that distance, head over heels down its steep cliff, he anxiously scanned the prospect to shorewards. His orders had not specified the direction in which he must keep watch.

The circular lens of the telescope drew in the distant picture of a small figure with a red flag. He watched until she faded from his sight, knowing that it would be a very long time until he saw her again. Reuben lowered the telescope and let the salt wind sting the tears from his eyes.

On the cliff, Damaris waved until the very last part of the *Pelican* disappeared behind the southern headland of the Bay, and tied the red kerchief neatly round her neck. She would wear it, she swore, every day until he returned, long after the familiar scent of him had faded from its fibres.

From the thick bushes on the cliff path, a figure with its right arm heavily bandaged and hidden within the thick fisherman's sweater with its rival pattern, watched Damaris with heavy emotions of anger, jealousy and pain.

Despite her exotic good looks and charismatic presence, Jiddy Vardy was at heart a down-to-earth, clear headed and very sensible young woman. She had experienced enough difficulties in her own life to understand all that Damaris was suffering, and from her own past unhappinesses she knew that life must go on, that there was nothing like hard work to pull body and soul together again. So it was with these thoughts in mind one chilly November morning some couple of weeks after the departure of Reuben, that she re-packed her sewing basket with an extra set of everything required, and headed down the hill to the Storms' cottage.

'Mornin' Liz!' she called cheerfully, as she knocked and entered the warm but unusually gloomy-atmosphered cottage. Sitting down at the table, and pushing her long hair back over her shoulder, she outlined her plans to Liz. 'Ah've bin thinkin' aboot young Damaris,' she said, and asked if Liz would agree for her to become her apprentice, and go out on sewing jobs with her. 'She's a skilled lass wi' her needle, and Ah really could mek use of her. T'would get her oot of t'house and her mind fixed on doin' summat positive. What does tha say?'

'Ah think it's a wonderful idea, and very kind and thoughtful of tha, Jiddy,' said Liz with a warm smile. 'Let's ask her.'

Damaris needed little persuading, for in truth life was very dull and sad without Reuben's daily presence. Damaris had never realised how much she had taken for granted the fact that whenever she walked out in the village she would be sure to glimpse the handsome young fisherman somewhere, and to have him snatched away out of her life just as the romance was flowering was a cruel turn of fate.

The weeks leading up to Christmas opened up new doors in Damaris' life. Not only did she genuinely enjoy her work and unexpected access to the wealthy households for whom Jiddy regularly sewed, but her natural artistic flair for design frequently brought looks of keen appreciation and approval from Jiddy. This was clearly to develop into a partnership of advantage to them both. Best of all for Damaris was the friendship that quickly bonded between them. Never before had Damaris had a friend like Jiddy, mature, amusing, and full of exciting stories. Knowing Damaris and her smuggling background, Jiddy gradually tested her trustworthiness, and soon realised that she dared safely reveal some of her own most personal and private experiences. Damaris glowed with pride at the confidences shared with her and no other living soul. However, even with this close and trusting friendship, Jiddy, true to character, never disclosed information that could harm anyone but herself.

During the weeks following Reuben's arrest, Baytown's smugglers kept a low profile. In a small community, dependent largely on fishing and the extra earnings from 'the revenue,' the loss of a strong pair of hands was serious and the men could not afford to run more risks just at present.

Without Reub's partnership in the boat, life would have been hard for Zack, but fortunately Matt was growing strong and able, and felt a degree of pride in his new manly relationship with his father. Zack sensed with apprehension that the sea skills he was quickly teaching his growing son would tear him away from the family even sooner, as Matt was determined to join the Navy as an officer as soon as ever possible. Already he spent many long hours poring over books, puzzling out the mysteries of navigation.

The 'snivs' were still keenly vigilant, following up their success in ridding the place of one important smuggler, so it was wise to pass messages on that the next major run should divert a little way north to the steep cliffs known as Hawsker Bottoms, where the only access down to the shore was a treacherous, zigzagging path known as the donkey road, definitely not a place for the unwary, especially on a slippery, wet, foggy November night.

November was a dull month at the best of times, a kind of seasonal no-man's-land between the festivities of Hallowe'en and Christmas, with late-dark mornings and early-dark nights, the intervening hours dim with lack of light and enthusiasm for anything much as the year dragged on greyly towards its close.

Fishing was poor that year, for the weather turned constantly against the struggling little community trying to wrest a living from the sea. Dense fogs were dispersed by squally gales carrying battering sleet and hailstones. Heavy seas roared up the slipway, spilling torn seaweed far up the village street.

Fishermen huddled desultorily round their boats, idly and unenthusiastically picking at blisters of flaking paint, ready for the spring re-varnishing, or gathered in small groups in cellars or outhouses, bored with mending tears in nets or meshes in lobster pots. An uneasy feeling permeated the entire village. The men became restless with lack of activity, for normally November with its long dark nights was a good month for smuggling and the extra earnings compensated for the lack of fishing and lined pockets with money for the Christmas extras which all families liked to provide for their children. They feared that this year Christmas would be of necessity as dull as the present miserable November unless something unexpected turned up. Rumours of a prospective landing at Hawsker only made them even more unsettled and discontented, knowing that most of them were unlikely to be part of it.

Zack stretched his aching back with a sigh, put down his netting needle, and said to Matthew, 'Coom on, lad. Let's tek a break and gan and have a leuk at t'boat.' Matt jumped up with alacrity. Anything for a change from the hated net mending. He was too young to have developed the patient resignation needed for this very necessary and time-consuming task. Climbing the ladder from their cellar, they heard voices in the kitchen above and the unmistakable sultry laugh of Jiddy Vardy. Hastening his steps, Zack's heartbeats quickened with anticipation.

The kitchen was filled with the pungent smell of the traditional Christmas pudding, rich with delicious fruit and liberally laced with rum, spirited by Zack from the hidden store in his cellar. Unobserved, behind the partially open door, Zack hastily smothered a smile as he watched the three women. Jiddy was vigorously stirring the pudding in the large earthenware bowl, eyes tightly closed, her full red lips pursed seductively as she made her secret wish. Damaris had evidently already made hers, and was thoughtfully licking the sticky sweet mixture from her fingers. Liz stood by the hot stove, a streak of flour stark white across her flushed cheek.

'Now then! Caught you!' shouted Zack, suddenly flinging open the door, and grabbing Jiddy tightly round the waist. Three pairs of startled eyes, two sky blue, one Mediterranean brown, shot open in surprise and alarm.

'Zack! Don't *do* that!' exclaimed Liz with a touch of real annoyance, as he attempted to grab the spoon from Jiddy. Jiddy, however, had not finished stirring and hung on tightly as Zack playfully chased her round the crowded kitchen. Liz's affection overcame the pang of jealousy caused by Jiddy's blush at the close physical contact with her husband. Her big fisherman was still a boy at times, smiled Liz to herself. 'Stop it, you two! Tha'll have t'bowl on t'floor, and then tha'll have no Christmas puddin,' and it'll serve thi reet!'

'Sorry, Liz,' apologised Zack with a grin, as he caught his wife and gave her a hearty kiss. He only half meant the apology, as he had thoroughly enjoyed the brief playful moment, the close warmth of contact with Jiddy's exciting lithe body, and the consequent break in his mental melancholy. He plunged the spoon into the mixture and stirred slowly and thoughtfully, opening one eye to slyly wink at Jiddy when Liz wasn't looking.

'Yes, my lad. I know what you're wishing for,' thought Jiddy. But she was wrong. In spite of his playful attitude, Zack was, and always would be, entirely faithful to Liz; what he *had* wished for was to be involved in the Hawsker run.

'Damaris, mek us a mug o' tea, there's a good lass,' requested Zack, as Liz put aside the pudding basin, waiting for Matt to come in and take his turn. Matt had seized the opportunity for a little freedom and fresh air after being cooped up all afternoon in the dark cellar with endless piles of holed nets. It seemed to him that as soon as one hole was mended another even larger one appeared, as if deliberately to stretch his patience to breaking point. So, as Zack and the three women settled down to tea and freshly baked hot scones gleaming with golden butter, Matt raced down the street, boots ringing on the cobbles, until he reached the slipway and onto the wet and windy beach. Revelling in the cold wind and stinging sleet, Matt galloped along the deserted shore, alone with the elements that were an integral part of his heritage. He ran until exhaustion beat him to a standstill then, cold and wet, but glowing with the taste of freedom, yet resentful that he was chained to his present existence, he turned for home, banged noisily into the cottage and rudely slumped down at the table.

'Matt! Wheer on earth hast tha bin? Jest leuk at t'state o' thee!' remonstrated Liz.

'Out!' retorted Matt, sulkily.

'Yes, Ah can see that. Ah'm not blind. But wheer?'

'Just out, Ah said!'

Liz turned away with a resigned sigh. Matt was so moody these days, but no wonder.

Jiddy, always sensitive to situations, pulled up her chair along side, pushed a steaming mug of tea and a scone in front of him and said, adult to adult, ignoring the rebellious teenager behind the sulky eyes and scowling mouth, 'Matt! Am I glad to see thee! Zack and I was wonderin' wheer tha'd disappeared to as Ah've got summat ti ask thee.'

'Oh? What?' Matt fiddled with the mug of tea and eyed the tempting scone disinterestedly.

'Well, as Ah've just bin tellin' thi faither, and would 'ave told thee, if tha'd bin 'ere......'

Matt rose furiously and banged the table with his fist. The tea slopped and puddled his scone. 'Hell!' he exclaimed. 'Can't a man even go outside wi'out asking permission from a lot of bloody women! Ah'm sick of all this. Ah'm gannin away ti sea!'

Jiddy took his arm, raised her eyes to Zack, and said calmly, 'Now Matt, if tha can be'ave like a man and not like a spoilt bairn, Ah can do wi' tha help. But Ah need men, reliable, cool headed men. This ain't a job fer spoiled brats.'

Matt shrugged off her arm and slumped back into his chair, half ashamed at his outburst but not yet man enough to admit it.

'All reet then,' he said reluctantly. 'What does tha want?' Lowering her voice and gazing straight into his young rebellious eyes, Jiddy quietly and calmly outlined the plan she had just been disclosing to his father.

Matt trudged sulkily along the narrow cliff path, kicking his boots moodily against the loose stones. It was bitterly cold, pitch dark and raining steadily. Zack, walking up ahead, hunched into his coat collar, was not in the best of tempers. Matt's open threat of running away to sea had been the protest of a petulant teenager, but that night's activities were men's work and Zack was not willing for Matt's childish behaviour to run them into any possible danger. So it was the ruthless smuggler and not the father who turned on him angrily.

'Keep up wi' me, and give over kicking them stones!' he hissed crossly at his son. 'If tha's goin' to join us as a man, then tha's got to be obedient, same as t'rest of us. And silent. If tha's not prepared to, then gan on back home. To thi mother,' he added scornfully.

Matt slowly crept up behind his father, deliberately tiptoeing with his heavy boots, and scowling in the dark under heavy eyelids. 'That quiet enough?' he whispered gruffly. Matt knew that Zack's threats were never idle, and, truth to tell, he doubted whether he could find his way back home in the dark. Zack had eyes like a night owl, so practiced was he in nocturnal excursions, but the cliff path so far from Baytown was unfamiliar territory to Matt and any false step could be highly dangerous, if not fatal.

'How much further is it? Ah'm bloody frozzen!' he grumbled. Somehow, swearing made him feel more like a man. That evening his confusion between boy and man seemed especially unnerving.

'Not far now; then tha'll be too busy to feel cold!'

Below them the rolling waves broke at the cliff foot, echoing up the sheer drop of some hundred feet; not a place for the unwary. Jiddy's instructions were that they should pick up the goods concealed by Jonas Chaplow and James

Linskill where the old donkey road zig-zagged perilously up the sheer cliff some half mile or so from where they now stood. James and Jonas would already have hauled the goods up and hidden them in the mass of thick gorse bushes.

Having already been involved, it was unlikely, but still possible, that James and Jonas's activities may have been noticed, so the next stage was safest in new hands. Zack and Matthew had been chosen as the best men for the job, as it was assumed by the Bay Preventives that they would be playing safe and lying low after the capture of Reuben, and at Matt's young age, they would not suspect his adult involvement. The attention of the three new 'snivs,' Henry Downsham, John Wellow and David Evans, would be fixed firmly on the remaining Bay men and any suspicious movements keenly followed. So it was important that Matthew realized the real value of his presence on the cliff.

James and Jonas were both big, strong men, farm-workers at Spring Hill which lay just inland of the cliff path, between Baytown and the village of Hawsker, northwards on the way to the port of Whitby. Unbeknown to the farmer they had a handy hideaway in a cellar underneath the stable where they cared for the horses. Being stablemen, James and Jonas were exceedingly valuable members of the local smuggling community, as they could turn a blind eye to the borrowing of a good strong horse at night. All they had to do was to ensure that the animal required had been well fed and watered, that the harness was readily to hand, and the cart or sledge placed where it could be utilised without undue noise. In many country districts, a horse found sweating in the stable in the morning was said to have been 'hag ridden' by witches, but whether the horse had been used instead of a broomstick for a midnight ride, or out on some other nefarious business, was a matter for its owner to decide. Country fear of the supernatural was exploited in the interests of secrecy, as no right minded person would risk meeting the local witch on her way back from a mysterious excursion. Stables were fairly safe ground for smugglers' activities, especially when the deterrent 'witch stone' hung over the stable door issued a frightening warning to keep clear.

Jonas lived in the village of Hawsker itself, and James with his sister Alys in a neat little cottage in the village of Stainsacre a little further on. Beyond both villages dense woods ran down to the valley of the River Esk, ideal for the dispersal of run goods, but not so ideal for the landing, the cliffs being steep and treacherous with but the one path leading down to the shore. Even that was hazardous as a sheer overhang near the top made it extremely difficult to negotiate in safety. In the dark it could be a fearsome experience.

Up to now this had been regarded as a reasonably safe area, being both so remote and so dangerous. The Preventives hardly ever made an appearance but Zack realised he could take no chances. One just never knew.

The rain which had started as a soft drizzle as he and Matt left the village had, during the course of their three mile walk, intensified until it was driving in relentlessly, blown by the strong easterly wind.

The night was dark and moonless, and Zack used his hooded lantern with caution, opening the shutter to shed a dim light only when absolutely necessary. Jiddy had informed him that Jonas would have placed a large white stone exactly twenty paces to the south of the bush which concealed the evening's haul. Nearing the top of the donkey road, it was this landmark that they sought. Instructing Matt to carefully watch one side of the path whilst he took the other, they slowed their pace and kept eyes firmly fixed to the ground. Matt was amazed how much he could discern once his vision had adjusted to the darkness of the night. Suddenly he saw it - a large ghostly white blur, and tugged his father's gansey excitedly. Finger to lips, he pointed, and Zack carefully confirmed with a glimmer of light from his lantern.

'Well done, lad!' he whispered. 'Now, count along o' me. One, two, three....' he measured until the twentieth stride brought them abreast of a great thicket of gorse bushes. 'This must be it. Let's tek a closer look.'

Matt hesitated as the sharp thorns pricked his hands and arms painfully. 'If it's in theer, we'll tear oursens to shreds afore we reach it,' he complained, not unreasonably.

''Ang on a moment! Look 'ere!' Zack bent down and picked up a loose end of rope that seemed to grow right from the root of the bush. 'Come on, Matt, let's give this the old heave-ho and see what's on t'other end!' Grasping the loose rope, they both pulled slowly and steadily, taking the strain and every few moments glancing anxiously over their shoulders, the rain lashing their exposed faces as they turned into the wind. After Zack's insistence on silence, it seemed to Matt that they were making a heck of a noise now!

It was unlikely that they would have company in that remote spot and on such an evilly foul night, but as Zack knew only too well, one could never be certain.

Gradually the dense bush parted and revealed its secret, a large iron-skidded sled, borrowed from its usual jobs on the farm. Sleds were frequently used on rough tracks where wheeled carts would just bog down or upset their loads bouncing over deep ruts. Earlier that evening, James and Jonas had taken three loads of barrels of spirits into the Esk valley; the remaining kegs were to be hidden in the deep hay of a lonely sheep shelter near the cliff, to be collected when convenient and distributed as a reward to those involved in the landing. James and Jonas, to avoid attracting attention by their unusual absence from their nightly visit to the Hare and Hounds, were warm and dry, pints of ale in their hands, and enjoying the company of their usual drinking companions. James appeared to have other matters on his mind, and caused his friend to comment, 'Hey up, Jim lad! What's amiss with 'ee? Got thy eye on a noice lass to mek thee a wife at last? Mind, Alys won't tek well to the idea of anither woman in t'house.' James jerked his mind back from its wanderings, not with an attractive young female, but with the barrels under the gorse bush, wondering whether Zack had found them, and got them safely away.

'Aye, wake up!' Jonas gave him a warning kick under the table. 'Drink up, and let's have another. Landlord!' he bawled loudly, as heads turned from all corners of the bar. He was certain he had drawn attention to their presence so no suspicion would fall on them in the morning.

The evening passed pleasantly enough, even though their minds were not fully on enjoying the beer. Eventually, they had to make a move, and go to recover the goods. In a way, it was fortunate that the rain, which had started earlier as a drizzle, now bucketed down. It was genuinely a foul night, and a cold draught blew in to the comfortable inn bar, to the annoyance of the customers, as James and Jonas, bitterly complaining about the atrocious weather, finally bade a good night to their friends within. They would not be suspected of going anywhere but straight home. Unpleasant though the rain was, it provided good cover for the two men who now headed back to the cliff and the sheep shelter where Zack and Matt should now have concealed the contraband.

A rope over each shoulder, Zack and Matthew sweated in spite of the cold as they slowly hauled the heavy sled across the muddy field to where the lonely sheep shelter rose in solid silhouette on their horizon. Matt had no idea it would be so heavy, but struggled on manfully, determined to make up to his father for his puerile behaviour earlier in the day, of which he was now secretly thoroughly ashamed.

'Phew! Nearly there!' whispered Zack, stopping a moment to wipe his wet face and straighten his aching back. 'Alreet, Matt?' he enquired. Matt smiled and flexed his sore shoulders and numb fingers. 'Aye, Ah'm fine, though Ah hope it's not much further!'

Shouldering the ropes, father and son hauled the last few hundred yards, took a cautious look around, and carefully rolled each barrel off the sled, through the stout oak door into the shelter. Loose hay piled generously over the top, the barrels lay hidden from sight, and father and son grinned companionably at each other - a job well done.

Outside, the rain torrented down mercilessly. Zack and Matt, resting a moment from their exertions, became aware of the warm itchiness of their sweating bodies steaming under rain-sodden ganseys. A fitful, childish petulance returning, Matt was all for stripping off and staying warm and dry in the sheep-shelter until the rain eased. Zack was uneasy and anxious to get away as quickly as possible, for who knew who was hiding in the dark and spying on them. Following the capture of Reuben and the increased vigilance of the Preventives, Zack was decidedly twitchy. Experience and commonsense prevailing, he dragged his protesting son out into the rain and set off back along the cliff path.

Had they but known it, Zack and Matt had had a very narrow escape.

They had not long left the safety of the shelter, and were only a dangerously short way on their homeward trek, when three dark-cloaked, tricorne-hatted figures approached the building. The Preventives were on patrol. Having found nothing to report on this horrible wet night, all three were anxious to have a few moments in the warm and dry, and comfort themselves with a quick smoke. Thankfully they forced their way in, shook off their wet cloaks, sat down in the warm hay, and settled down for a well earned rest. Stretching out his aching legs, David Evans' boot hit something hard. Reaching forward, he parted the hay, and there, right in front of his eyes was one of the kegs, so recently left by Zack and Matt, and which they thought had been adequately hidden. This was an added bonus, for the Preventives had not yet found anything to report.

'Way-hey! Look at this!' he exclaimed. 'Right under our very noses!' John Wellow came over and scrabbled under the hay. 'Here's another!' he shouted. 'And another!' chimed in Henry Downsham, diving in and throwing the hay aside. 'Now then, let's think about this,' said David. 'We'd better get back to Whitby straight away, and bring a cart.'

'We can't leave this unattended,' said John, the more cautious of the three. 'Henry and I will have to stand guard, while David goes for help.'

'Wait on,' said David. 'There's more chance of us being set upon on the way to Whitby than there is here. I say two of us should go together in case of attack.'

Henry, being the older of the three, and less agile, agreed to stand guard, and reluctantly watched as David and John pulled up their cloak collars, crammed their hats low over their eyebrows, and set off into the dark.

The silence, broken only by the sound of the rain beating on the roof, was almost tangible. The atmosphere was lonely and eerie, and Henry shuddered as he realized he would be alone for quite some time until the others returned. He took a cautious look outside; all was quiet. Not a soul about. He settled himself in the hay, and the warmth creeping over him, gradually fell asleep.

Some time later, he awoke with a jump. The rain had stopped, but there was another, different sound disturbing the silence of the night. Voices! Cart wheels! Horses hooves!

'They're back quickly!' he thought. Then realized that although he had lost sense of time through nodding off, it would not have been possible for John and David to have got back so soon. It must be, it only *could* be, the smugglers returning for their booty. 'Help!' he thought, and quickly hoisted himself into the loft. It did not feel too safe, so he lay very still.

The door pushed open, and in came James Linskill and Jonas Chaplow.

The kegs under the nearest piles of hay were soon recovered, but James thought there should be more. 'I'll jest tek a leuk up 'ere,' he said, and hauled himself onto the overhanging ledge. He was a heavy man, and the ledge, supported only sufficiently to bear the weight of the hay, and not two hefty men, collapsed, hurtling James and poor Henry onto the hard floor. James was lucky, only bruising a shoulder, but Henry fell awkwardly, and broke his leg. It was difficult to say who was the most surprised.

Jonas acted quickly, and before Henry had time to identify either of the smugglers, he hefted a piece of wood and delivered a well aimed rabbit punch to the back of Henry's head.

'No more trouble from *him!*' declared Jonas. 'But let's get oot o' 'ere, quick! I'll bet he was set on guard, and more o' them damned snivs will be comin' back.'

They loaded the remaining kegs, and were only just nicely away when John and David, with two more officers and a cart arrived back at the sheep shelter to find Henry unconscious and with a broken leg, and of the contraband no sign at all.

To avoid looking foolish and inefficient, they agreed on a tale whereby they were all attacked by a vicious gang, who beat them up and robbed them of their captures. The head office believed them, but James and Jonas were the only two who really knew the true story, and had a good laugh for many a year.

With the excitement of the evening over, a long trek home in the rain ahead of him, Matt trudged along, grumbling morosely, hands in pockets, trying to keep up with Zack's shielded lantern. Suddenly, he became aware of a strange sound rising above the crash of the waves below. Faint at first, he pushed away the sound from the forefront of his imagination. Then it became clearer, the pitiful cry for help was undeniable. Quickening his foorsteps, Matt reached for Zack's shoulder and halted him in his tracks, fingers on lips.

'Listen, Da! Can tha hear owt?'

Zack shook his head impatiently. 'Come on, Matt, get a move on. Ah thowt tha wanted ti get home?'

In the pause that followed, as Matt held his father with a restraining hand on his arm, another faint cry penetrated the darkness. This was no seagull shriek, but a distressed human sound. Zack was now all attention.

Sure enough, far below on a precarious ledge poised high above the pounding sea, a small figure could be discerned in the dim light of the moon.

'It's a lad! What the blazes is he doin' there?' queried Zack. Forgetting the danger of pursuit, Zack uncoiled the rope he still had over his shoulder, and fastening it firmly round his waist, the other end round Matt's, he carefully stood, feet braced firmly, and slowly lowered his son over the sheer cliff edge. Matt had no time to be scared, sensing the need in a fellow creature. Slowly and surely he reached the shivering boy, and carefully wedging himself on the narrow ledge, with trembling fingers, untied the rope from his own waist and attached it to the terrified stranger.

'Whoa, there!' said Matt, as if he was soothing Reuben's horse. 'Steady on, and tha'll soon be safe.'

Putting his fingers in his mouth, Matt's sharp whistle drew Zack's attention and slowly the youngster reached the cliff path, wet, frightened and still sobbing with terror. Matt clung tight to his ledge, not daring to look down, and for the first time that night felt his knees go weak with fear, and his forehead chill over with a faint sweat. Just as he felt he could cling on no longer, the comforting end of the rope touched his shoulder, and without planning his moves, he grabbed the end suddenly, lurched out into the terrifying black void, and nearly jerked Zack off the cliff.

Zack staggered and swore, and dug his heels in, leaning back with all his strength, but felt himself hopelessly slipping towards the edge. Suddenly a small wet form flung itself round Zack's waist and pulled with all his small might, gathering an amazing strength considering his size and condition.

Panic slowly left Zack as he steadied and Matt slowly made his way back to safety. This time it was his son who lay wet, panting and frightened at Zack's feet. In relief, the rugged fisherman had to smile as two very bedraggled young faces met each other head on in the gleam of the lantern.

Matt sniffed and wiped his nose on his gansey. Relief flooded his whole being and a sense of heroism made him grasp the hand of the small stranger. 'I'm Matt,' he introduced himself. 'Who on earth are you?'

'I'm Jan,' said a small voice with a foreign accent. 'I'm Dutch. I fell off the ship when they were landing the goods. They did not see me fall. I swam ashore and climbed out of reach of the sea, but I couldn't get any further up. They've sailed away and left me. I thought I would die.'

'Well, lad. Welcome to England!' Zack greeted him with a friendly pat on the head. 'But coom on and get up, and let's get thi back tiv our home, a decent fire and some warm, dry clothes. Liz'll be a bit tekken aback, like, but she's a good sort and likely won't mind getting anither son!' He grinned and the three of them set off in a spirit of cheerful adventure.

Zack did not know how prophetic his careless words of greeting were to be, and that young Jan would remain part of their family for many years to come. He added a wonderful sense of practical usefulness to a cheerfulness of spirit, along with a great talent for entertaining with song and story, and his presence cheered many a long winter evening. Zack and Matt had come home with treasure after all!

Christmas was coming. The long, dismal month of November had finally passed and even though the early days of December were no lighter or brighter, they brought with them the first hints of anticipation. It was a season of many old traditions, which the country folk had kept since time immemorial, and the children of the present generation made sure they were perpetuated and would still be there for their own children years hence. The infectious excitement amongst the younger ones rubbed off on the older folk, who were, deep down, only too glad to be drawn into the preparations to celebrate this beacon of light in the dark and often depressing winter. As the long, grey, wet November days gave way to an even darker December, families anticipated and prepared with varying degrees of enthusiasm.

All round the village, children began Wassailing, singing the traditional carol in tuneless but excited voices, carrying with them elaborately decorated boxes holding a replica of the Virgin Mary and baby Jesus. The streets rang to the sound of the words 'Here we come a-wassailing, among the leaves so green....,' and the many verses requesting money and refreshments were greeted with much good humour and as much generosity as the householder could afford. Jan had tried to teach them a traditional Dutch carol, but his native language came out from the young ones with such an extraordinary Yorkshire accent, that he fell about laughing and gave up. At the end of a tiring but successful day, the children huddled together to share their earnings and discuss the forthcoming spending.

Damaris, facing long hollow day after long hollow day, could raise little enthusiasm, though only last year she had been leader of the singers. What a lifetime ago that seemed now, in this lonely December. On the days she was not out with Jiddy, she trailed miserably from one room to another, slowly touching and moving pictures and ornaments until Liz could stand it no longer. Damaris had good reason for feeling so depressed and unsettled, but as yet she did not know why. Matthew, also, showed little excitement, though inside he longed to be out with the younger children, but since his acceptance into the smuggling ring, and thus into manhood, he reluctantly disdained the childish games.

Now firmly settled in his new home, Jan had lost all traces of homesickness. He had lost his parents so long ago that he could hardly remember them, and his recent years had been spent as cabin boy on a number of different Dutch trading vessels before his last ship, which had been one of the regular smuggling boats. He was a sunny-natured lad, willing to help Liz with daily chores, and at night, sharing Matthew's bunk, planned all kinds of harmless pranks to cheer up the somber Damaris. Liz smiled as she heard the muffled giggles behind the closed doors. Jan had certainly loosened up Matt's dour temperament.

He was a young lad full of surprises. His capable hands could carve beautiful model ships, he was clever at drawing, and made some very observant caricatures of the family, which had them all laughing. Being used on board ship to turning his hand at many tasks, he was also helpful in the kitchen. One morning he asked Liz if she could spare some butter, flour, sugar, and a little of the very precious cinnamon which he knew she kept for special dishes. 'I just want to make you something for Christmas – something we have in Holland. Please. I think you will like it.' He gave her a winning smile, Liz generously came up with the ingredients and Jan set to work. He would not show her the result, but from the fragrant aroma, it certainly seemed good. On Christmas morning, he presented a beautifully packaged box, with a hand drawn card, thanking Liz for her kindness to him since his rescue. Inside she found the delicate cinnamon shortbread, traditional to all Dutch Christmases. 'You like?' he asked. 'I remember my grandmother she make this for us. It is a taste of my home for you.'

'This is your home now, Jan, for as long as you want it.' Liz hugged him to her, and both their eyes sparkled with happy tears.

Up at the farm Jane and William Barnard viewed their first Christmas together with a calm happiness in the joyful prospect of the birth of their child, due in the late spring. For Jane this birthday season held a particular significance, as she identified with Mary, and on Christmas Eve, she promised herself, she would spend a quiet time of reflection in the stable, alone with William, and away from the noisy family, just sharing the moment with the farm animals, as Mary had done almost two thousand years ago. All through her childhood, Jane had been charmed by the country tradition that at midnight all the animals in the stable would kneel in homage to the Christ Child. This year, she promised herself, she would be there with them, and witness this miracle of nature.

Jane had settled well into her new life on the farm, and William's mother, having borne only sons, delighted in the company of her new daughter. Many a time William and his father had come into the warm farm kitchen at the end of a long, hard day's labour, to find the two of them, laughing and rosy cheeked with the exertion of their day's baking and with the heat of the ovens from which the most tantalising odours wafted across the stone-flagged floor. On the hob simmered a great shining copper pan of frummety, the traditional dish of wheat boiled in milk flavoured with sugar and spices. This year's brew was especially tasty, thanks to the chest of assorted spices William had found in the stable, left as a thank-you after the adventure of the sheep.

Jiddy Vardy's approach to the festive season was one of hard work and long hours of sewing, which brought prosperity to enable her to celebrate in some style, and also to set her up financially through the winter. At the big houses of the Squire and the gentry, new dresses for the ladies and jackets for the men were an essential part of the seasonal celebrations. Jiddy's creations of rich silks, velvets and laces, obtained at some risk from France, swished, swirled and rustled at many a Christmas and New Year Ball. She made the effort to make each one different, knowing the jealous glances that would be exchanged if two ladies attended the same party wearing identical gowns! Jiddy enjoyed this festive sewing. Humming happily at her work, mouth full of pins, she sat surrounded by trimmings of a rainbow hue, as the scraps from her skillful cutting fell to her polished floor. She suddenly found herself extremely popular amongst the little girls of the village, who crowded, squirrel like, peering bright eyed and expectantly round her door, hoping to collect and hide away any off-cuts to make their own Christmas gifts or new clothes for their dolls. Many a Baytown mother received these loving gifts with gentle smiles, speculating which fine lady of the parish would be wearing the rest of the fabric which had made the lace-trimmed handkerchief sachet, or the humble pincushion.

Damaris, called in to help at this, Jiddy's busiest season, was truly grateful for the company and diversion on the long winter evenings. Instead of brooding at home, she worked alongside Jiddy in the candle-light and glowing warmth of her peat fire, sharing not only the quietly sympathetic com-panionship, but also a great sense of amusement and admi-ration as Jiddy whiled away the time with stories of her past adventures. On the small lace-making stool which stood near to their work chairs, three small glasses filled with water reflected and concentrated spots of bright light, nec-essary for the finer parts of their work. Reuben had made Jiddy this beautiful and useful piece of small furniture. Under the present sensitive circumstances of Reuben's absence, his thoughtfulness and craftsmanship brought his presence closer to the two young women to whom he was very special.

Liz and Zack were grateful for Jiddy's understanding and compassion. The hours Damaris spent at home tended to be glum for she cast a depressed mood over the festive preparations. Grieving over the absence of Reuben, she still blamed herself for his capture. Reflecting on the past year, especially the carefree happiness of the last Christmas before her love for Reuben had flowered, brought such sadness to cloud her joy.

Away up in the strange stone cottage at the foot of the moor, now almost hidden by the tall autumnal bracken, Jennet and the cat were quietly contented. Christmas made little difference to their distant lives, but with plenty of food brought up by Liz and a good supply of neatly chopped wood carried in by Matthew and Jan she and the cat would winter well enough. On Christmas Eve Jennet would venture out to the bottom of her garden to visit the hives where, according to tradition, the bees woke from their hibernation, and hummed in celebration of the Saviour's birth. The bees were closely involved in human activities, for they had to be the first to be told of any changes in the family situation. At times of birth and death, the bee-master must knock on the hive and inform them before any human being was told the news. Jennet did not differentiate between the more recent customs of Christianity and those dating back to pagan times, for when she had visited the bees she would return to the house and enjoy her Christmas dinner. A roast fowl, sweet mashed turnips, potatoes in their jackets, and a small plum pudding made from the same mixture as Liz's, which her cat shared with equal delight. With a bit of luck, she would find enough brandy left to make a tasty sauce for the pudding. His yearly treat was a dish of brandy sauce, after which he spent several minutes cleaning every drop off his whiskers and from round his ears, after which he would totter unsteadily to Jennet's bed, and snooze contentedly for the rest of the day.

At midnight on New Years Eve Jennet would worship the Earth Mother, Demeter, and ensure a good crop of apples the following year by chanting a strange incantation and pouring a generous libation of cider over the roots of the oldest apple tree in her small orchard.

Rebecca would shake her head reproachfully at what she regarded as the old woman's nonsense. But then Rebecca had neither Jennet's skills nor her deep intuition. Isaac and Rebecca usually spent Christmas Day with Liz and Zack and the children. Whilst Jennet was out in the garden talking to the bees, Rebecca enjoyed the experience of attending the midnight service in the Chapel. Coming home to a warm fireside, she would find the comfortable presence of Isaac, smoking a fragrant pipe, ensconced by the hearth on which the traditional Yule Log burned brightly. The few moments of solitude whilst walking slowly home in the cold clarity of the midnight air, gave her time to reflect on the past and remain sensibly contented with her present lot. Next morning, she and Isaac would dress in their best clothes, Isaac wearing once again the 'bridal' shirt which still caused amusement and pride as Rebecca recalled how well she had made it and how perfectly it yet fitted old Isaac's still strong and upright body. The small gifts she had made for the family would be packed securely in her basket, then away they two would walk arm in arm, to the home of their last remaining son. After dinner Rebecca generally snoozed contentedly, though denying all accusations that she had nodded off whilst, feet comfortably on the fender, Zack and Isaac enjoyed a companionable pipe or two of tobacco.

Young Matthew could hardly contain his excitement over the Christmas gift he had received from his grandfather. Isaac's old well-thumbed copy of his Theory of Navigation had waited in his sea chest until the time was right to give it to his grandson. Liz observed the way in which Matt had holed himself up in a quiet corner with the book, and realised with a pang that old Isaac's gift had brought her son's departure a considerable step closer. Looking at the situation wisely, however, Liz accepted that Matthew's future would be far more satisfying and rewarding than Zack's present life style. Successful fishing depended entirely on the weather; if the seas were rough, the boats could not put out; if the boats did not put out to fish, there was no money coming into the house, and without regular money, the family could not be fed. This was why so many of the fisher-folk turned to smuggling, when in a single night running contraband they could earn more than in a whole week's legitimate labour. The risks were great, that she had always accepted, so now that the opportunity was presenting itself for Matthew to study and obtain a commission in the Navy, she would not be the one to stand in his way. She knew only too well from personal experience the hardship of bringing up a young family in such circumstances. No matter what it cost her emotionally she, like all good mothers, wanted the very best for her son.

Her thoughts naturally turned to Reuben. If he had had better opportunities as a child, he might well not be where he was at this present moment. Although his living conditions were cramped, with headroom in the men's eating and sleeping quarters between decks so low that not even the shortest man among them could even remotely stand upright, Reuben's Christmas Day was not as bad as it might have been. Naturally, he missed his family sorely, and grieved at his absence from Damaris on this, which should have been their first Christmas together. Reub's skills as a seaman had rapidly been noticed by his Captain, and although he was nominally a prisoner serving a sentence, he had found life under a fair-minded and appreciative Captain not too unpleasant. It was fortunate for all on board the *Pelican* that they were on coastal patrol and had managed to put into harbour for fresh supplies only a few days previously. A substantial meal of fresh poultry, with good vegetables, a helping of the ship's cook's solid fruit pudding and with an additional tot of rum the day would pass pleasantly enough. Those of the crew off watch passed the time with games of cards, and an atmosphere of good-humoured bonhomie in the mess deck helped take their minds off Christmas at home by their own firesides with their loved ones. Reuben had kept a careful check on the ship's position in the chart room, and calculated that by midnight on New Year's Eve, they would not be far off Robin Hood's Bay. If only.......

Peter Maxwell had ridden home for the festive season, leaving the village in the charge of James Herbert who, having no family commitments, was content to eat his dinner and down pints of ale in the Fisherman's Arms. It being the season of goodwill to all men, Richard Tindale somewhat grudgingly served him as he sat in a warm corner by the fire, long legs outstretched, boots comfortably on the fender. It seemed a lifetime ago since his embarrassing encounter with Peter Maxwell when the brandy kegs had so mysteriously vanished from his cellar.

Christmas was the only time of year when Peter and his brothers managed to find time to meet together and exchange news. Each succeeding year he found himself in reflective mood, expecting to be given orders to move on to a new post. He had already stayed in Baytown longer than most Riding Officers, and debated whether this was because he now knew the people and the village with all its secret nooks and crannies so well. On the other hand, this was generally the reason for Officers being moved on, so that familiarity did not breed contempt or they found themselves open to bribery. Perhaps this year would be his last. After the happenings of the past few months he could not make up his mind whether he would be sorry or not. He certainly found his thoughts frequently straying to the Storm family and his sympathies for Damaris in particular were strong. He was pleased that he had not been instrumental in the capture of

Reuben, as so easily could have been the case. With this thought taking root, perhaps it was time for moving on.

After observing his brothers' delight in their growing families, Peter found himself ruminating on marriage. If he left the Bay he would keenly miss his contacts with Jiddy. His thoughts kept returning to her, as far from her presence he missed her more than he liked to admit. They had already found themselves in several situations where it had been all too obvious that she found him, as a person, attractive, and if he was to leave the Preventive Service who knew what exciting future they may have together. It was a very tempting thought.

After a late party, a small group of friends departed in twos and threes on their homeward way under the dark blanket of sky studded with brilliant stars. Young Annie Harrison shyly allowed Richard Bedlington to hold her close while they observed the bright star of Bethlehem hovering in timeless wonder over an unseen stable.

The flocks of black-faced moorland sheep were all safely folded, the shepherds keeping watch as shepherds of old had done since time immemorial. In this country district, however, no kings travelled these lonely roads. The three men Annie and Richard observed silhouetted against the dark sky were no magi, but simple farmers making their way homewards.

In the distance, the sound of the hand-bell ringers pierced the darkness with their sweet tones. 'Down in yon forest', a traditional country carol with a very appropriate chorus, 'The bells of paradise I heard them ring', pealed on the crisp night air. For Annie, wrapped closely in Richard's arms, the moment for her was paradise indeed. All across the landscape the night flickered with lighted candles in distant windows, welcoming any stranger abroad that night. The old people still believed that the Christ Child, homeless in a stable, may see their candle and make their home His own. For Annie and Richard, time stood still, and then was now and now was then.

At Thorpe Hall, Squire Farsyde presided over the most elegant and stylish party in the village. The beautiful Elizabethan building had witnessed many such celebrations as each generation passed through its sturdy stone walls. Traditions held firm here also. Great ceremony was always made of bearing in the Yule Log, placing it in the huge stone fireplace and lighting the Yule Candle which would burn continuously throughout the twelve days of Christmas. The Hall's gardeners scoured the grounds for the finest boughs of holly and assisted the indoor staff in swathing the rooms in garlands of evergreens and scarlet berries. From the ancient oak tree in the woodland, sprays of the mistletoe, worshipped aeons ago by the Druids, now formed a 'kissing ring' under which any unsuspecting maiden would be made to pay the forfeit.

In the great kitchen, once the work of preparing the Christmas and New Year feasts was over, the staff celebrated in their own fashion, carrying on the tradition of the Lord of Misrule, where for the days until Epiphany, all would be turned topsy-turvy, the humblest servant became 'king' in his domain, and the Squire, joining in with all good humour, became as the lowest menial.

In his grand manor house over in the Dales, Jocelyn Whyteacre headed a large dinner party in his oak panelled dining room. His table, laden with old family silver laid on a pristine damask cloth, echoed with the laughter of happy and well contented guests. Tonight he finally related his experiences, dramatising with elegant poses, the story of his turning parson. The rich golden brandy swirling round crystal balloon glasses was of the finest quality, and the toasts drunk 'To the parson!' carried a high degree of appreciation from the discerning guests. Candle-light reflected from the shimmering dresses of silk and lace; claret reds, forest greens, golden ambers, and midnight blues all blurred in a rich rainbow as the dancers whirled to the music of flute and fiddle. All the best of county society were present, celebrating the festive season in an opulent manner that rewarded all the efforts of Jocelyn's young wife, Phillippa as she paused at the head of the stairs, her young son in her arms, on his way to bed. Jocelyn glanced up, and they exchanged knowing and loving glances. Each was proud of the other, but for different reasons. The coming year would be good for both of them, he was certain.

Thomas Duke sat alone on the quayside at Yarmouth, kicking his heels discontentedly against the strong harbour wall. A cold east wind gnawed hungrily at his back, poking and penetrating every gap in his clothing. He shrugged himself more closely into his pea-jacket, and took out his clay pipe. With his left hand, he awkwardly tamped down the tobacco into the bowl. Reaching for his tinder box, he struck a light, but the wind blew out the spark. With only one hand he could not shelter the pipe and light it. After several fruitless attempts he flung it to the ground in sheer frustration. It shattered into tiny pieces. Angrily he kicked the broken bowl into the dark waters of the harbour where, like his once-bright hopes, it sank without trace.

From the dimly lighted tavern came sounds of festive merrymaking. Seafarers roistered noisily and he longed to be among them. His maimed hand pained him still, he had no money in his pocket, no prospect of a decent job ever again, and the furthest his hopes of travel to glorious foreign parts with a new life of riches and luxury had got him, was a few hundred miles south to the desolate and windswept coast of East Anglia.

His hatred of Reuben simmered nastily in his heart. Because of him, mused Thomas, he had been attacked and assaulted, crippled and forced to leave the village of his birth, and lose all that he formerly had owned. He refused to concede that it was all his own fault, caused solely by his own greed and jealousy. No, it was all the fault of that cursed Reuben Granger. One day, he vowed, viciously kicking away the scraggy harbour cat, the only creature that showed any interest in him whatsoever on this depressing December day, he would get even with that Reuben Granger. Be damned to him! He spat angrily into the water, shrugged deeper into his coat, and turned back in solitude towards the bleak, empty landscape.

It was almost midnight. The old year would soon be gone. From the church tower above the village the muffled bell pealed the last few seconds of the old year, before the clear chimes of the New Year midnight joyfully swept through the still air.

The sound of the bells would penetrate right across the landscape, and would be heard by many people, in many differing moods. The moment of change from one year to the next was a strange one. The minute before and after midnight was the same as on every other night of the year, and mostly went unmarked and unnoticed, so why did those passing seconds on New Year's Eve have such significance? By some they were heard with sadness as loved ones, no longer celebrating, were with them no more; by some, with joy and hope for things to come, and by others with perhaps a sense of uncertainty and even fear of what the coming year would hold for them. Those moments held the truth of man's mortality as yet another year came and went with the relentless march of time.

In Baytown, as the midnight bells rang out, a slender figure stood alone on the slipway leading to the shore. At her neck she tenderly fingered a red kerchief. The sharp wind blew her long golden hair across her sad blue eyes. As she pushed the straying strands away, her vision blurred. Silhouetted against the full moon, the topmasts of a tall ship broke the horizon. As she sailed closer in, she was clearly recognisable as the *Pelican*. Reub was aboard, and within sight, but never had the distance between them seemed greater.

Damaris gazed on the tall ship and wept with longing. She watched until the dark sky once more took the ship from her sight. Sadly, she turned and began to make her way homewards.

Overhead the desolate mocking cry of the gulls as they wheeled above her seemed to echo the loneliness of her spirit.

A tall figure emerged from the shadows from where he had been watching her with a heavy heart. Slowly he walked up to her and put his arms round her shoulder. It was her father.

'Dinna fear, my lass. We'll look after thee 'til Reub gets free.'

He placed his hand on her waist and moved it gently downwards, letting it rest where he felt the first stirrings of the child within her.

'We'll tek care of thee – thoo and thi bairn.'

Damaris snuggled into his shoulder.

'Oh, Da!' she sniffed, and brushing away the tears, she gave him a watery smile. 'Oh, Da! What should I do without thee?'

'That's what family's all aboot, lass. Good times and bad. Coom along home and lets get thee a nice hot drink. Thi mither'll be fair chuffed ti be a grandma!'

She laid her head on his shoulder and, arms around each other, they turned homewards and walked up the slipway. Damaris knew that all would be alright, and that when Reuben returned, it would be to his own loving family.